BLACK GIRL UNLIMITED

ECHO BROWN

BLACK

GIRL

UNLIMITED

The Remarkable Story of a Teenage Wizard

WITHDRAWN

Christy Ottaviano Books

HENRY HOLT AND COMPANY | NEW YORK

Henry Holt and Company, *Publishers since 1866*
Henry Holt® is a registered trademark of Macmillan Publishing Group, LLC
120 Broadway, New York, NY 10271 • fiercereads.com

Library of Congress Cataloging-in-Publication Data
Names: Brown, Echo, author.
Title: Black girl unlimited : the remarkable story of a teenage wizard / Echo Brown.
Description: First edition. | New York : Christy Ottaviano Books, Henry Holt and
    Company, 2020. | Summary: From age six through her high school valedictory speech,
    believing she and her mother are wizards helps young Echo cope with poverty, hunger,
    her mother's drug abuse, and much more.
Identifiers: LCCN 2019018533 | ISBN 978-1-250-30985-3 (hardcover : alk. paper)
Subjects: | CYAC: African Americans—Fiction. | Poverty—Fiction. | Family Problems—
    Fiction. | Cleveland (Ohio)—History—20th century—Fiction.
Classification: LCC PZ7.1.B794 Bl 2020 | DDC [Fic]—dc23
LC record available at https://lccn.loc.gov/2019018533

Our books may be purchased in bulk for promotional, educational, or business use. Please
contact your local bookseller or the Macmillan Corporate and Premium Sales Department
at (800) 221-7945 ext. 5442 or by email at MacmillanSpecialMarkets@macmillan.com.

First Edition, 2020 / Designed by Carol Ly
Printed in the United States of America

10 9 8 7 6 5 4 3

For Day Day

CONTENTS

I rise
Up from a past that's rooted in pain

— MAYA ANGELOU
("Still I Rise")

LESSON 1

Building the Perfect Shell

My mother is a wizard. Wizards can freeze time and sit on ceilings. My mother isn't doing either of those things right now, however, because she's passed out on the bathroom floor, where she's been all day. I can see her bare brown ass; it's protruding awkwardly in the air since her pants are down, ruffled around her ankles. I'm embarrassed for her. I want simultaneously to cover her and to cuddle up next to her. I have tried to wake her up. She is needed in this moment. The smoke is pouring into the apartment through the windows and looks like thunderclouds, dark and puffy. Both my brothers are in their cribs in the next room crying. Screaming. Coughing. I keep hoping my mother will pop up off the floor somehow, perform one of her miracles, and save us all from the smoke. I have tried, but I am only six and I don't know if I'm a wizard like my mother. In fact, the only special power I seem to have is rising from the dead.

I rise from the dead every morning, excited to go to school. School is no ordinary place; it is an extraordinary place for extraordinary little boys and girls. At least that's what my kindergarten teacher, Mrs. Jackson-Randolph, tells us. We begin every morning by twirling on the magic carpet. It's old and falling apart like the rest of our school, but Mrs. Jackson-Randolph says we shouldn't focus on the negatives; we should search for the positives in every situation so we don't become bitter or discouraged. When the ceiling tiles leak during a big storm, or our toys fall apart, or a mouse darts across the classroom, Mrs. Jackson-Randolph shouts, "But look at how much of the ceiling isn't leaking! Look how many toys we still have! We are blessed and bountiful!" We shriek with glee. We clap. She is right, we still have so much. I know that even more is on the way thanks to the wishes we make while twirling on the magic carpet.

Every morning, we twirl and twirl around one another until Mrs. Jackson-Randolph tells us to "Freeze!" Then we all freeze in whatever position we find ourselves. "Now make a wish," Mrs. Jackson-Randolph says. "Think about someone you really, really love and make a wish for them. We shouldn't only wish for things for ourselves. We also have to think about others." I'm happy to wish for someone else this time since I have already wished everything for myself: a pink motorized Barbie truck that I can drive down the sidewalk like I see the girls do in the commercials on TV; an Easy-Bake Oven so I can make cakes like my mother does; more red bows and ponytail holders so I can make my hair look better (it never looks right); and lots of crayons, markers, and colored pencils so I can color all the coloring books in the world.

I make other wishes also, secret wishes, but don't tell anyone about those. Like wishing I was just a little more light-skinned like my best friend, Jessie Stewart. Jessie and I hold hands, walk to school together, and sit next to each other in class. I only just met Jessie at the beginning of the school year, but we have already become like brother and sister. When Mrs. Jackson-Randolph isn't looking, we pass candy and make funny faces at each other. Sometimes we even cover our ears and scream at the top of our lungs to see if our voices can reach all the way to outer space where the aliens live. Maybe they will hear us and come twirl with us on the magic carpet. We wonder what wishes the aliens would make. Mrs. Jackson-Randolph does not like when we scream and wrinkles her face while telling us to use our inside voices. We nod yes, but start screaming again as soon as she turns around. Screaming, like yawning and sneezing, is contagious. Soon, almost everyone in the class starts screaming, including my two other friends, Tiffany and Davante. None of us can out-scream Tiffany. Her high-pitched shrills cause Mrs. Jackson-Randolph to cover her own ears and shout, "Enough!" We all stop midscream, mouths wide open, and stare awkwardly around the room at one another until she tells us to close our little pie holes.

"But I don't like pie, so mine gotta be anotha kinda hole, don't it?" says Davante, who always has something smart to say. Mrs. Jackson-Randolph slowly turns around and stares intensely at Davante, until he lowers his eyes in shame. No one says another word.

Davante's parents are Black Panthers. I don't know exactly what that means, but they have large Afros and are always dressed in black, including black sunglasses, which they keep on all the time, even inside the school when they pick up Davante. I wonder if they always wear sunglasses because they secretly don't have eyes. People without eyes would be scary, so I hope they never take off the sunglasses if they really don't have eyes. The sunglasses inside are not the only strange thing about Davante's parents. They also raise their fists all the time, like they're going to punch someone, but I never see them hit anyone. Davante raises his fist like his parents, but only sometimes, like on picture day.

I wish Jessie, Mrs. Jackson-Randolph, Davante's Black Panther parents, or any of my friends were here right now to help stop the smoke and save us. I stare at my brothers in their cribs. I put my hands through the bars and pat their foreheads to try to get them to stop crying, but tears are pouring out of their eyes and their little arms and legs are shaking. They know something is wrong, too. I am shaking like my brothers. There is a pinching in my throat, like someone is squeezing it closed so no air can get in. I have only felt like this one other time, when Tiffany and I almost drowned at the beach.

Mrs. Jackson-Randolph takes us on a class field trip to see the gray lighthouse at Lake Erie. "Each of us is a lighthouse,"

Mrs. Jackson-Randolph says, "shining our light and purpose out into the world. Your purpose can be as big and vast as the water in front of you. It's never too early to start thinking about what you want to do in this world, deep down in your heart. Whatever it is, make sure it helps other people in some way. We have to take care of each other." When Mrs. Jackson-Randolph says this, Tiffany grins and gives me a big hug. I squeeze her back tightly until she starts squirming. If I had a sister, I imagine she would probably look like Tiffany. I stare at the lighthouse across the water, close my eyes, and scrunch my face up trying to look inside my brain to see what my purpose is, but I can't think of anything. My mother is always saying, "This ain't no place for a girl chile. Lawd, I prays fo da day when someone heps da lil girl chiles of dis worl', 'specially da black ones." I don't know why the "lil girl chiles" need so much help, but maybe that can be my purpose, to help the other "lil girl chiles." I'm not sure yet. I will have to scrunch my face up and look inside my brain again to see if there are any answers in there.

When Mrs. Jackson-Randolph isn't looking, a few of us run excitedly toward the water, trying to get to the lighthouse and see for ourselves what's inside. We sprint ahead until Mrs. Jackson-Randolph yells at the top of her lungs, "Stop!" Everyone freezes except me and Tiffany. We can't stop. The water calls us forward as we try to outrun each other, splashing and splashing. I look over and see that Tiffany, my almost-sister, is laughing and smiling just like me, until the water begins to swallow us, pulling us way down. Tiffany's and pulls him away from the girls, saying he's her "baby." She says it like a mother would say about their child, but we all know she means boyfriend. I want Jessie to be my boyfriend, like all the other girls in the class do, but Tiffany is bigger and stronger than all of us so I guess she can have him.

My mother calls Jessie "the little high-yellow boy that lives 'round the corna on Foster Street." Jessie is the only high-yellow kid in the class. The rest of us range in color from caramel to dark brown, like wet dirt. Everyone says Jessie has "that good hair" because he's mixed with black and white. His hair is curly and falls in thick black ringlets down the sides of his face. He looks like he could be Middle Eastern or Latino. I ask my mother repeatedly if I can get a relaxer so my hair can look like Jessie's. Tiffany already has a relaxer, and now her hair is silky smooth and not knotted and nappy like mine. My mother thinks I'm too young to get a relaxer and tells me to stop asking her about it. Even though she says no, I still wish for a relaxer every morning on the magic carpet.

When it's time to take the class picture, we all stand, wobbling and smiling on the bleachers. Jessie stands next to me and grabs my hand, like he always does. Tiffany tries to kiss Jessie on the cheek, like she always does, but he turns his face in disgust. Davante raises his fist like his parents, which blocks the faces of two people standing behind him. Mrs. Jackson-Randolph shakes her head when she looks at the photo on the cameraman's camera and says we will have to take another one. This time we must stand still, look directly ahead, and smile proudly. We nod yes, but when the photographer says "One, two, three . . . cheese!" we sprint around the bleachers, make funny faces, and hug and hit each other. After eight pictures, Mrs. Jackson-Randolph finally gets one she's satisfied with. Frazzled and exhausted, she walks us outside to where our parents are waiting. The end of the school day is a relief for all of us. We scatter, like marbles in a pinball machine, into the arms of our parents. My mother doesn't gallop, like most of the men in my neighborhood, but instead streaks forward with the fury of a thousand panthers, grabs my and Jessie's hands, and drags us along the concrete sidewalk all the way home.

As soon as we get home, it's reading time, which is a very special time. My mother opens the pink box sitting on the dresser with the black spinning ballerina inside who twirls to the song "What a Wonderful World" and has a bright white light in the middle of her stomach, which my mother says symbolizes the light we all have inside. I don't see any lights inside myself or anyone else, so I don't know what she's talking about. My mother says she will let me have the pink ballerina box when I'm old enough not to break it. Once everything is quiet and cozy, my mother gathers Jessie and me in the big armchair and reads several of the books piled by the chair. Books like *Green Eggs and Ham*, *Goldilocks and the Three Bears*, and *The Cat in the Hat*. Reading time is my favorite. I can't read yet, but I love listening to the adventures of all the characters in the stories. Plus, reading time is really the only time my mother softens. Her voice and eyes grow warm, and she kisses us on the forehead after each story. I secretly wish reading time would never end.

Staring down at my mother unconscious on the floor, I think about who will bring me home after school and read to me if she doesn't get up. My stepfather is never around, and Jessie's parents are very mean. What if no one takes me to school again? I will miss all my friends and Mrs. Jackson-Randolph. I look intensely at my mother and begin to worry that she is dead.

———— ⸺ ∘O∘ ⸺ ————

I have seen only one other dead person in my life, at Mr. Casey's funeral last year. I ask my mother why he isn't moving. Why he won't get up out of the box in front of the church. My mother calls the box a "casket" and says he won't get up because "he's dead and gone to the in-between wit' da rest of da ancestors. He ain't neva comin' back ta dis worle."

I tell my mother I die every night also, but I've never seen Mr. Casey in my dreams.

"Sleepin' ain't da same thang as dyin', chile. You don't neva wake up when you dead and gone."

I feel sad that Mr. Casey will never wake up again. He used to give me and my brothers candy every time he saw us and say, "Children are the bravest of all, so they deserve special, sweet treats," and pat us on the head. And now he's gone to the in-between, which is a place I have never been, but my mother says we will all go there one day. I hope not anytime soon. I'm still getting used to this world.

I want to ask her what the in-between is, but the pastor starts preaching all about Mr. Casey's life and accomplishments. Mr. Casey's family starts whooping and hollering all around the church. It sounds like the feral cats that roam the streets by our apartment when they are in heat. One of Mr. Casey's relatives runs up to his coffin and throws her whole body over the casket while yelling in a shrill, high-pitched voice, "Why? Why? Why ya hafta take 'im so soon?"

My mother shakes her head and says, "So soon? Lawd, dat man was ninety-three years old. I don't know why people's got to be so dramatic and act a damn fool. Jus' be wantin' attention."

I watch the ushers work to pull away three people who have made their way to the front of the church. They continue their feral-cat screaming and claw feverishly at Mr. Casey's casket. I wonder if all funerals are this chaotic.

Right now, my mother looks like Mr. Casey did in his casket that day. I tell her that she can't go to the in-between yet. She is still needed here. I tell her I wished for her at school today on the magic carpet. I wished that she would take down her shell more often and show us the warm parts underneath.

My mother has had her shell since she was a little girl like me. She spent years "gettin' it jus' right and makin' doubly sho it was strong enough," which is why she never likes to take it down. I am shocked when I find out my mother wasn't born with her shell—that she had to learn how to build it. Being a wizard is not what you think. In fact, it requires serious training. The first lesson is how to build a shell. My mother is a master at this. She flips a switch and—*bam!*—she's gone. A million miles away. And what's left is a hard shell. She started developing this shell when she was a young girl, after her uncle started doing bad things to her in the bathroom in the middle of the night. I ask her what things he did, but she tells me not to worry about it because those things will never happen to me. I'm glad. I don't want bad things to happen to me, either.

The bad things happened from the time she was my age until she was ten. Every time he came to her room late at night, she would hide under the covers. She would pull them up over her head and wish she was invisible. (Unfortunately, wizards don't have the power of invisibility.) Her uncle would come and carry her to the bathroom and do the bad things. She would leave her body and sit on the ceiling until he finished. Leaving her body wasn't enough, however. At the end, she always had to come back down because "you cain't stay on the ceiling foreva," she said. She would cry alone in her bed after it was all over, her small body sulking and shaking in the dark.

So she learned how to build a shell around herself. When

she put the shell up, she didn't feel anything, and that's what she needed to protect her warm parts inside. She knew that the shell would have to be hard enough to keep out the rest of the bad things coming her way. She didn't make just any shell. She made a double-layered shell that was impenetrable. Airtight.

The shell couldn't stop the sinking, however. My mother said she sank all the way down to the bottom of herself, after what her uncle did to her. "So fuh down, my mama had to come get me and brang me back, but I don't wanna talk 'bout huh, my mama. You heah? I ain't neva got ova what happn'd . . . Don't ask me no mo questions 'bout huh. You heah? Chi'run is too damn nosy. Got a question fo ev'rythang. I sweah ta God." Every time we ask my mother about her mother, her shell flies up and she gets so mad. I wish I could have met my grandmother so I could ask her myself what happened, but she, like Mr. Casey, is no longer in this world.

Besides reading time, my mother rarely takes down her shell. I want her to take it down more often because I need the warm parts underneath that she keeps hidden. I have been trying to build my own shell, to protect my warm parts also, but it's hard. I just want to twirl on the magic carpet with all the people in the world, but I know that's not possible. Some people are dangerous.

I wish I had a shell right now to protect me from all this smoke. It keeps pouring in and is getting thicker. I know if my mother doesn't get up soon, it will fill the entire apartment.

I waddle back to the living room, where my brothers are still crying. I have an overwhelming urge to save them. I can't figure out what to do. I look around the room for help. The lights are off. The TV is on. The glare disturbs me. The people on the TV are not helping. Neither is the sad-looking man with brown hair and blue eyes hanging in a picture frame on the wall. I reach toward him and the people on the TV, trying to grab them and show them we need help, but my arms are too short. I'm wearing a long T-shirt and my hair is in braids like Ms. Celie's from *The Color Purple*. I'm trying not to cry, but the tears fall from my eyes and I start to panic. I wonder where my stepfather is. Maybe he can come and save us from the smoke. I listen for his keys jingling at the door. I pray for the sound but hear only the TV.

— — —— ———◦○◦——— —— — —

The men can build shells, too, but they are not wizards. I never see them make miracles. I only see them make chaos. My father is not my biological father—he's my stepfather, but my brothers' biological father. I still call him father and not stepfather because he's raising me. My mother said my real father is a "lyin'-ass, conniving-ass, no-good-ass mothafucka wit' thirteen kids"—all girls—"by different womens, and he don't take care a' none of 'em." My mother tells me to forget about him, but I still wonder where he is and what he looks like and if he drinks like my stepfather, who is drunk all the time. My brothers and I love it when my stepfather gets drunk. He comes to life, gleefully bouncing us on his knees and telling us stories about what a great man he is. He tells us he's a member of the T-Man Trivilization. We don't know what it means because they never teach us about the T-Man Trivilization in school. We later learn that *trivilization* is not a real word and that he actually means *civilization*. He's been out of the South for almost twenty years, but his Alabama accent is so thick, he sounds like he has a mouthful of cotton when he talks. He stretches out his words and talks slow, like molasses running down a maple tree, except when he cusses, which is the only time he ever talks fast. He loves to cuss and often forms entire sentences with just cuss words. I once heard him say "Goddammit, hell naw, shit, hell naw, shit, goddammit, hell naw!"

My brothers and I enjoy my father's drunken antics, but we know they won't last long. Eventually, after the glow of the alcohol has worn off, there will be a fight. There is always a fight. My father will begin making his fast cuss-word sentences, directing them at my mother, shooting them into her like bullets. My mother will raise her shell, and the chaos will begin. She will spin around the apartment like a tornado, destroying everything in her path. I don't understand how she can make so many miracles and yet cause so much chaos. How she can be so dazzling and destructive at the same time.

Making Something Out of Nothing

I am always astonished by my mother's spectacular miracles. Even though she can't do it right now because she's lying facedown on the bathroom floor, I see her make miracles all the time. Like making something out of nothing, which is the second lesson of wizard training. I don't understand how she does it, how she is able to make things appear out of thin air. My mother is truly gifted at this.

One day, when we are much older, my brothers and I sit at the kitchen table, starving. We have each already eaten a bowl of dry cornflakes (we refuse to add water and there is no milk). We have also eaten Miracle Whip and cheese sandwiches on white bread, but we are still hungry. We don't dare say we are hungry. By now, we also have shells and hide behind them like we have been taught. We sit quietly at the table poking and prodding one another. We are never quiet unless we are hungry or at one of my mother's Saturday-night grown folks' spades parties. We don't make a peep as we glance out of the corner of our eyes at our mother, waiting for the miracle. She stands, hunched over the sink, smoking a cigarette, pretending like she doesn't see, but we know she does. We can feel the electricity of the approaching miracle coursing through her body. And then, from her hunched position, she rises and calls out my name, "Ecka, watch yo brothas, I'ma be right back. Don't let nobody in, you heah?" I nod faithfully. We quietly watch her leave.

As soon as she's gone, we run to Ms. Patty's apartment in the front of the building. Ms. Patty is sixty-eight years old, lives alone, has lived in the apartment building since before we were born, and has a lot of health problems. Her voice is very hollow and scratchy because she had throat cancer many years ago and they had to remove one of her vocal cords. She sounds like Marge Simpson's sister from *The Simpsons*. Her back is also hunched over because she has sciatica. She's always drinking from a plastic purple Kool-Aid cup. No matter what time of day you knock on her door, she has that purple cup in her hand. Ms. Patty feeds us constantly. She tells us she knows our mother "been goin' thru some thangs," so she has to make sure we don't start looking like "dem little po', big-belly babies in Africa we always see on the late-night TV commercials." She makes us peanut butter and jelly sandwiches or gives us big hulking slices of lemon pound cake that she makes from scratch.

Our apartment is behind Ms. Patty's in the back of the building on the top floor and doesn't face the street, so we can't see what happens on the sidewalks, which is why we always run to her apartment when one of our parents leaves, to see in which direction they go.

"Ms. Patty! Ms. Patty!" we yell while banging on her door. "Let us come sit on da porch wit' you!"

Ms. Patty pulls open the door and says, "Lawd, if y'all ain't the loudest chi'runs in dis buildin'! Go on, but don't touch nothin'. Nothin'! You hear me?!"

We nod our heads yes and then run through her apartment touching everything we can on the way to the porch while giggling uproariously.

Ms. Patty hit the lottery many years ago, but no one knows how much she won for. She has the nicest apartment in the building, and it's full of strange fancy items like painted glass vases; a cabinet with white porcelain dishes on display; the biggest TV we've ever seen in our lives; and, taking up an entire wall, framed paintings of black people picking cotton and getting whipped in various positions. My brothers and I wonder why anyone would want pictures like that all around their apartment. Ms. Patty says it's to honor the struggles of the ancestors so that she never forgets where she came from.

"But you don't come from no cotton field, Ms. Patty. You come from Philadelphia," Rone says when she tells us about the paintings.

"Aww hush, boy! I swear y'all have da fas'est and freshest lil mouths, jus' like dem damn Bébé's kids!"

She's right. At this age, we are like Bébé's kids—the characters in a popular animated movie that run around making a ruckus. Nobody can stop Bébé's kids from wreaking havoc and destruction wherever they go. Bébé's kids would have broken all the nice things in Ms. Patty's apartment, but we don't break anything on our sprint to the porch. We just run our hands over as many surfaces as possible, including her glass vases and the china cabinet. Later Ms. Patty will tell our mother, "Dey cain't neva come back to my apartment 'cause dey leave greasy handprints all ova my shit." But she always lets us back in.

When we finally arrive on the porch, we see our mother drive off in a red Buick with a man we don't know. A few minutes later, Ms. Patty emerges with her purple cup and tells us to "sit down somewhere until ya mama get back." I wonder if she knows my mother is a wizard and that she is going to perform one of her miracles. I search Ms. Patty's eyes for a glimmer of knowing, but I don't see any flashes of insight. My brothers and I sit on plastic chairs on the left side of the porch and stare up and down the street. This porch is the epicenter of social life for the apartment building in the summer. My parents, Ms. Patty, and their friends sit there for hours on warm summer days, talking about everything: politics, the old days, the future, and the people on the sidewalk. Ms. Patty is notorious for making comments about people passing by, whether she knows them or not. My mother says, "Ms. Patty talks about er'body. She jus' cain't hep huhself. She got ta be observin' and commentin' on ev'rythang."

Shortly after Ms. Patty joins us on the porch, she begins her observations: "Ooooh, look at huh. Got all dem damn kids dat she cain't take care of. Ooooh, what's happenin' to da young folks today, Lawd? Wearin' all dese tight dresses and thangs." Ms. Patty suddenly turns to us and tells us, "Cova up y'all's eyes," so we won't see what Danielle, the woman across the street, is wearing. We've already seen, but we still cover our eyes. We peek through our fingers and watch Danielle, who lives down the street and has five kids, saunter up the sidewalk. All the men parked in vans on the side of the street yell out to her, "You lookin' mighty fine today, Ms. Danielle. When you gon' let one a' us have a piece of dat?"

After Ms. Patty has done all her secret observing, she yells down in a syrupy-sweet but fake voice, "All right, Ms. Danielle, how you doin' today? I like dat outfit. You lookin' mighty good, gurl! And how dem kids?"

Danielle hollers back, "Er'body doin' good, by da grace of God."

Ms. Patty responds, "I know that's right. All we got is grace. Well, I'm glad you doin' good. Have a blessed day, now."

As Danielle walks away, we uncover our eyes and Ms. Patty continues her commenting.

"Ooooh, dat girl jus' ain't done nothin' wit' her life 'cept single-handedly repopulate da whole damn earf. Ooooh, Lawd keep her high in yo favor, 'cause she shole gon' need as much grace as you can give. If dat ain't da truf, I don't know what is." Ms. Patty takes a sip out of her purple cup while chuckling to herself.

My brothers, Jerone and Teandre—Rone and Dre, and I sit for the next hour on Ms. Patty's porch while she drinks and talks about everybody who walks by. She must be taking the smallest sips known to man because she never seems to run out of liquid. When we finally see the red Buick back on the street and turning into the driveway, we run down the hall to our apartment and sit quietly at the table, putting our shells back up.

Our mother bursts through the door with McDonald's, our favorite, and two bags of groceries. We are astonished. *How did she do it?* With no money. With no job. She has turned air into food. Amazed, we sit at the kitchen table feasting upon her miracle. We gobble the cheeseburgers and fries, and gulp down the sodas. She stands, leaning against the sink, smoking a cigarette, watching us. Her eyes are dead. Her clothes and hair are disheveled. She doesn't say anything. She is cold and detached. Behind her shell again. I ask, "Momma, do you want some?" Suddenly, the shell breaks and tears begin pouring out of her eyes. We stop eating. We are shocked. We are disturbed. We don't understand. Why is she crying after she has produced such a marvelous miracle? "No, baby," she says. "I'm awright."

She's not "awright" now, though. She's lying on the bathroom floor, not moving. And the house is burning. I don't know that the house is burning. I am only six and don't know what smoke means, but I know something is wrong. I see several birds chirping frantically outside the open window. As soon as I notice them, everything starts to move in slow motion. The people on the TV talk much slower. The black clouds of smoke roll in slower and slower. The birds seem to know something is wrong. They fly in circles right outside the window. I want to tell them to fly far, far away before the smoke swallows them, too, but before I can, I hear muffled voices shouting, "Is there anyone inside? Is there anyone up there?" I hear sirens blaring, right outside the apartment. I don't have many words yet. So I start crying. I stand in the middle of the room and cry as loud as I can. I try to push all the energy of my body into my voice. I amplify myself, attempt to become just sound. A sound so big it can reach the voices outside.

It works! I hear someone coming up the stairs. I hear Ms. Patty's voice. I hear my father's voice. I hear other voices. I hear pounding. I hear keys jingling at the door. Suddenly, my father bursts into the apartment and in one fell swoop grabs us all—my mother, Rone, Dre, and me—in his big, drunken arms. He is not cussing now. He is quiet and focused. More quiet and focused than he's ever been in his entire life. He transforms himself into a nest and carries us all away from the smoke. It is the only miracle I have ever seen him make. Our tiny hands grip the back of his neck as he gallops forward, unstoppable, until he emerges outside into the crisp, stinging air. I rest my head on his shoulder and watch as the birds fly away north into the night sky.

— - — ——o◦o—— — - -

When I am older, I ask my mother what she was dreaming about when she was lying on the floor while our apartment building was on fire. She said she wasn't dreaming, she was praying. She was in a crack cocaine–induced coma that almost took her life. She could hear me nearby and wanted desperately to help, but she couldn't activate her body. Instead she lay there and prayed the whole time. She said she had no choice but to surrender to the beyond. It was out of her hands. So when she was lying there, in a puddle of her own vomit, with pants down and her body paralyzed, she prayed, "Dear God, please let my chi'run be diff'rnt. Please, God. This ain't no kind of life. It might be too late fo me, but it ain't too late fo dem. Make a way, God. Make a way out of no way."

She spiraled those prayers so far and deep into the universe, she felt like she left her body altogether and traveled to the in-between: the quantum field of infinite possibility where miracles originate, where the ancestors live, and which exists between this world and the beyond. In that place, outside the limitations of time and space, she begged for mercy, for another way, and the whole quantum field vibrated from the impact of her desire. In fact, the universe began to reimagine the trajectory of what was possible. Unforeseen realities for me and my brothers began to take shape. My mother is no ordinary wizard. She is a quantum wizard with the power to disrupt the future by spiraling her prayers far beyond the man-made barriers of this world.

Reaching the In-Between

I wonder if I came from the in-between, if that's where I was before I was born. My mother said that's where she went on the night of the fire and that's where all the dead people are. I wonder if that's where all the born people are as well, before they are born. Nobody will answer my questions about the in-between—where it is, who lives there, how to get there—so I make up my own stories. It's at the top of the sky, way above, where the blue part ends. And aliens, not ancestors, live there. I stare up at the sky with my notebook, trying to see where it is. I squint my eyes, which causes the sides of my mouth to pull up, like I'm smiling, but I'm not. I bend my head all the way back until it feels like it's going to fall off. I still don't see anything but clouds and sun rays. *God has hidden it well*, I think.

I ask my third-grade teacher, Mrs. Samuels, if she has ever seen the in-between at the top of the sky where the aliens live and where we spiral our prayers. She cranes her head confusedly to the side and says there's no such thing as the in-between. "There's nothing but empty space, other planets, and the sun above the sky."

I stare at her doubtfully. "But my mother went there," I say definitively. "So it has to be hidden somewhere we can't see."

"Sweetie, I don't know what you're asking me. No one knows what's above all of that, but I very much like your curiosity."

On the first day of school, Mrs. Samuels gives us all notebooks and tells us we have to be scientists in our own lives, curious about our surroundings. Like scientists, we should write down our observations about the world around us. She doesn't need to tell me that, however, because I'm already very curious about everything. In addition to my curiosities about the in-between, I am also curious about my parents and the other adults in my neighborhood. I observe them carefully and take notes about my findings in the small notebook. I figure out that the adults are very strange, and not like us children. For example, they seem to be angry all the time, even at little things like when we forget to close the screen door, or when we come running up the stairs in excitement. And when there is food in the house, my mother gets very angry when we don't eat every single bite on our plates. Sometimes, I get so stuffed, I feel like my belly will explode. I feel like the white Pillsbury Doughboy who's always on TV. I don't want to eat another bite, but there is still so much food on my plate. I try to sneak the plate past my mother, who is talking on the phone, but she sees me and tells me to "sit right on down and scrape dat plate. You thank food grows on trees?! Well, some of it do . . . But dat ain't da point. Ain't gon' be nothin' wasted in dis house!" I sit for another hour taking small bites until all my food is finally gone.

I tell my brothers we have to observe our parents like they are specimens in the laboratory to figure out why they are so strange. My brothers hate school, but they love observing. The only time I ever see them focus all the attention in their brains is when we are secretly observing the adults. I have tried to convince them of how important school is, even setting up a pretend school on the weekends to teach them everything Mrs. Samuels has taught me, but they wiggle and squirm and eventually run around the living room screaming, "Noooo!" They sit as quiet and still as rocks when we are observing, however, like they are about to learn the most important lesson in the world.

Our favorite place to secretly observe adults is at the Saturday-night spades game. My parents dress up and invite all their rowdy friends over. Spades is a popular card game for black people in America that involves lots of trash-talking, like "Who taught you how to play spades, nigga, Stevie Wonder?" At first, my brothers and I think the adults will begin fighting when they start their trash-talking, but two minutes later they are laughing and joking, slapping the table in glee, and patting one another on the shoulder. The trash-talking seems to be how they bond and build community during the game. My brothers and I practice trash-talking after the party by hurling insults we hear during the game at each other. We know we are not supposed to say cuss words, so we cover our mouths and giggle while mocking the strange adults.

The process of setting up the game is the same every time. First, my father assembles two white plastic foldout tables, one in the middle of the room and one by the window. Next, my mother sets out an assortment of snacks and drinks: potato chips, fried pig skins, peanuts, cans of Pepsi, and fresh Kool-Aid. Their friends bring bottles of Colt 45, packs of cigarettes, and small plastic bags filled with white rocks. Later, they will all be crawling around on the floor searching for any white rocks that might have fallen. I don't understand why anyone would crawl around on the floor picking up rocks, so I write it down in my notebook as part of their strange behavior. After everything has been set up, my mother puts a record on. She always plays old-people songs by Marvin Gaye, Aretha Franklin, Al Green, Sam Cooke, Otis Redding, and the Temptations. She rotates the records throughout the night until all her favorite hits have been played.

My brothers and I wish she would play newer music like Tupac or Immature or Mariah Carey instead. We don't understand the significance of the music my parents play at the Saturday-night parties. To us, the singers sound ancient and out of touch. We don't know that the music is pregnant with the pain and suffering of our parents' generation. That it's a soundtrack to their lives. When Sam Cooke cries, "A change is gonna come," or when Marvin Gaye asks, "What's going on?" my parents and their friends lament their own conditions. They complain about how "the government don't give a fuck 'bout da niggas." How it's all designed for them to fail and how things "gotta get betta in da future. The Lawd'a see to it." I write it all down in my notebook, including how sad they get when their old-people music plays.

They don't just tell sad stories and complain about the government, however. They also recount raucous tales from when they were young. The first boy or girl they liked. Their proms and school dances and how they was "the sharpest looking one at da whole dance." They remember all the things their parents told them about how to live in the world. "Man, my momma use'ta say don't neva give up, no matta how hard life get. She use'ta say if there's a will, there's a way. I shole do miss my momma, man." Everyone sits in silence for a moment to honor all those that "done gone on home to da glory." They smoke cigars and cigarettes and talk about the good ol' days in the "hot-ass, cotton-picking South," which is what my father calls it and is where most of them are from. They had no idea how hard their lives would be in the North, about all the obstacles to come. So they left the South in droves, headed north, unstoppably north, before landing in Ohio, the Buckeye State, nestled on the shores of the great Lake Erie.

My father calls it the Shotgun State and says, "Ain't nothin' but hillbillies and honkies wit' big-ole shotguns soon as you step foot anywhere outside a' Cleveland into one a' dem yella co'nfields. Have you hopin' and prayin' one of 'em don't decide to send yo black ass on home to da good Lawd way befo' yo time. Show up at da pearly gates a' heav'n, and da good Lawd'll tell ya you ain't 'spected fo anotha thirty yeahs. 'Not accordin' to dem white folks,' you tell 'im wit' sorrow in yo eyes and pity in yo soul. And dat's when you really realize dat da only thang standin' between you and da good Lawd is a praya and da mercy of da white man. But I guess it's always been dat way, ain't it?" Everyone at the table nods in prodigious agreement.

I notice that they talk a lot about God and prayer during their spades games; it's almost like a second church. Everyone seems to believe in "da good Lawd," except my mother, who always tells them to "stop talkin' all dat religion talk, 'cause God ain't comin' to save none of you niggas." But they don't listen to her.

Ms. Patty, who has a different wig for every occasion, wears her Tina Turner wig to the spades games, and says she stays in prayer "fo ev'rythang and er'body," even though she talks about "er'body and dey mama."

"I still pray fo 'em afta I talk about 'em," Ms. Patty says while cackling to herself. Ms. Patty says she's received everything she ever wanted thanks to the power of prayer.

"Well, Ms. Patty, you must be doin' somethin' right. How many times you done hit the lottery?" Quincy, one of my father's friends, asks.

"Don't worry about my money, nigga. Worry 'bout da power of yo own prayers," Ms. Patty shouts playfully, drinking from her purple cup while everyone laughs in the background.

Despite their prayers and all their talk about God, it does not stop them from sinning, which is something else I write down in my notebook—how often they say one thing but do another. Pastor Aily, whom we only see in church on Sunday mornings, says you are not supposed to curse, hit each other, drink, do drugs, or go to bars, "which are the devil's playgrounds," but my parents and their friends do all those things.

Pastor Aily says, "Da only reason God don't strike us all down fo our sins is 'cause he's good and merciful. Anybody can repent and beg for forgiveness for their sins."

I want to believe Pastor Aily, but my mother says, "Ain't no mercy here." After what happened to her mother, which she still refuses to tell us about, she stopped believing in anything. I am only a kid, but I know you have to believe in something to make sure you have a story in your head that explains the world. There seem to be many things to believe in, and I believe them all: God, the in-between, heaven, hell, and the devil. So I have many stories in my head to explain the world. I haven't conducted enough observations yet to prove any of them wrong. I figure I better just believe in them all in case they are all true.

After the adults finish talking about God and the good ol' days at their spades game, someone turns the music up and they start dancing and swaying and singing and clapping to the beat. It is the happiest we ever see them. My brothers and I watch from our secret hiding place on the side of the couch. We tuck our heads beneath a blanket and peek in amusement as the adults begin their wild spinning around the room. They remind me of kindergarten when me and my friends used to twirl on the magic carpet, but the adults don't just spin, they also dance very close together, which we were never allowed to do on the magic carpet. Soon, my father, in his purple velvet suit and matching fedora with a green feather on the side, and my mother, with her purple silk dress that has a slit all the way up her leg, will be dancing in the middle of the living room while their slow old-people music plays in the background. I don't know why, but I feel funny inside watching them dance like this. So funny, I cover Dre's and Rone's eyes so they don't see. My mother melts her whole body into my father, as if he is a big tall tree that will shelter and protect her forever. It's strange to see them like this, especially since they are usually in chaos, but I prefer this over their chaos.

Others slow-dance also or sit smoking cigars and cigarettes, watching the slow dancers while blowing large plumes of thick smoke up toward the ceiling. I watch it rise, remembering the smoke from the night of the fire three years ago. I look toward the window and watch as a bird, just like on the night of the fire, lands on the windowsill, crouches under the cracked window, and attempts to come inside. I wonder if he is trying to grab some of the potato chips that lie scattered on the table near the window. Someone sees him and swats at him with a broom before he has any chance to peck at the chips. I watch as he flies off into the night sky, wondering where he is headed.

wear her big brown fur coat made of coyote that she says her "daddy hunted and killed his self when we was down in Alabamy." Then she will take up all the space and oxygen in the room to tell us all about Jesus and how he saved her and how she "don't pa'ticipate in Saturday-night parties no mo, 'cause I done let all dat sinning go." She continues, "Yes, Lawd. I done seen da light, and da light is da man upstairs, Mr. Jesus Christ! You betta get right if you ain't, 'cause da rapture is a-comin'! You heah me?! Dis worl' gon' end befo' not too long." My mother will tell Ms. Jannie to save the preaching for church and just enjoy the food. I look up at the picture of Mr. Jesus Christ, who hangs over the stove now and not in the living room anymore. He always looks sad, with his hands resting in prayer in front of his chest and his eyes rolled up toward the heavens. I sometimes talk to him when I'm alone in the kitchen. I ask him what he thinks about our unruly family and what he thinks about people constantly praising him or constantly calling out his full name. Does it make him feel good even though he's no longer here? I wish more people would call me by my full name, Echo Unique Ladadrian Brown, instead of calling me "chile," "girl," or "Bébé's kid."

As the Sunday-morning breakfast rolls on, usually my father, who is always the last one up, will come shuffling into the kitchen still wearing one of his colorful velvet suits from the night before and say, "A'ight, Ms. Jannie, you got it," in recognition of Ms. Jannie's standing in the community. "How you feelin' dis mornin'?" he'll ask. Ms. Jannie responds that she's feeling better than how he looks. "Lookin' like you done been run ova by a truck dis mornin', Ed." She will ask him when he will be ready to give up sinning and get right with Jesus Christ. My father will smile to himself, give her a hug, and change the subject by commenting on the excellence of the food. "Dis bre'fast shole do look good dis mornin', Aprah. Thank you, darlin'." My mother's name is April, but everyone calls her Aprah. My father will then give my mother a kiss on the cheek, shifting the focus entirely away from his sinning. None of that happens this morning, however, because my father is not home. He left at eight, and none of us know where he went.

After my mother finishes cooking breakfast, Ms. Jannie, the most righteous among us, will lead us in prayer before we can eat. I hate when she starts her praying, because we never know how long it will last and I can smell the bacon the entire time. I peek out from underneath my eyelids to see if it looks like she's almost done, but she just keeps going and going and going, like the Energizer Bunny. She never runs out of words for her Lord. I mark that down in my observation notebook— how the adults always seem to have endless words in every situation, even when more words are not needed. Ms. Jannie continues with her never-ending prayer for what feels like forever. When I hear the word "finally," I know she's almost done. "And finally, Lawd, watch ova us. Clean us, Lawd. So many of us done gone astray. Bring us back in yo favor and grace. Bring us back. Tho we know da end of times may be upon us, restore all those who suffer ta health and good for-tune. In yo name I pray, amen."

We all rise as if on cue and eat our breakfast, which has almost gone cold. After we finish breakfast, we prepare to leave for church. Right as we are about to walk out the door, my father comes stumbling in drunk and shooting his cuss-word sentences everywhere.

"Goddammit, hell naw! Ain't nobody goin' no goddamn, motherfuckin' goddamn where! I got somethin' ta say." My mother immediately bristles and puts up her shell, but not her normal shell. Her combat shell, which means she is pre-paring to fight. My brothers and I are surprised since she never puts up her combat shell in front of righteous people like Ms. Jannie, but my mother has been on edge all morning. She has been nervous, agitated, and jittery. I wonder if it's because of what happened last night. I wonder if she has not fully returned to her normal self or if she is still stuck in the other realm,

where the procession in and out of the bathroom has finally concluded. Eventually, my mother gets up again and starts dancing in the middle of the room, alone this time. Someone puts on Marvin, her favorite, and dims the lights. She starts off slowly, winding and twisting her hips, pulling at the edges of her purple dress until it rides up her thighs and threatens to reveal the very round behind it is struggling to cover.

Everyone in the room is mostly quiet now. The bottles of Colt 45 are empty. The cards lie strewn about the table, some wrinkled, some folded. Two people are passed out on the couch. Another on the floor. My brothers and I are falling asleep but have managed to sit undetected in the corner of the room beside the couch the whole night. Two of my mother's friends see us at one point, but instead of giving up our secret location, they smile and sneak us a few pieces of candy and potato chips. We are supposed to be sleeping, and would get a whooping if our parents knew we were watching, so we are grateful for the candy-gifting mercy of my mother's friends.

My father and his friends watch my mother dance alone in the middle of the room while they take long, slow drawls from their cigars and cigarettes. Quincy leans over and tells my father, "You sho got yo'self a good woman. A damn good woman." My father nods and marvels at the sight of her. They focus all the attention in their brains on her body. None of them see

my mother grab a knife from the kitchen drawer suddenly and press it into my father's neck. Ms. Jannie recoils in shock and cries out, "Aprah! Now, come on, Aprah! Put dat knife down! Come on, Aprah, now! You don't wanna do this! Trust me, Aprah, I knows! You don't wanna do dis!" Ms. Jannie gathers all the kids in her big arms covered in coyote fur and pushes us behind her. Ms. Patty, who has a fear in her eyes I've never seen, runs to stand behind Ms. Jannie also, purple cup still securely in hand. I peek anxiously between Ms. Jannie's arms and legs at the events unfolding. Ms. Patty repeats everything Ms. Jannie says out of the shock of not knowing what else to do. "Our father who art in heaven.

Hallow' be thy name. Stop huh, Lawd. Stop huh!" Ms. Jannie prays loudly and Ms. Patty repeats.

I watch my father's skin fold and stretch unnaturally around the point of the knife. I watch the blood furtively slip out and run down the blade. First in drops, but eventually the drops combine to form a small red stream. "Ask him where he went last night afta da party, Ms. Jannie!" my mother shouts, enraged. "Ask 'im who he was wit'! I swear dese niggas is all da same. Ain't worth da spit on da bottom of yo goddamn shoe. You ain't shit, nigga, and ain't no reason why I shouldn't send yo black ass to meet yo maka right now. You know what I'm talkin' 'bout! You know exactly what

"I'm talkin' 'bout. C'mon, baby . . . Let's get it on," Marvin croons in the background. My brothers have fallen asleep, but I, like my father and his friends, can't stop watching. My mother is mesmerizing. She moves in perfect sync with Marvin's words. Her body glows brighter than anything else in the room, even the candles, which suddenly begin to flicker as if someone is trying to blow them out.

Marvin is on repeat. "Let's Get It On" starts again, but this time Marvin sounds like he is singing in slow motion. I look at my father to see if he notices. I wonder if it is my imagination, if I'm just sleepy, but Marvin slows down even more. His words become stretched out, and it sounds like he has a mouthful of cotton: "T h e r e ' s n o t h i n g w r o n g w i t h m e l o v i n g y o u . . ." I am afraid and astonished. I wake my brothers up. I want to know if they hear, but when I tell them the music is playing in slow motion, they rub their eyes in confusion. "Listen," I tell them. "Listen!" They look at me as if they don't understand. I sit up at full alert watching my mother

as she twists the knife farther into my father's throat and again demands he tell us what he did last night. "Tell 'em how much of a no-good dog you is, Ed! Where was you last night, huh? Afta da party?! Speak up, nigga! You ain't neva been quiet befo'! Tell 'em! Den we'a get on ta church and get ta prayin' and shoutin' and repentin' sins we gon' repeat soon as we step foot outside dat church. Now, go on 'head, nigga! Confess yo sins!" Everybody in the room

begins

to move in slow motion, including my father and his friends, until they freeze in space and time. My father's fingers are wrapped, unmoving, around the cigar in his mouth. I start to wonder if they are still breathing. I suddenly look to see that Dre and Rone are also freezing. I become terrified at the sight of my frozen brothers. I try to shake them, but their bodies are stiff and their eyes stare, glazed and unmoving straight ahead. Just like the night of the fire, time begins to wind itself down. My mother starts chanting something I've never heard before—"Habercito nyucatana sumacsinchi machainini . . . Cielo, cielo"—and crying out, "I'm so sorry, Mama! I'm so sorry! I didn't know, Mama! I didn't know! I'd take it all back if I could, trade myself fo you. I tole you I ain't want no girl chile, 'cause I know'd. I know'd she was gon' be one, too, but it don't do none a' us no good to be what we is. I don't want dat fo huh, Mama! I don't want it!" my mother cries out in distress. I look to see whom she is talking to, but everyone in the room is frozen except her and me.

Suddenly, she looks over toward me as if she is looking directly at me, but it's almost as though she is looking past me, way past me. I am still covered by the blanket, but I feel like she can see me. Her head starts to roll slowly up toward the ceiling. I follow her gaze and am shocked that the ceiling seems to have dissolved. I stare in disbelief at the dark space above. I've never seen anything like it. There are dazzling, shimmering specks of light that rain down periodically, stopping just at the top of the room, and there are puffy colorful clouds that float slowly across the space. I also hear some kind of noise that sounds like a thousand people humming quietly in the background.

I stare up, way up, the way I do when I'm conducting my observations outside, but I don't understand what I'm looking at. I'm completely hypnotized by the colors and the light. I try to turn my head and look back over at my mother, but I can't move my head or close my eyes. I see the specks of light start to wrap around one another, spiraling and spiraling until they form a light beam that streaks across the dark space and then down directly into my forehead. I feel a small jolt, as if something has been downloaded into my brain. There are no thoughts in my head. I am blank, like an empty piece of paper. Until a single thought comes: *Mrs. Samuels was wrong.*

Suddenly, a flood of other thoughts pours into my brain and my whole head is full of words, too many words, like Ms. Jannie's never-ending prayers. Words that I don't completely understand wash over me: *Your mother is a wizard. So are you. She can open a portal to the in-between, like the one you saw just now, when she's high on the white rocks. She does it to try to contact her mother. She doesn't want to be a wizard, because of what happened, what she did to her mother. You'll come to know what happened when the time is right. For now, don't worry. She will be a very difficult mother, but she loves you and your brothers more than life itself. You and they are her single purpose here. You cannot make miracles yet. Not until you realize the unbreakable. Don't worry, for now you'll forget all of this. Just keep watch for the birds: they are messengers. Keep watch.*

The third lesson of wizard training is that the in-between cannot be found or discovered. Instead, it reveals itself to unsuspecting wizards. It cannot be hoped, prayed, or called for the first time. You can only wait for the portal to finally open. Then, after first contact, you can grow to reach it at will. A wizard's path through life is greatly impacted by their relationship with the in-between, whether they choose to run from its immense power or whether they learn to cultivate it to better navigate the future. Each choice has consequences that ripple, ultimately determining if they will become a broken wizard or an enlightened one.

The spiral of light retracts, and when I open my eyes I see that the ceiling has returned but everyone else is still frozen.

I look back over at my mother in confusion, but she is still looking past me. I try to remember all the words that were just in my head, but they're falling out. I open my notebook to write down some of them before they're all gone. All I can remember is *birds*. I write it down and notice that my brothers, my father, and my parents' friends start slowly moving again, but my mother still looks suspended in the other realm. Her eyes are dull and glazed over, but the rest of her is glowing. All the light in the room bends toward her. She looks ethereal, like she is possessed

with fury and rage. The knife presses so deeply into my father's throat, I'm afraid she will pierce his windpipe. Suddenly, she drops the knife, which hits the floor with a disturbing *thunk*. We all watch as she whispers in my father's ear loud enough for everyone to hear, "If you eva go near dat bitch again, I'a kill you. I'a kill you dead, nigga. Afta ev'rythang I done fo you and dis family." She then looks sharply at Ms. Jannie and Ms. Patty and tells them to "stop all dat cryin' and prayin'. Wasn't y'all's prayin' or y'all's white Jesus dat saved dat nigga's life. It was dem kids and only dem kids. Now, let's get ta goin' befo' we miss da mornin' service."

LESSON 4

Stopping the Time

Pastor Aily preaches about the importance of fighting evil spirits in the morning service, but I barely hear anything he says. I'm too busy staring at Jessie, who sits on the side of the church with his mother and father. Jessie and I are both twelve years old now, but something about him has changed. He is no longer just a curly-haired kid who I've made fun of since we were in kindergarten. Now he towers over me, his voice has deepened, and his body has spread out in all the right directions. He is stunning. He looks like those models I always see in Calvin Klein commercials, with perfect eyes, hair, and lips. I think about kissing him all the time, like I see the girls do in all my favorite shows. But I'm not D.J. Tanner with pretty blond hair from *Full House*, or Laura Winslow with flawless skin from *Family Matters*, or Brandy with effortless popularity from *Moesha*. I like D.J. and Laura, but I'm obsessed with Brandy. She's the only black girl I ever see on TV who looks kind of like me. Hopefully Jessie thinks I look like her, too, instead of the beast I feel like I'm turning into. I have already figured out that my dark skin and nappy hair, which is chemically relaxed now, means I'm ugly. Not just regular ugly, but beastly. Untouchable. I have started to feel bad about the way I look, like very sad inside. I desperately wish I looked different. But even if I did, it wouldn't matter because Tiffany is still telling everyone that Jessie is her boyfriend. He always denies it, but it doesn't stop her from claiming him. I'm afraid of Tiffany, even though we still hang out sometimes. She is turning into a bully who takes what she wants. I don't want her to come after me, so I try to push Jessie out of my mind. But no matter what I do, I can't stop thinking about how much I want to press my lips on Jessie's.

After the service, everyone gathers on the front lawn of the church to release black balloons that have prayers and blessing cards inside. The prayers are supposed to float to people who need the blessings the most and in the process ward off evil spirits that may be surrounding them. It's a ceremony to celebrate Easter and the rising of our Lord and Savior, Jesus Christ. The balloons rise as Jesus did, with blessings and wisdom for anyone lucky enough to find one.

I grab two of the balloons, which are all loosely tied to a rail on the side lawn of the church, and hold them while waiting for the ceremony to begin. The balloons were supposed to be pink and white, but Davante's Black Panther parents bought all black balloons despite Pastor Aily's wishes. They stand to the far left, holding black balloons and smiling mischievously in their black clothes and sunglasses. They look like characters from a horror movie set in the hood. I look over at Davante, who holds his head down in embarrassment, and shake my head playfully at him when he finally looks up.

Pastor Aily begins reading from a small red book that has the words TIMELESS CHRISTIAN WISDOM written along the spine: "'And so, as a man soweth the seeds in the Earth, so he must sow the seeds of light in his own heart to prevent darkness from washing over him, and he must submerge himself in the holiest of waters to ensure his safe passage into the Kingdom of Heaven.'" I scan the crowd and see my mother by the rail, holding a black balloon while staring ahead blankly and smoking a cigarette. Per usual, she looks irritated with the pomp and circumstance of church rituals. My brothers, who are both bored, begin shadowboxing some of the balloons. Tiffany keeps trying to grab Jessie's hand, but he swats her away and comes to stand next to me. Ms. Patty, Ms. Jannie, and my father all stare obediently at Pastor Aily, nodding in prodigious agreement at everything he says. Pastor Aily finishes reading and shouts, "Rejoice!" We release our balloons and watch as they float up around the church. I stare up and watch as the smattering of black balloons scatter across the big, open blue sky. Everyone starts clapping and talking as the balloons float away.

I look up one more time and am surprised to see that one balloon is still lingering right above me. I suddenly feel paralyzed and very heavy, like my body weighs a thousand pounds. And I have a sinking feeling in my stomach, like everything is all wrong. I try to yell for others to look up at the lingering balloon, but it's hard for me to get my words out. "Hey!" I say, pinned in place and pointing to the sky in confusion. "Hey, look! That balloon isn't floating away!" A few people standing near me look up but don't see anything. One of them replies, "All da balloons is gone, girl. What's wrong wit' you?" My mother sees me standing there, pointing and frozen, and comes running across the church lawn toward me. She pulls my arm down and says, "Dat ain't no balloon. Now, be quiet! Don't look at it. Jus' hush up, you heah me? Hush!"

I look back up and realize she is right. It isn't a balloon. I keep staring and see that it looks like a black piece of thick lace fabric flying in the wind, or a spinning black Frisbee. As soon as I look back at it, I become paralyzed and transfixed again. "Why nobody else don't see it?" I ask my mother in confusion, even though she has told me to hush.

"Ain't nothin' dere, okay? You don't see nothin,' you heah me? Now, go on up to da field wit Jessie and yo brothas and dem, and play kickball or sumthin'. Don't worry 'bout dis. I'a see y'all when you get home lata."

I try to ask her more questions, but she dismissively waves me away, turns her back, and starts talking to Ms. Patty and Ms. Jannie.

Jessie suddenly grabs my hand, jerking me along as we both run toward the field. Tiffany, Dre, Rone, and Davante chase after us. We all stop at home first to change clothes, and then meet at the penny candy store, where we buy an assortment of Jolly Ranchers, Tootsie Rolls, bubble gum, lollipops, and gummy bears. We stuff the candy in our pockets and continue running until we reach the big open field near the train tracks.

Once we get there, we sprawl out in the prickly dead grass and begin spiraling our prayers. I don't know if our prayers vibrate the quantum field like my mother's do, but we spiral prayers anyways for all kinds of things, including new cars, new clothes, more money, and bigger houses. We each claim cars as they drive up and down the street. "That's my car," Rone shouts at a shiny red Cadillac slowly cruising down the street, blasting "Gin and Juice" by Snoop Dogg. "I'm going to LA when I grow up and I'ma buy a big house by the ocean," Rone says confidently. "And I'ma be the best rapper alive, just like Tupac. And," he continues, "I'ma be a pilot."

"A rapper-pilot? Nigga, dat's dope," Jessie chimes in while fist-bumping Rone.

I ask Rone where he will get the money to do all that. He says he doesn't know, but he's going to park his plane right in his driveway. I tell him I don't think you can park planes in a driveway.

"Where you park 'em, den?" he asks.

"At the airport, I guess."

Outside the unrelenting gaze of our parents, the field is the only place where we feel free to dream and talk about whatever we want. There used to be an old textile factory here before they tore it down. Now there's only the vast, empty field enclosed by a rusted fence with several gaping holes, which we crawl through to enter. I wish there were some trees to help shield us from the sun, but there aren't, so on hot summer days we bake like potato chips. There are no trees, but there is tons of trash scattered all across the field, including broken bottles, crack needles, and bags full of dirty old clothes and random objects that someone has thrown out. We search through the bags to see if we can find anything valuable. We never do. It's all worthless stuff that nobody wants, including us.

After we are done spiraling prayers and looking through discarded items (and there are new items every week), we start asking each other all the questions we can think of: How many black people you think is in the world? "Like eight billion, I guess." Who you like more: Tupac or Biggie Smalls? "Man, definitely Tupac. He da best dat eva did it." What you think da aliens be doin' up dere all day? "Shit, chillin', watchin' space TV, or some shit like dat, I guess." Where you think we goin' when we die? "To heaven." What you think people be doin' ova in da otha countries? "I'on' know, but I hope I get to go to another country one day."

On some days, like today, we gather up all the stray dogs in the neighborhood after we leave the penny candy store and go searching through garbage pails on the sides of people's houses for scraps of food. Right now, there are only nine stray dogs in our neighborhood. There were thirteen two months ago, but we don't know what happened to the other four. When there aren't many scraps in the garbage pails, we collect discarded pop cans and pieces of scrap metal that we find scattered around the neighborhood and take them to the scrap-yard down the street. The scrap man, named Mr. Jimmie James, is always dressed in a navy-blue jumpsuit and has a half-smoked cigar hanging out of his mouth. Whenever he sees us coming, he always says, "Here comes Bébé's kids and da little Mexican boy."

Even though everyone knows Jessie is mixed with black and white, people still regularly call him the little Mexican, little Hispanic, or little Indian boy to highlight the racial ambiguity of his features. Davante, who is secretly jealous of Jessie's light skin and curly hair and all the attention he constantly receives, despite his Black Panther upbringing, always teases Jessie for "not being a real black person." Davante's parents have convinced him that light-skinned people are not "real" black people. Davante and Jessie constantly get in arguments that mostly center around Davante questioning Jessie's blackness:

"What you know about rap music, boy? Light-skinned niggas cain't undastand or relate to da music of da struggle."

"Nigga, er'body always complimentin' you, which means you on' know how hard life really is."

"Man, if I looked like you or at least had good hair, bet my life would be ten times better than it is right now. Prolly wouldn't be stopped by da cops all da time, even though I ain't doin' nothin' wrong. Prolly wouldn't have my teachers tryna put me in special ed all da time. And prolly would be in the Gifted and Talented Program wit' you and Echo."

Davante's questioning of Jessie pushes him to the edge,

and he finally snaps one day, aggressively barking at Davante, "Nigga, fuck you! I'm jus' as black as you! Bet you I'm black where it counts, nigga!" Jessie points to his pants and everyone laughs, but I can tell he is really upset, more upset than usual.

And I can tell Jessie is really upset when he responds to Mr. Jimmie James, "I ain't Mexican, Mr. Jimmie, and I don't speak no Spanish. *No hablo español*, okay?" he says in frustration.

"Sounds like *español* ta me, José," Mr. Jimmie James says mockingly, further irritating Jessie. He then pats each one of us on the head, including Jessie, and asks if we are doing well in school. "Y'all betta stay in school so y'all don't end up in a scrapyard like me. Ecka and da lil Mexican boy is ova dere at dat white school, so I know they gon' be jus' fine. I'on' know about the rest of y'all lil Negroes. Betta say yo prayers, 'cause you cain't make it nowhere in dis world witout dem honkies," he says, laughing wryly to himself. When he notices the looks of disappointment on Davante's, Tiffany's, Dre's, and Rone's faces, he quickly changes his tone and tries to smooth over the low expectations buried in his words. "Hey, anythang is possible, right? Jus' keep believin' in yo'self, and it'll all work out. Jimmie believe in ya. Jimmie luv da kids." But the damage has been done. The seed has been planted, and I watch as it takes root in their minds. I watch as it sinks in that, somehow, we are not all on the same path. Somehow, though we started in the same place, we are heading in different directions.

Rone and Dre are only eleven and ten, but they are already falling apart and starting to spin the same webs of chaos as our parents. They regularly get into fights, skip school, and smoke cigarettes. They are both in the special education program for kids with learning disabilities at the black school on the East Side, which is one of the worst schools in the district. It's run-down and looks like an old factory or juvenile detention center, which it probably was at one point. The black school doesn't have new books or computers like my school, nor does it have enough teachers, so there are usually thirty to forty students per class. The mayor says, "That school is a disaster that needs to be repaired and restored immediately, but the city is broke and who pays the price for an inadequate education? You guessed it, the students."

I try to think of ways to get Dre and Rone to follow me, to understand that what they do now will affect the trajectory of their lives, but they cannot seem to connect their current actions to their future realities. I don't understand everything, either, but I know there will come a time when we are all adults, when I won't recognize them. When their self-destruction will conclude in tragedy. I can't yet imagine the pain that will befall my brothers: the long stints in prison, addiction to the white rocks, schizophrenia, intense bouts of depression, and suicide attempts. I still have hope that something will come along and return things to how they used to be when we didn't understand the brutality of the conditions around us.

I think about how just two or three years ago, we all were

still innocent. We created whole worlds in our imaginations out of everything we found. We held hands and sang together while walking down the street, usually singing along to "Billie Jean" or the theme song from *Fresh Prince of Bel-Air*. We were free. We were unlimited. We didn't yet know or understand race and class and all the intersections between them, so we were not yet black, at least not on the inside. Our psyches were still free from the troubles of the world. We reached our tiny hands up toward the sky, trying to imagine what was up there, beyond the blue part. "Where you think we go when we die?" we asked each other curiously. "You think we go up there? You think we turn into aliens?" We dissolved into the sky and all the mystery it hides.

But it's not like that anymore. We are not like that anymore. My brothers are no longer children, and they're already trapped in a school system that is failing them, just like the mayor says.

In contrast, the white school on the West Side has state-of-the-art facilities, all the books you could ever want to read, a pool, and the best playground in the district. I wish we could all go to the white school. I glance over at Rone, Dre, Jessie, Tiffany, and Davante laughing hysterically while bouncing up the sidewalk, with the nine stray dogs following closely behind. I'm sad that one day it won't be like this. When we get older, we'll all be in different places.

We use the ten dollars Mr. Jimmie James gives us to buy two large bags of dog kibble. We walk the kibble and the nine dogs several blocks to the open field. Ms. Patty, watching from her porch, says we look like "the little black-ass cousins of Shaka Zulu walking all dem damn dogs up and down the street like dat." She says we belong on an African prairie or in the jungle somewhere with the rest of the wild, badass kids. We don't care what she says. We know it is our duty to look after these dogs. Otherwise they might all starve to death and that would be terrible.

When we get to the field, we pour both bags of dog food into the grass and watch the dogs gobble and gobble until it's all gone. By the time the sun starts going down, none of us want to leave the field. We know we have to be home before dark, but we linger until the last drop of light leaves the sky. The dogs scurry and roll around, gobbling up any remaining kibbles that lie scattered in the grass.

Jessie and I are standing in a small wooden shack, watching the sun go down, as Tiffany, Davante, and my brothers play fetch with the dogs. The shack used to be some kind of watch post for the old textile factory. All the windows have been busted out and the wood is deteriorated. There are beer cans, used condoms, and crack needles strewn about on the floor. We kick the needles out of the way and lean against one of the walls. I watch as the sun starts to make its final descent, just behind the bridge. I think about the black Frisbee thing I saw in the sky earlier and try to avoid looking at Jessie since we are standing shoulder to shoulder right next to each other. I feel awkward and tingly inside standing so close to him.

I am very aware of his body, which I have been watching

all day. He is wearing a sleeveless white undershirt, and I enjoy watching his muscles flex every time he moves. I continue staring out of the busted window frames while shifting my shoulders nervously from side to side. Jessie seems nervous also and joins me in staring out the window.

"Hey, what you was pointin' at dis mornin' at da church? I seen you pointin', but ain't see nothin' up in da sky."

I look over at Jessie and say, "I don't really know what it was, but it wasn't no balloon."

Jessie turns his body toward me and says, "Hmph, maybe it was a bird or sum'in' like dat."

As soon as he says the word "bird" I am transported, sucked back in time. Words that I don't recognize start rolling through my mind: *Your mother is a wizard and so are you. Keep watch and start your miracles. Your mother can't help right now. She will remain difficult until she rectifies the past. Beware of her rage. A wizard with unresolved rage will keep unleashing terror*

into our tiny bodies. I wonder what could make a person this angry. All we did was try to get rid of the roaches, which are taking over the apartment, and now my mother and father are whooping us like slaves on the TV show *Roots*. My mother raises and lands the belt decisively against our bare arms and legs several times. Then she gives the belt to my father, who does not hit us as hard as my mother does, even though he's stronger than her. It's an act of mercy on his part. They take turns hitting us with the belt, and while one whoops, the other smokes a cigarette. This whooping is worse than usual because we accidentally set the carpet in our bedroom on fire while trying to burn the roaches. Both our parents come running when they smell smoke. It reminds them of that night, the night they almost let their three children burn to death. My father throws one of the blankets over the fire and stomps it out. My mother says in the calmest, coolest voice, "Go get a belt," and then the whooping starts.

Rone and I have learned how to put our shells up immediately when a whooping starts. We shut down our emotions like we have been taught. I try to think about happy memories like Christmas three years ago when we got all the presents we wanted, thanks again to our mother's miracles. I picture her walking through the door with a bagful of gifts. We squeal and scream like we have just won cars on Oprah's TV show. "*You* get a present! And *you* get a present! And *you* get a present! *Everybody* gets a present!" Dre, Rone, and I jump around in a circle, smiling and giggling, giddy with a glee that only young children feel. We haven't had a Christmas like that since then. Now our parents spend all their money on Colt 45s and the white rocks. Instead of presents, for the past two years they have hung white envelopes, each containing a crisp one-dollar bill, on the Christmas tree. They can't bear to watch us open the envelopes, so we open them in our rooms. Before we open the envelopes, we spiral prayers and hope there is at least fifty or a hundred dollars in the envelope, not a dollar, but it's always just a dollar.

I can feel blood running down my legs now. I guess the

skin has finally broken. The goal is not to break our skin, but to break our shells, shells they have taught us to build. It's a wicked kind of irony. The longer we keep our shells up, the longer they whoop us, until they finally break us. But I am determined not to break this time.

Dre is watching and crying already. He knows he will be next. But he is so soft. His eyes and heart are always so soft, begging for love. He is still too young. He hasn't learned how to build a good shell yet. So it is especially cruel to watch him get a whooping. His is always the shortest. My father can never give him more than five or six lashes. I wonder why they can't see how they are destroying him. He is so soft. The damage will never be repaired. They are trying to make him strong. Prepare him for the whoopings the world will give him, but they are destroying him, too. I spiral prayers for Dre, that he might be spared. I keep my shell up for as long as I can to absorb most of the impact of their rage for his sake. I turn away from his sobbing face and instead think of all the times I've seen him smiling, laughing, running

in wide, gaping circles around the shack where Jessie and I are now pressed firmly against each other. Tiffany, Rone, and Davante all join Dre playing while the dogs wallow in the dry, brittle grass. I try not to look into Jessie's eyes out of fear he will see the beast inside me and run away. The highlights of his skin are illuminated by the setting sun, making him glow like a high-yellow Mexican god. The entire scene reminds me of an impressionist painting, which we learn about in school: warm, alive, and colorful. I could have stood there silently in Jessie's arms forever, but he suddenly starts speaking.

"Maybe it was God dat you saw up dere in da sky earlier today? Maybe God *is* black like Davante parents be sayin'."

I don't respond. I am mesmerized by the Vincent van Gogh moment unfolding around us and still thinking about the words that were just rolling through my mind. *Your mother is a wizard and so are you. Keep watch and start your miracles.* What does it mean? Why am I suddenly receiving messages?

Jessie interrupts my train of thought and asks, "Why you get quiet all of a sudden? What you thinkin' 'bout?"

I don't want him to think I'm a freak, so I smile nervously while trying to think of something to say. I open my mouth to speak, but I'm so overwhelmed, no words come out. I'm embarrassed and want to go home and hide in my room, but Jessie keeps holding me tightly. "It's cool. Girls be quiet sometime. My mother and sister be like dat, where dey jus' stop talkin', like for hours. I'on' be knowin' what to do, so I just leave 'em alone till dey start talkin' again. Y'all girls be confusin' sometimes." Jessie laughs to himself.

I smile, but feel increasingly awkward. When I still don't say anything, Jessie starts speaking again, but in a much softer voice.

"Ey, you know what I was thinkin' 'bout da otha day? 'Bout how when we was kids, we use'ta spin around on dat magic carpet and make all dem wishes. Man, ain't hardly none a' my wishes came true, doe. I'm still in da same house, ain't got no money, and my momma and daddy still fightin' all da time . . . I be wishin' life could be like it was den, befo' all da pain and stuff started, you know? Like when we still believed in magic and Santa Claus and da tooth fairy and dat magic carpet . . . Mrs. Jackson-Randolph knew all dat stuff about magic wasn't true, but she still made us believe in it. I be missin' her some-times . . . You know what else I use'ta wish for, doe, on dat magic carpet?"

Jessie whispers to me in a barely audible voice. He is pressed so firmly against me, I can smell the Laffy Taffy and Jolly Rancher on his breath. There is so much conflict-ing energy coursing through my body, I feel like I'm going to explode. I want to scream with joy, fear, and confusion, but I manage to contain myself.

My shell drops partially and I soften. I am glowing. I know Jessie can see it, because he starts smiling. I have never been looked at like this before. It is the most intense, amazing, warm, enveloping smile I've ever seen. I look down. I look around. I look at my brothers. I look anywhere to try to avoid the radiance of his smile. I feel exposed. I haven't been exposed in so long. I try to put my shell back up, but I am increasingly disarmed. I like how it feels to be disarmed, how it feels to touch another human. I realize the paradox of the shell: that it keeps out all the bad stuff, but it also keeps out all the good stuff. Jessie drops his shell also and I notice he looks different now. Softer. Warmer. But also on fire. He is burning somehow, and I am overcome by the heat.

"When we was kids, on dat magic carpet, I use'ta wish dat

I could kiss you," he says finally after just staring and smiling at me.

My shell

shatters totally and I start screaming at the top of my lungs for them to "stop it! Stop it, please! We won't burn any more roaches!"

Rone, who always follows me, joins in and begins screaming at our parents to stop whooping Dre. All three of us are crying now. Rone and I pull Dre away from our parents and throw our bodies around him. We transform ourselves into a titanium shelter and absorb all the blows on our backs. Rone and I don't care about our pain anymore, but we cannot watch the decimation of our little brother any longer. Now I understand what Mr. Casey meant when he said, "Children are the bravest of all." We would have died, Rone and me, to save Dre. Our parents realize this. They see that we have grown in power, that they can't break us like they used to. *I am unbreakable*, I think to myself. *I am unbreakable*, I repeat over and over, until suddenly, just like on the night of the spades game, time starts to slow down. I watch as my father's arm moves slower and slower until it is suspended in midair, belt in hand. Dre and Rone, who are both pinned underneath me, stop squirming and freeze. Only my mother and I are not frozen.

I stand up, with tears running down my face and my shirt stained with blood, and ask her what's happening.

My mother looks panicked and starts saying, "Aw no, no,

no! Ecka, you got to turn away from dis. It don't brang nothin' but trouble."

I look at my mother in confusion and ask her what she's talking about. She drops to her knees and grabs the sides of my arms and starts shaking me. I've never seen such a look of desperation in my mother's eyes. They bulge out of their sockets, and all the blood vessels swell and pop. I feel myself grow increasingly afraid.

"Listen, baby, you stopped da time just now. You just didn't know it. It happn'd 'cause you done realized the unbreakable, that you cain't be broken, no matter what. It's da first thang dat happens when you ready ta become a wizard. Dat, and you start seein' thangs otha people don't see, like dat thang you saw in da sky da otha day, da black veil. Dat veil start comin' 'round when you start to feel bad inside. I'on' know why ya feelin' like dat, but we got to fix it and get rid of it. But listen to me: You ain't gon' be no wizard! You heah me? Don't nothin' but bad thangs happ'n when dat kinda power get inside ya. It can make you do thangs you don't wanna do. Dat's how I ended up hurtin' my mama. Dat's how I ended up killin' huh. I killed huh! You hear me?! I killed huh! I didn't mean to, but I did, and it done ruined me and I don't want you to be ruined, okay, baby? Jus' trust me. You got ta turn away from dis." The time starts unfreezing, and she starts speaking faster, so fast she stumbles over her words.

I stare directly into my mother's despairing, bulging eyes in disbelief. "You killed your own mother?" I say slowly. "But why would you do somethin' like dat?"

I wait for an answer, but she closes her eyes and stops speaking.

The fourth lesson of wizard training is learning to stop the time. Once a wizard realizes they are unbreakable, their ability to perform miracles is unlocked. The first step to performing a miracle is stopping the time, since all miracles occur outside of space and time—in another realm of reality. Miracles happen in this world, but they originate in the in-between, like how rain is made in the clouds before eventually falling to the earth.

My father, Dre, and Rone all unfreeze. Dre and Rone start squirming and wincing, until they realize they are no longer being hit. My father asks my mother, who is still on her knees with her eyes closed, what's she doing down on the floor. "Put dat belt down," my mother responds. "It's finished. It done started. Lawd, it done started and we brought it down on huh." My father looks at my mother in confusion. Only I know what she's talking about. We all get up off the floor. My brothers wipe the tears off their cheeks and

start running closer to the shack, screaming at the top of their lungs: "Jessie and Echo sitting in a shack. K-I-S-S-I-N-G." They laugh out loud and run in circles around us. Tiffany, who is not laughing but scowling, starts throwing rocks at the shack. I can see the glowing rage in her eyes. When one of the rocks narrowly misses my head, Jessie releases me, un-kissed, and chases all of them far into the distance toward the train tracks.

LESSON 5

Unburying Yourself

I tiptoe around my mother, observing her cautiously from the corner of my eyes. I ask my father if he knew my mother killed her own mother.

"Yeah, I know'd," he says. "Everybody knows, but don't nobody talk about it. She ain't neva got ova it. Dat's why she crazy as hell. Best if you don't ask huh nothin' 'bout it, neitha. Jus' don't worry 'bout it. She ain't killed nobody else, fuh as I know." He chuckles to himself as if this is funny. I stare at him stone-faced until he stops chuckling. I don't tell my brothers, Jessie, Tiffany, or Davante about my mother. I don't want them to know. I'm embarrassed to have a mother who killed her own mother. I don't understand. I don't know how to make sense of it. I always knew my mother was harsh, but I didn't know she was capable of something like that. I try to push it out of my mind, make up stories about why she might have done it: Maybe her mother was abusive, maybe her mother was trying to kill her, maybe her mother was a very bad person. I choose the third story and stick to it. *My mother's mother must have been a very bad person*, I tell myself over and over.

My mother says baptism will stop me from becoming a wizard. It will somehow change the direction of my energy and turn me toward the light of the Lord. Even though my mother has always been anti-religion, anti-church, and anti-God, I don't question her sudden insistence on me being baptized. I'm too afraid of her to question anything she says. If I defy her and become a wizard, will she kill me, too? And if becoming a wizard makes you do bad things, I don't want to become a wizard anyway. I don't tell anyone, even my brothers, about me being a wizard and stopping the time, so that nothing bad happens to them.

I begin attending Bible study every Tuesday and Thursday. I follow Ms. Jannie all around the church, watching her tidy and straighten things before eventually setting up the Bible study classroom. Ms. Jannie seems very sure of herself and at peace, so maybe it's not such a bad thing to become religious and proud like her.

"My mother says I have to get baptized, like you, as soon as possible," I tell Ms. Jannie.

"Yo momma? Ms. Aprah-ain't-believed-in-God-since-I-don't-know-when tole you ta get baptized? Well, I guess hell done froze ova and dese really is da end a' times. Dat's very interestin', ain't it? Yo momma wantin' you to be baptized?"

I don't know how to answer her, so I just stare in silence.

"Well, what's mo impo'tant is dat you be ready to turn yo'self ova to da Lawd. Dis not 'bout playin' no games, and it's a lifetime commitment. Once you get baptized, you become a servant of Mr. Jesus Christ. Is dat what you want fo yo'self?"

Again, I don't know how to answer her, since I'm unsure I want to be a servant of Mr. Jesus Christ. I stare at her in silence before placidly nodding my head. "Yes."

Ms. Jannie is delighted I have "taken such a keen interest in da Lawd" and immediately takes me under her wing. Every time I walk into the church, she smiles with her big ham-hock teeth and gives me a bear hug, covering my entire body in the smell of her old-lady perfume.

Eventually, I meet all the deacons and Bible study teachers and try to force myself to pay keen attention, like I do in school, but it's hard because I don't believe everything they are saying. I wonder if this is how my brothers feel in school. If they don't believe what the teachers are saying, do they mentally check out? For example, the more the Bible study teachers tell me about hell, the less I believe it's true. Why would a loving, merciful God damn most of the people on the planet to hell for eternity even though he made them that way? Why would he make so many Muslims and Buddhists and other people who aren't Christians just to send them all to hell? I want to ask the Bible study teacher, but I can tell these kinds of questions are not allowed.

My favorite part of coming to church is the bologna-and-cheese sandwiches. The sandwiches have usually been sitting out for hours, which means they are warm and slightly soggy, just how I like them. The mayonnaise and yellow American cheese meld seamlessly and dissolve instantly in my mouth.

I think about those sandwiches throughout the entire class. The Bible study teacher says we are only allowed to have one sandwich each after class, but I secretly eat two or three every time, which means there usually isn't enough for everyone, prompting the Bible study teacher to scold the entire class for our "shameful dishonesty and wickedness."

"Remember, the Lord is always watching," she says, scowling.

I feel guilty when she says the Lord is watching, but I plan to repent all my sins after my baptism.

The biggest sin I plan to repent is having sex with Jessie outside of marriage. Jessie and I haven't even kissed yet, but ever since that day in the shack, I can't stop thinking about what it would be like to have sex with him. I don't even really know what happens during sex, but I remember how good it felt to touch him, and remember the warm, tingling sensations in my underwear, which happen every time I think about him. Jessie and I have both avoided getting too close again, out of fear of what comes next. So now we just smile and hit each other playfully, but I know it's only a matter of time before we stand close to each other again.

They talk a lot in Bible study about how bad sex is. The Bible school teacher says we can get pregnant or get diseases from having sex. I wonder if Jessie thinks about having sex with me, even though I'm ugly, which I've figured out with certainty now. I don't have big breasts or a nice round behind, like the girls in rap videos. My skin is too dark (I really hate how dark it is), and my hair is short, brittle, and broken from the constant relaxing. I look like a beast. *Men don't want to sleep with beasts*, I think to myself. Once Jessie figures out that I'm a beast, I know he'll stop liking me. I hope he doesn't figure it out anytime soon. And I hope my baptism will allow me to repent all the "unholy and impure" thoughts and fantasies I've already had about him.

- – — ——o○o—— — – -

On the day of my baptism, three crows circle above the church lawn. My mother sees them and bristles. She doesn't say anything, but I watch her glance up nervously as we enter the church.

"Well, it's mighty fine to see you in da church on a mornin' otha dan Sunday, Ms. Aprah. How you been doin'?" Pastor Aily says while warmly placing a hand on my mother's back.

"Oh, well, you know, I'm survivin', Pastor, but then ain't we all?"

"Yes, Lawd, ain't we all. Some of us a lil better than others wit' da hep of da Lord," he says jovially.

My mother rolls her eyes and heads to sit in one of the pews in the back of the church.

"Now, you don't have to sit all da way back dere, Aprah. You can come on up to da front wit' da rest of us. Everyone is welcome, even nonbelievers such as yo'self," Pastor Aily shouts to my mother.

"Naw, naw, I'm awright. Don't worry 'bout me. I'a be jus' fine back here."

There are six people at my baptism: Ms. Jannie; my mother; Pastor Aily; the Bible study teacher; Mrs. Dorothy Althea, the church pianist; and the deacon, who will dip me under the water when Pastor Aily tells him. Mrs. Althea begins playing the piano on the side of the room and singing a gospel song called "Come to Jesus." We all bow our heads and hold our hands in prayer while she sings. Mrs. Althea has a beautiful voice that reaches out and grabs you by the heart when you least expect it. We are all in tears before she finishes the song, due to the emotion and spirit she infuses into every note. We clap as Pastor Aily stands and makes his way to the front of the church.

The fluidity of Pastor Aily's movements, combined with his stature and very round body, gives the appearance that he is not walking but rolling everywhere. I can't help but giggle while he walks. Ms. Jannie sees me giggling and shoots a sharp look in my direction, silencing my laughter and forcing me to return to the seriousness of the moment. I am wearing a black one-piece bathing suit beneath a robe. I look down at my skinny frame and wish it were more filled in, like my mother's. My hair is covered with a black swimming cap to protect it from getting wet, but it doesn't matter whether I wear the cap or not. My hair looks awful either way.

Pastor Aily and the deacon stand in front of the circular tub full of tepid water that I wish was warmer. I test it beforehand, when no one is looking, and decide it's too cold. Secretly, I would just like to take a nice long bath and relax, but I know this won't be anything like a bath. Ms. Jannie tells me to kneel before the pastor and the deacon, and I comply. My mother jumps up and protests, saying her daughter "will not kneel before no man."

Pastor Aily scolds my mother again and says, "Aprah, Aprah, please relax in the house of the Lord. You have chosen your path; let this sweet girl choose hers."

My mother bristles and raises her combat shell. "Why y'all church niggas gots to be so damn uppity? How you know what path I'm on? Don't talk to me like I'm da devil walkin' da earth. Did you fo'get I'm da reason she in here gettin' baptized in da first place, Pastor?" She stresses the *P* and stretches out the *a* to mock the Pastor so it sounds like *Paaastor*.

Pastor Aily softens and agrees to let me sit on the bench with Ms. Jannie and Mrs. Althea instead of kneeling while my mother fumes in the back of the church. Pastor Aily bows his head, takes a deep breath, murmurs something to himself, and then opens his black Bible, which is frosted with gold paint on the sides. He begins, "Galatians chapter five, verse seventeen: 'For the flesh sets its desire against the Spirit, and the Spirit against the flesh; for these are in opposition to one another, so that you may not do the things that you please.'"

As soon as he says the word "flesh," the tingling sensations start and I am transported. I feel like some part of me leaves my body, my own flesh still sitting there with Pastor Aily and his deacon, but I am not there, my mind has gone somewhere else. I am lying in my bed with Jessie. We are looking into each other's eyes. He tells me I'm the prettiest girl he ever saw and he can't stop looking at me. I stare deeply into his dark brown irises. I want to lose myself in them. I tell him about the warm tingling, and he tells me he can help me with that. I ask him how, and he starts to run his hand slowly down my stomach toward the tingling. The closer he gets, the faster and louder I start to breathe until I hear Pastor Aily shout:

"Are you all right, girl? What's going on? Why are you breathing like that?"

I tell Pastor Aily I'm just nervous and I don't know how to swim and what if I drown in that pool that is supposed to set my soul free. I ask, "If I drown, will it still count as a baptism and will my soul still be set free?"

Pastor Aily looks bewildered at my question. I am bewildered I asked, but I can't tell him what I was thinking about while he was reading from the Bible.

"I won't let you drown," Pastor Aily says assuredly. "Just take a deep breath, relax, and bow your head while I finish reading the necessary verses.

"Now, where was I? Oh, yes, here . . . 'For the one who sows to his own flesh will from the flesh reap corruption, but the one who sows to the Spirit will from the Spirit reap eternal life.'" The tingling starts again when I hear the word "flesh," and I am back with Jessie. He pushes his hand down into my underwear. I try not to breathe fast or loud, so that Pastor Aily won't know, but it's hard to hold my breath in. Jessie starts rubbing me down there. I haven't been touched like that since I was seven years old by the man down the street who takes me to his house when my mother isn't looking.

That's when I learn about the tingling sensations, at seven, from the man who also rubbed me down there. I am confused at the time. It feels good and it feels bad all at once. At seven, I don't understand how that is possible. The man whispers to me while he rubs me, "I like your pretty little flesh," over and over. He smells like alcohol and musk and the whiskers of his beard graze my face every time he whispers into my ear. I ask him what the word "flesh" means, but he tells me not to worry about that and to just lie back and relax.

Sitting now on the edge of the tub in church, having moved from the front pew at the command of Pastor Aily, I still don't know what the word "flesh" means, but it has power over me. The deacon helps me take off my robe, tells me to relax, and then dips me back into the lukewarm, but too-cold water. I hear Pastor Aily say, "Relax your body," but instead of "body," I hear the word "flesh" again. As soon as I am submerged under the water, I begin flailing and splashing. Suddenly, Jessie turns into the flesh man down the street and we are outside and not in my bedroom anymore. I run away from him and tell him to stop. I tell him to bring Jessie back, that only Jessie can touch me like that. I scream at the top of my lungs, "Leave me alone!" I turn around, stop stark in the middle of the sidewalk, and try to direct all the energy in my body toward him. I put my hands up in front of me, palms facing him, as if lightning will come shooting out of my hands. I scream one more time for him to leave me alone. I watch in shock as a car suddenly comes barreling up on the sidewalk, striking him from behind. I whip my head up toward the sky and watch as he floats way up in the sky, far,

far away from me. When he finally falls back to the earth and lands on the ground with a disturbing *thud*, I run over to him and am surprised by what I see. I cover my mouth with both hands in shock as Jessie's lifeless eyes stare back up at me. I shake my head in disbelief and scream, "No, no, no!"

When I open my eyes, I am still submerged. I have stopped flailing and screaming now, but I hold myself underwater at the shock of what I have seen. The deacon tries to pull me out while shouting, "It's ova now! Come on now, girl! You can get out!" When he is unable to pull me out alone, Pastor Aily, my mother, and Ms. Jannie all come running and forcefully pull me from the tub. Everyone looks stunned. My mother wraps me in a towel and drops to her knees. "Ecka, baby, what happn'd? What you kept yellin' fo? What you mean stop touching you? Did sumthin' happen to you, baby? Ecka, look at me and tell me what you mean by 'stop touching me'?" I don't say anything to my mother, but she reads the terror in my eyes and she knows. She grabs my hand and yanks me forward before eventually pulling me out of the church, dripping wet, wearing only a swimsuit and wrapped in a towel. Pastor Aily, the deacon, the Bible study teacher, Mrs. Althea, and Ms. Jannie all stand and stare, mouths agape, not having words or biblical verses to mask the shock of the moment.

— — — ——o○o—— — — —

When we get home, I sit quietly in a chair at the kitchen table while my mother paces angrily back and forth, calling all her friends and cussing and crying. "Lord I'ma kill 'im. Naw, I ain't gon' calm down, Regina! Ain't no way ta protect a girl chile in this world. Jus' ain't no way! I swore on my soul dis wann't never gon' happ'n to huh. And look it done happened right under my goddamn nose. I'ma kill 'im, I swear 'fo God!" She is so angry, she goes outside and paces the length of the driveway while shouting into the phone.

I sit alone at the kitchen table, trying to figure it all out. Trying to understand. I stare up at the picture of Jesus hanging over the stove. I am shocked to see that he has somehow changed positions. Instead of his normal hands-in-prayer, head-rolled-up position, now his arms extend out in front of him and he stares down compassionately as if he's looking right at me. I rub my eyes, but when I look up, he's still in his new celestial position. I wonder how much stranger this day will get. I stare at new Jesus and blur everything else out. I ask Jesus when he's coming back to save us from all this chaos and tell him how much I wish he was real because I need a Savior to help get me through all of this. I will Jesus to wake up, to uncurl from his celestial position and live up to all the stories they tell about him in church, but he doesn't.

I push everything that happened out of my mind, including the vision of Jessie being hit by a car. I would never want that to be true, not in a million years. Not in a billion, trillion years. I decide I won't tell Jessie what I saw. I won't ever speak of it, so it never comes true. I merge into a hazy filter that softens the entire room and the sound of my mother's voice from outside. If my life were a movie, we would be in a dream sequence surrounded by white haze, with the volume of my mother steadily turned down until you couldn't hear her at all. Then the camera would focus on me, sitting in sadness at the kitchen table in a white towel and a black swim cap with my hands clasped on my lap, eyes closed, trying to make it all go away, trying to bury it again. I thought I had buried the pain so far down that it would never come back.

The fifth lesson of wizard training is everything you have buried inside will rise from the dead one day. Nothing can stop you from bleeding over into the corridors of your own flesh. Everything must eventually exist in the light. You cannot become an enlightened wizard until you exorcise your demons.

Now I understand why my mother is always on the verge of collapse, why she is always suspended in a state of destruction rather than transformation. She has left too much buried. She has refused to release her pain and face herself. This whole time she has been trying to liberate a graveyard, but not even a quantum wizard has the power to do that.

Evading the Black Veil

And not even a quantum wizard can change what has really happened to Jessie. Tiffany is standing in my kitchen, speaking in slow motion. I don't know if she is really speaking slowly or if I'm imagining it, but as soon as she says, "Jessie's in the hospital," everything stops and the hazy filter bursts. It all bursts. Tiffany's tears fall out everywhere. All over the kitchen floor. I have never seen her like this. I have never seen her cry. Not even after Mrs. Jackson-Randolph pulled us from the water. I couldn't stop crying after Mrs. Jackson-Randolph saved me, but Tiffany just sat stone-faced, staring at the same water that almost drowned her. She could not cry for her own life, even then, but she is weeping now for Jessie's. We all love Jessie, especially her. Especially me. Tears pour out of my eyes also, even though I don't make a sound. I just stare at her with streams of tears gushing down my face while she yells, "He cain't die! He cain't die, Echo!"

When we get to the hospital, a day after my baptism, and I see him unconscious, with tubes coming out of his mouth, a bandage around his head, and an IV stuck in his arm, I decide for certain there is no God. What God would do this? We wanted to rush to the hospital yesterday, right after it happened, but Jessie's parents told my mother he was in surgery, to come the next day. Tiffany and I stayed in the kitchen, weeping, inconsolable. My mother wrapped her arms around both of us. Her shell had dropped and she became a nest, like my father on the night of the fire. She is rarely a nest. I wish she were always a nest.

Jessie's parents are nests now, too. I wonder why only tragedy seems to transform our parents into nests? Warm and supportive. Loving and kind. His parents kiss his forehead and pray over him, calling upon a God who will never come. Have they not noticed that Jesus never actually intervenes, no matter what kind of chaos is happening in our poor, tiny apartments? He just watches it all, helpless. I think about the Jesus hanging in our kitchen, who appeared to change positions. I convince myself that I imagined it, even though the picture of Jesus in Jessie's hospital room is oddly in the same new position. I ignore him and his open arms. I decide I won't try to talk to him anymore—not after this.

Initially, I try to be strong when I see Jessie in his hospital bed, since everyone else is dissolved in grief. *Someone has to be strong for Jessie.* I try to suck my own tears back up into the center of my spirit, but they just keep falling, endlessly falling. I choke on the sound of my own wails. I cry like a future widow. Jessie was going to be mine. My one person in the world who wanted me despite the fact that I'm an ugly beast.

And now I have been left with nothing. I become aware that I'm crying for myself also, for the fact that I will always be alone in the world. The thought of it is almost unbearable. I buckle over from the pain. I spiral prayers. I ask what I can give to make it all go back to the way it was.

Everyone is here: Davante, Tiffany, my brothers, our mother and father, Jessie's parents and sister. All the eyes in the room are wet, running with endless tears. Even Davante, who has teased Jessie relentlessly since we were young, has been brought to his knees. He sits, holding Jessie's hand, solemnly staring straight ahead. And Dre, sweet Dre, turns to me and asks, "Is he gonna be awright?" I want to be strong for Dre, too, but I can't. His question hits me right in the center, causing more tears to fall from my eyes. "I don't know," I say finally. "I don't know."

The doctor says it's very unlikely Jessie will regain full mobility. They did all they could, but when he wakes up, he will likely be paralyzed, or "neurologically compromised," or both. He has several contusions in his brain, which they call a "traumatic brain injury." He also has a spinal cord injury. His spine was broken in three places. "It was a very long operation," the doctor says, "but we think he's going to pull through. He's in a coma right now and we don't know how long he'll be in it. All we can do is hope he comes out on the other side of this in the best shape possible. My deepest sympathies to you all." The doctor's lips stretch and curl up at the sides into a warm half smile as he soberly drops his head before leaving the room. I keep looking at him, waiting for him to turn around and say something else. Waiting for him to say, *Actually, I changed my mind. Everything's gonna be just fine.* But he doesn't. As he walks out of the room, my last bit of hope leaves with him. I sink into the deepest sadness I have ever known.

Later Rone and Davante, who were both there, tell me what happened. They were playing in the field until the sun went down. On the way home, they decided to play Ghetto Superman, where they try to do something to prove their strength, like jumping down a flight of stairs or running into a wall at high speed or racing across the street while a car is coming, which is what they were doing when Jessie got hit. I have told them so many times not to do things like this. But they are boys trying to become men, and they think this is what men do to prove their manliness. I am learning that boys do so many stupid things to prove their manliness.

As soon as Jessie gets hit by the car, Rone runs home, calls the police, and gets the adults while Davante stays with Jessie, holding his hand right there in the middle of the street. Minutes later, Jessie's father and our father and so many other fathers from the neighborhood come running at top speed. The mothers run three or four paces behind. Jessie's father screams at the top of his lungs, "No, no, no, no! Goddammit, not my boy!" All the fathers and mothers gather around Jessie's body, which is twisted awkwardly in an unnatural position. They know he can't be moved until the ambulance arrives.

The ambulance and two police cars come whirring onto the scene. The police ask my brother and Davante questions: What happened? How did he get hit? Were you playing in the street? But they say nothing. They are in shock. Their brains stop producing words that they can speak out loud. They stand there in silence watching the whole thing play out: the medics carefully lifting Jessie up onto a stretcher; the three crows circling above and cawing mercilessly at the top of their lungs; the dark, low-hanging clouds; Jessie's father continuing to shout, "No, no, no!" at the top of his lungs. His mother crying while climbing into the back of the ambulance. The tragedy of the day will be forever burned into them.

The nurse says visiting hours for non–family members are almost over, but I don't want to leave. I want to remain with Jessie's parents and sister, who will all stay overnight. I ask my mother if I can stay. If we can tell the doctor I'm one of his sisters, too, even though I'm not light-skinned with good hair. My mother thinks to herself and says, "Naw, baby, I know how much Jessie means to you and yo brothas, but I thank da family should have some alone time wit' him now. If anythang like dat eva happ'n to you, God forbid, I'd wanna jus' be wit' da family at some point.

"And I want you ta know, dat afta all dis pass ova, we need ta talk about what happn'd yesteday in dat church. I needs to know what happn'd, baby."

I am too full of emotion to speak and am overwhelmed by her sudden warmth and compassion. My body immediately locks up, though, when I think about the fact that I still don't know why or how she killed her own mother. I look up at her with renewed suspicion. She sees it but remains soft and keeps her shell lowered to stay warm toward me.

My family and I begin hugging and saying goodbye to everyone in the room. Davante and Tiffany also get up to say their goodbyes. I turn toward Jessie and reach down to give him a hug without disturbing the various medical devices tucked in and around his body. I look at his closed eyes and yearn for them to open and look at me like they did that day in the field. When they don't open, I give him a kiss on the forehead.

Just as I start to pull away, I notice something on the windowsill, which is slightly cracked. At first, I assume it's a bird, but it doesn't move like a bird. It moves like a spinning disk, like the thing I saw in the air that day at church. I start walking toward the window to get a better look while everyone else continues to say their goodbyes. My mother sees me and comes running over. I lift the window and then recoil in shock, covering my mouth with both hands. I see it, the black veil, right outside, hovering in the dark of night. I see clearly now that it looks like an ominous black creature with no face, shaped like a rectangular piece of fabric, that ruffles and moves like a flag in the wind. I hold my hands over my mouth so tightly, the pressure might crush my jaws. I am infused with terror. Just like that day on the church lawn when we released the black balloons, I feel heavy, a thousand pounds, like I can't move. And there is an awful sinking feeling in my stomach.

My mother quickly closes the window, puts her hands on both my shoulders, and nudges me toward the door. "She just very upset," my mother says to others in the room who have been watching me in confusion. "Dat's all it is. She upset. Jessie been her little buddy since kindergarten, so she takin' it hard. And it's been a tough coupl'a days fo huh even befo' dis happn'd."

We all rush out onto the street in the dark of night, each heading to our respective apartments. My family and I shove ourselves into a nearby taxi. I turn my head backward, unnaturally so, craning my neck to see if the black veil is still there. It is. I see it, hovering outside Jessie's window. I shudder, turn back around, and sink into the warm arms of my parents and brothers.

— – —— ———◦◇◦——— —— – –

I first seen it when I'as ten years old," my mother tells me, "da black veil." She is smoking a cigarette while we sit across from each other at the kitchen table. It's Saturday morning, a week after Jessie's accident. No one else is home. Dre and Rone have both run off to collect cans and scrap metal that they will later sell to Mr. Jimmie James for their own pleasures, not to buy dog food. My father is at Rockets, an after-hours bar that opens at eight for those who like to start drinking at the crack of dawn, like him. He drinks even more when bad stuff happens, like Jessie's accident. Alcohol is the only way he knows how to process and hide his feelings. I've never seen my father cry, but I know he must be a deeply feeling person if he needs to drink that much. So it's just me and my mother as she recounts memories from her past. My mother has never talked to me like this before, so real and direct, like I'm an adult. I listen intently to everything she says.

"I was a lil thang. Had curly pigtails in my hair, like how I use'ta do yo hair when you was a lil girl. I'as runnin' 'round witout a care in dis world. I'as free den, befo' ev'rythang went down. I memba da first time it happn'd. I'as jus' in my room colorin' or playin' wit' my dolls. And he come in dere, my uncle, and sat on the edge of my bed. I know'd as soon as he walked in, somethin' wasn't right. Said he got a special gift fo me. Said I cain't tell nobody 'bout it . . . And I was a chile, so I liked da idea of special gifts dat was jus' fo me. Gave me a pink teddy bear wit' a big ol' white bow 'round da neck. I was so happy to have it, I jump up and give him da biggest hug." She pauses to blot some of the ash from her cigarette into the tray before blowing out a big plume of smoke. "But den, he jus' . . . he jus' started puttin' his hands er'ywhere. Befo' I know'd what was happ'n, he was on top of me. I'as only six or seven, but I jus' kept thankin' to myself, *Dis ain't right. Dis ain't right at all.* Next thang I know'd, I was up on da ceilin', just sittin' up dere watchin' da whole thang. Sittin' up dere was da only way I survived it. I thought dat'd be it. Won't be no mo 'cause he done took what he wanted, but dat was jus' da beginnin'. Kept goin' like dat fo four years. Lawd, four long years."

My mother rests her cigarette on the rim of the ashtray, abruptly gets up from the table, and pours two glasses of cherry Kool-Aid—my favorite. She also grabs a can of Vienna sausages and empties them onto a small saucer sitting in the middle of the table. She motions for me to eat some. I don't want to eat in this moment. I am overwhelmed by what she is telling me. But I don't want to upset her, so I grab one and

"When my momma finally come home from work da next mornin' and seen me collapsed on my bed, strangled by da black veil and da rest of me sittin' up on da ceilin' watchin', she went and got Ms. Mary Jacobs and Ms. Corrine Turner, the two most powerful quantum wizards she knew. They had to do a special ceremony to brang me back. I had done all but died inside myself, so dey had to do a special kind a' cer'mony only quantum wizards can do ta brang somebody back from da dead. And I was 'bout nearly dead by da time dey got to me. All three of 'em worked to get me off da ceiling and ta get da thang, da veil, off me. Da only problem is, dat veil can get inside yo head, make you see and believe thangs dat ain't true. So when dey finally got it off me and sucked me down off da ceilin' back into my body, I come to, heavin' and coughin', but I still wasn't myself. All I seen was demons, like da pastor had tole me in church, I seen demons all around me. I thought my momma, Mary Jacobs, and Ms. Corrine was demons dat was gon' hurt me like he did. So I grabbed da knife I had up unda my pillow. I had put it dere intendin' to kill my uncle 'cause I jus' couldn't take it no mo. I grabbed dat knife and . . ."

My mother stops talking. I see now that tears are streaming, running down her face, but her eyes are dead, lifeless. She looks up at me, directly into my eyes. I see the pain now, the tremendous well of pain just on the other side of the coldness of her eyes. "I ain't mean ta do it. I . . . I . . ." She starts stumbling over her words. The words begin stomping out of her mouth with such grief and intensity, I grab the sides of my own face to try to steady myself and remain present. "I . . .

see 'em. It ain't on you yet, and you got to fight to keep it off. Only way you can keep it off is to stay lifted. Got to stay spirited and in da light. Dat's why I was tryin' so hard to protect you and yo brothas. I didn't want none of dis to happ'n to y'all. Only way I can get mine off now is drankin' and druggin', othawise it's always on me. I done learned how ta live in it mostly, but sometimes, I jus' cain't control it, the darkness inside me. I knows I ain't done nothin' right by y'all. I knows how much I done messed up. And I knows you sad and devastated 'bout what happened wit' Jessie. You cain't let his accident sink you, tho. You gotta fight. You got ta keep goin' ta keep it off ya. If ya keep goin', stay spirited and stay up, it'a stay away from ya, okay? It needs you to be sinkin' inside befo' it come around."

The sixth lesson of wizard training is that the black veil haunts the darkness and pain inside of you. Once it begins its ominous descent, the only way to keep it off you is to stay spirited, lifted, and internally risen.

My mother sees me staring at the black veil wrapped around her and says, "Just close yo eyes and thank to yo'self, *Show me da light*, and you'a stop seein' 'em. You'a see da light in people again instead of da darkness. And if you wanna see people's darkness, if dat's somethin' you feel like you wanna see, just close yo eyes and thank to yo'self, *Show me da darkness*, and dere dey'll be, all da black veils, as plain as day."

I take my mother's suggestion, close my eyes, and ask to see the light. When I open them, I am stunned. My mother is glowing, like on the night of the spades party. She is radiant, warm, ethereal. The sight of her this close up brings tears to my eyes. "Dis who I am, too, who I was befo' it all happn'd," she says. "I done spent my whole life tryna get back, tryna come home . . . I want you ta remember me like dis. I want you ta think a' me like dis when da veil take ova me, okay? Can you do dat fo me, baby?" I nod my head emphatically yes and lunge across the table, giving her the biggest hug I can muster.

— – — —— –∘O∘– —— — – —

I walk around the neighborhood switching between the two ways of seeing. I am shocked at how many people around us have a black veil wrapped around their heads. Now I understand why so many of them drink and drug like my mother, to try to lift it. I start walking toward the hospital to visit Jessie. My brothers and Tiffany are supposed to meet me there. Davante and I usually walk to the hospital together after school, but today he had to stay to work on a group project, which I find out later. Sometimes on our walks to the hospital, he even holds my hand. I never say anything when he does because I don't know if he's holding my hand as a friend or more than friends. I haven't figured it out, but I like holding his hand. I am smiling to myself, thinking about Davante, when I round the corner of the church and see Tiffany walking toward me. My smile widens as I yell, "Hey, Tiffany! Do you want to walk to the hospital together?" My smile fades as I see she looks irritated.

She walks right up to me and says with hostility, "I just came from da hospital."

"Oh, that's cool," I respond. "I thought we was all supposed to meet there. I'm heading up there now."

Tiffany rolls her eyes and says, "I wanted ta be alone wit' him, finally. Since you was always on his dick. Always following him around like a lost puppy."

I don't know how to respond to Tiffany, so I remain silent.

"What, you don't got nothin' to say? You jus' gon' stand dere looking dumb?"

I open my mouth to try to form words, but nothing comes out. Suddenly, I close my eyes and think to myself, *Show me the darkness*. When I open my eyes, I see that Tiffany has a black veil wrapped tightly around her. I wonder if it comes from all the pressure she's under to take care of herself and her little brother since her mother is heavily strung out. Or if she has a flesh man down the street, like me. Or an uncle who brings her special gifts, like my mother. I wonder what has caused her black veil.

"I'm sorry if I did anything wrong to you, Tiffany. I don't know what I did, but I just want Jessie to get better, like I'm sure you do also."

Tiffany rolls her eyes again and says, "Yeah, whatever. I'll see you around."

I watch her walk away. I hurry toward the hospital, spiraling prayers to the beyond to rid us of all our despair.

Killing the Imposter

My classmate, Elena Farahmand, has two black veils. I stare at her from across the classroom trying to make sense of it. A year has passed since Jessie's accident. An entire year. I used to think a year was a long time, but this past year flew faster than the speed of light. Now here I am, thirteen years old in my last year of middle school, carefully observing Elena, who moved here eight months ago from Iran. I don't know where Iran is, but it sounds very far away. The teacher introduces her as "a new student from the Middle East." The only thing I know about the Middle East is what they say on the news: that Muslims and terrorists live there, and the United States is always bombing it for oil. I want to ask Elena what it's really like where she comes from since my parents say "ya cain't trust nothin' you see on TV."

I've never seen anyone who looks like Elena. She's white, but not white like the other white people in the school. She will later explain that she's Persian, which makes her an "ethnic minority, like Hispanics and black people," but she still looks more like a white person to me. She has olive skin, green eyes, and long, silky black hair, which is covered today with a black headscarf, her second veil. She only started wearing the headscarf a couple of weeks ago. She shifts nervously in her seat and seems shrunken and small, avoiding eye contact with everyone in the class, which is shocking to me. She usually bounces down the hallway with a full face of makeup like the other white girls. Today, with the headscarf covering her hair and the ominous black veil hovering right above her, threatening to latch on at any moment, Elena doesn't seem like her normal confident self, and I want to understand why.

My own black veil hasn't returned since I saw it outside Jessie's hospital room. I've been trying to stay lifted and spirited, like my mother said, even though I'm not really sure what that means. I mostly just stay busy and hope that's enough. I'm so afraid of the black veil returning, I even try to stay busy in my dreams. I keep having dreams where I'm running. I never reach a destination, but I'm always running, hiding, and looking over my shoulder. I never see the black veil in my dreams, either, but I know that's what I'm running from. I hope with all the cells in my body it never returns for me.

I especially have to stay spirited and lifted when I visit Jessie. I still can't believe how different he is since the accident. Every time I visit him, I have to amp myself up with a pep talk before. Otherwise it makes me very sad. As soon as I walk into his room at the rehab center, I summon all the positivity and good energy I can, unleashing the biggest "Jessie!" He lights up, grinning from ear to ear. Most of the doctor's worst predictions came true. He's paralyzed from the waist down, which means he'll never walk again. His right arm is functional, but he has very limited use of his left hand and arm, which hangs folded and stiff at his side. His cognitive abilities are restricted, which means he can't process and understand information like before. We can't talk about all the things we used to talk about: aliens in outer space, how many people are in the world, how great Tupac's music is. Instead, we watch cartoons together like *Pinky and the Brain*. He always shouts after, "What are we gonna do tomorrow?!"

I look at him before pausing dramatically and then saying, "The same thing we do every day, Pinky—try to take over the world!"

Jessie laughs. "Try to take over the world!" he says several times.

He sometimes repeats what the people around him say, as if he's trying to paint the words in front of him to make sure he understands. And the tone at the end of his repeated sentences is always raised, as if he's asking a question: We're gonna have lunch now, Jessie. "We're gonna have lunch now?" It's freezing outside. "It's freezing outside?"

There is also a blankness in Jessie's eyes now, like an empty white piece of paper. Everything that used to be written on that piece of paper—his curiosities, his frustrations, his fears—is no longer perceptible at the surface. But he's becoming an artist, with a clear passion for light, color, and music. He started painting soon after he came out of the coma. He can paint only with his right hand and paints elaborate, colorful pictures. He has a new picture just for me every time I come visit. He gives me pictures of trees, animals, his family, cartoon characters, or balloons. I have never liked art, but something about Jessie's paintings speak to me. They feel alive, radiating an exuberant energy. I hang several of his paintings around my room.

Jessie will be getting out of the rehab center soon, which was covered entirely by Jessie's father's insurance. Jessie's father doesn't make much money as a janitor in one of the downtown office buildings, but he gets excellent medical coverage for him and his family. At least, that's what my mother says: "Thank God dat boy's fatha got a good job wit' benefits. If it had happn'd to one a' y'all, I'on know what we woulda done. Da gov'nment insurance we got shole ain't gon' cova no year in rehab. I knows dat fo sho." Jessie has spent the last year regaining his ability to speak, read, write, and feed and wash himself, basically all the skills we learned as children. Now that he has learned to do all those things, the doctor says progress past his current level of understanding will be improbable. His parents plan to put him in a school for kids with special needs.

Everyone visits Jessie often, including Dre, Tiffany, Davante, and my parents. Rone doesn't come, because he's locked up in juvenile detention for stealing someone's car and crashing it into a mailbox. He has also dropped out of school. He's only twelve years old, but he's already making so many bad decisions influenced by what's around us. Maybe he doesn't realize different decisions can be made. And he has a black veil covering him now, fully covering him, but doesn't know it. I see it wrapped around him, suffocating him, every time I visit juvenile detention. I become even more determined to save him and Dre, from the other side of the world, so I just secretly observe her and try to imagine who she is and what she's like.

I'm slightly obsessed with figuring out Elena because she's so pretty and appears to be different from the other white girls at my school, who float carefree through the hallway with their long blond or brown hair flowing effortlessly behind them. I wonder if this is their way of stopping time, because all the boys freeze and stare at them the way my father's friends do at my mother on Saturday nights. Whenever I stand next to them, I can feel the blackness of my skin covering me all over, like a scar I can't remove. I wonder how it would feel to walk through the world as a white girl, if I would feel better about myself on the inside. I am envious of all that has been given to them and sad about everything that has not been given in the same way to me. I know everything must not be perfect for the white girls, either, however. When I switch views, to the darkness, I see that many of them are covered by black veils as well. I wonder why. I wonder what secrets and pain are haunting them, what they have left buried.

I know Elena must be burying something big, because the ominous black veil is even closer now, her shoulders are always slumped, and she doesn't hang out with anyone anymore. The girls she used to hang out with now snicker and roll their eyes when she walks by in the hallway.

I wonder if there is going to be any drama on the field trip to Cedar Point today. I love field trips because you get to observe the entire social web of the school: who hangs out with who, who doesn't like who, who *does* like who. My favorite thing to do on field trips is to watch how everyone interacts. Since I don't have any close friends at school, I entertain myself by secretly observing others, like I did when I was a kid with my brothers. Only this time, I don't just observe. I make up stories about who I think they are. I have a story for almost everyone. I pretend we are all on an episode of *Saved by the Bell*. Jake, the boy all the girls like, is our Zack Morris. He's blond with blue eyes, wears high-top sneakers, and talks to everybody in the hallway. Jamericka, the only other black kid in our class (out of forty black kids total in the school), is Lisa Turtle. She has curly brown hair and is rich and stylish just like Lisa on TV. Jamericka and I avoid each other, as do all the black kids at the school. We all know instinctively that if we stick together, the white kids will be threatened by our attempt to bond over our skin color, like they do. We remain separate and isolated even though we desperately need each other. We pass each other like strangers in the hallway, but I feel the pulse of their longing and I know they feel mine. Even though stylish Lisa Turtle hangs out with a group of white girls, I can tell she feels uncomfortable, too.

Our final guest star on *Saved by the Bell: The White School on the West Side Edition*, is Elena, the foreigner from the other side of the world. She was once one of the popular girls, but now, after a mysterious twist of fate, she's a loner who spends most of her time in her room watching *Little House on the*

Prairie reruns, secretly smoking cigarettes, and writing love letters she'll never send to boys she likes at school. She definitely watches *Little House on the Prairie*, which I assume all white people do. Except Elena doesn't. And she doesn't smoke cigarettes or write sad love letters to cute boys. It turns out we have a lot more in common than I could have ever imagined, which I learn on the field trip to Cedar Point.

We talk the entire time at the amusement park. While everyone else rushes onto thrill rides and roller coasters with names like Power Tower and Corkscrew, Elena and I are the only two who don't ride any of the rides. We are the designated coat holders and water distributors. Every time someone gets thirsty or wants their jacket, they come find us sitting on a bench like two old women reminiscing about the good ol' days. Neither of us sees the point of going on rides that give you a headache or make you vomit.

"Who would willingly choose to do that?" Elena says while we sit on the bench. "Humans are a mess, a failed species for sure."

I smile uneasily at the harshness of her comment and respond, "Well, there are some good ones—Nelson Mandela, Harriet Tubman, and Oprah! I mean, Oprah gives away cars and houses, so she's definitely not one of the failures, but I personally also don't understand a lot of things people do. Like, I don't see the point of trick-or-treating; dressing up for Halloween; riding skateboards, which are so dangerous; or drinking pop, which is basically like drinking a can of carbonated sugar water, and why would anyone want to do that? I mean, we have to make an obvious exception for Kool-Aid, but pop is basically poison."

Elena nods but asks what Kool-Aid is.

When I tell her, she says, "Ew, that's just sugar water, too, and preservatives."

I tell Elena I will show her the wonders of Kool-Aid in due time. We are like long-lost sisters, and we bond over our eclectic tastes while eating nachos and popcorn and talking about all the things in the world that don't make sense.

We talk about deeper stuff, too. I learn why Elena started wearing a hijab, which she tells me is a complicated religious and political symbol in her country. She didn't want to wear it, but when her mother found out she was taking it off when she got to school, she threatened to send Elena to live with her uncle in Turkey if she didn't obey. "Just because we are in America," her mother said, "does not mean you stop being Muslim. We will always be Muslim no matter where we are!"

Like me, Elena struggles to believe in religion. "I just don't understand why we have to listen to ancient men who died centuries ago or to those who use religion as an instrument of control. I'm just tired of living by all these meaningless rules, but if I disagree in any way, my parents will ship me off to Turkey, and I really want to stay in America. Anything is possible for women here. And there's more freedom here for people who . . ." Elena's voice trails off before she abruptly changes the subject. "Hey, have you ever seen *The Matrix*? I love that movie. It explains everything about our mind-controlled reality. I love a lot of movies, but that's my favorite. I want to be an actress, but my parents want me to be a doctor like them. There's no way I'm becoming a doctor. I just don't get it. Why can't you just be who you want and be left alone? That's why I stopped hanging out with the girls in the bathroom, too. They wanted me to be just like them. It got harder and harder to pretend." Elena pauses, glancing up at a roller coaster as it climbs to its highest peak before plunging down the tracks and back up again. "I thought if I did whatever they wanted, I would finally be 'in' with 'real' American girls, but I hated everything they liked. They always talk about boys and drink and watch cheesy movies like *Pretty Woman* or shows like *Little House on the Prairie*."—*I knew it!*—"God, kill me. My mother says the worst thing you can be in this world is an imposter, a fake person who just reflects what other people expect from them, but she can't see that the person she wants me to be is an imposter, too. It's painfully ironic." When Elena talks about imposters, I think about how out of place I feel at this white school, and how out of place I feel in my own neighborhood. I don't really fit in anywhere. I wonder when things will be different. When I'll finally find a place with other people like me, maybe even wizards like me. I am suddenly overcome by an urge to tell Elena all about the wizard stuff, but I don't know if she will believe me. I decide against it since she is the first person I have really connected with at school. *Better not give her any reason to believe I'm a freak*, I think to myself.

"So those girls just stopped talking to you?" I ask instead.

"Well, once they figured out I wasn't really drinking beer, and I kept 'accidentally' dropping cigarettes every time they gave me one, yes, they stopped talking to me," Elena responds. "And once I started wearing the hijab, there was no chance we'd ever different parts of the world can have so much in common. And I wonder how two people from the same neighborhood can be so different. How Tiffany, who is waiting at the bus stop smoking cigarettes with her friends when I get off, can be so mean, even though we grew up together and were almost-sisters. She lives in a roach-infested apartment like ours, with busted Goodwill furniture, bedsheets for curtains, and splintered floorboards. Tiffany's mother also smokes crack, drinks, and had a traumatic childhood just like my mother. When we used to play in the field, before Jessie's accident, Tiffany always complained about how much she hated her mother and how she wished her daddy wasn't in prison. Tiffany also works on the weekends, like me, to pay the bills her mother smokes up in crack and to help take care of her six-year-old brother, Lil Man. We really could have been sisters. But we're not.

And now she has made me the target of her rage. Maybe because I have chosen to not give up, like all the people around us, and it reminds her of everything she is sacrificing in her own self-destruction. Maybe she wants to destroy the reminder. She, like my brothers, also drinks, smokes cigarettes, and has given up on school. Maybe she feels like an imposter, too, trapped in a life she never wanted or imagined, and it's all too much to bear.

If and when she finally decides to attack me, I'll be the one who has to bear it. She and her friends have been following me home, hurling insults, for two weeks. "Stuck-up bitch," they say. "Goody Two-shoes. Wannabe white girl." I mostly just keep my head down and pretend like I don't hear them, but I know it's only a matter of time before their fists back up their words.

I start going to Elena's house after school to escape Tiffany and her friends. Elena lives on the West Side in a nice house on a tree-lined street. She lives in the kind of house I always wanted to live in. The first time I go there, I stand on the sidewalk and stare at it with my mouth wide open. There are big white pillars in front, all the windows are huge, and the lawn wraps around the whole house.

"What's wrong?" Elena asks concernedly.

"Nothing. I've just . . . I've never been inside a house this big before."

Inside is even more amazing than outside. I again look at everything with my mouth wide open. There is a grand staircase, like the ones you see on the house-hunting shows. At the top of the staircase there is a chandelier, and she even has a black piano in the foyer. I have never heard the word *foyer* until Elena's mother tells Elena to go and put the flower vases, which were previously resting on the dinner table, by the piano in the foyer. It's like a real life *Full House*, only they seem even richer than the people on *Full House*. I didn't know that people in real life could be richer than the people on TV.

"So what do your parents do, Echo? I'm sure they must be really proud of you," Elena's mother asks while we are all sitting around the dinner table. "Elena tells me you are really smart and are at the top of your class. Congratulations. I'm sure for someone with your background, that's no easy feat." I don't like the way she says "someone with your background," but I keep smiling and nodding cheerfully. "Well, my father is a welder and my mother is a seamstress," I respond to Elena's mother, which is only partially true. My mother *was* a seamstress right out of high school, but she hasn't sewn in years, and my father is a welder, but he drinks up most of his money, so we depend on food stamps and welfare to get by.

"Oh, well, those are nice jobs to have in the world. My husband, who's studying late at the university tonight, and I are doctors. Surgeons. We're both in the residency program at Case Western Reserve School of Medicine, getting recertified. It's a lot of work. Neither of us is thrilled about it, but we both believe a career in health care is one of the most noble jobs you can have. Saving lives. There's nothing more valuable. That's why we moved to Cleveland, for its well-known hospitals and to give Elena access to a top-notch education." Elena's mother glances toward Elena, but Elena ignores her and glares down at the food. "I miss many things about our country, but in America so much more is possible for Elena. Who knows, maybe one day we'll all be working at the same hospital as a family. That would be a dream. Elena doesn't realize how lucky she is. She takes all this for granted. Right now, in Iran, there is so much economic strife. The money doesn't come from oil anymore. We know all about oil, unfortunately. My father-in-law was in the oil business and passed down most of his wealth to my husband. We both feel guilty about that. 'Blood money,' my husband calls it because of how many people have died in the pursuit of oil and wealth. When you both get older, you'll see how complicated life can be." Elena's mother takes a deep, reflective sigh and continues talking. "Trade is down also. The government is corrupt. The regime bends everything, even using the sacred text of Islam to control the people, but Islam, at least our practice, has nothing to do with politics. I guess politics always smothers religion in the pursuit of power eventually." She shakes her head in disappointment. "Poverty is rising also," she continues. "There is so much money and yet, so many remain poor, embarrassingly poor in an ocean of wealth. I wonder if we will ever have true equality in this world. Now many are leaving, trying to find a way out of the madness. People will always do what is needed to survive. My brother went to Turkey. My cousins scattered across Europe. Only my mother is still there, living in the mountains somewhere."

I am surprised to hear from Elena's mother the same despair my parents exhibit during their spades games. I thought rich people were happy all the time, like on TV. Elena, who appears totally unmoved by what her mother has said, continues to look down at her plate angrily, pushing her food around with her fork and rolling her eyes.

After dinner, Elena and I head to her bedroom and sit on the floor by the side of her bed. I notice that Elena looks pale and sunken—more sad than usual. I ask her if everything is all right. "Oh yeah, I'm fine. It's fine," she says dismissively. We both sit in silence for a few seconds since I don't know what else to say. She's clearly not fine. "It's just . . . I mean . . . Why does life have to be so hard? How can she sit down there and talk about 'humanity' and 'equality' when she doesn't even accept her own daughter. She's such a hypocrite! If she knew . . ." Elena shakes her head and tears start to fill her eyes. "If she knew . . . ," Elena repeats, "she'd lose her shit for sure and all that equality hypocrisy would fly out the window!" Elena starts crying. I don't know how to comfort her, since no one ever comforts me when I'm sad, so I just look at her with a warm, partial smile. I want to reach out and put my hand on her shoulder; that seems like the right thing to do, but the gesture also feels awkward to me. So I just sit next to her without saying anything.

"If she knew what?" I ask gently, trying not to upset her again now that she's calmed down a little.

My gentleness doesn't work. Elena starts shaking her head and crying intensely again. "God, I'm such a freak!" she screams, while continuing to cry uncontrollably. "And I've been seeing all these things that I know aren't real. My parents want to put me on medication. They think something's wrong with me." When she says this, I switch views and see that the black veil is now even closer to her head. I watch as it extends to its full wingspan right above her.

I jump up and say, "Elena, Elena!"

I point at the black veil looming. She looks up and I watch terror roll across her eyes like dark clouds before a storm. She shrieks in fear right as the black veil makes its final descent. It suffocates her with such force, I'm afraid it's going to kill her. Elena passes out suddenly. Her limp body falls to the floor on the side of her bed. I stand up and look around the room in a panic, wondering what I should do. A million thoughts run through my mind. I try to yell for help, but my throat constricts. My words won't come out, but my mind races: *Please! We need help! Please somebody*

help me! Please! I think to myself while running as fast as I can up the sidewalk. Tiffany and her friends are chasing me. They have finally grown bored with only shouting insults. Tiffany flicked her lit cigarette at me. I could feel the heat of the lit tip on my cheek before it fell to the ground. I become so angry, I forget my fear and push her, watching as she falls backward into the bus shelter. She is stunned. Rage boils over in her eyes. And now I'm being chased, at high speed, by a group of ravenous girls who are going to shatter me if they catch me. I hear them hulking and barking behind me. I am drenched in sweat, and my lungs feel like they are going to explode, but I keep running until my legs almost give out. I know if I don't stop running soon, I'm going to pass

out again, but this time, Elena opens her eyes and stares straight up at the ceiling. Her head is lying in my lap. I have been gently patting her on both cheeks until she finally opens her eyes. Suddenly, time starts to slow down and the lights in the room grow dim. The second hand on Elena's big white clock on the wall in front of us winds down to a complete stop. I look up and see that the ceiling has dissolved like on the night of the spades party, and I hear the same hum in the background I heard that night. All the specks of light in the dark space above begin to coil around and around one another until they form two beams of light that shoot down from the dark space above directly into Elena and into my forehead. The light almost knocks me

to the ground. Tiffany's friends raise their fists and begin to land them decisively all over my body. I try to cover my face, but they still manage to hit me in the face several times. I notice that Tiffany is just watching and has not joined them in their attack. "Tiffany, stop this!" I yell at her. "We're practically sisters! Please don't do this to me. We have to take care of each other!" As soon as I say this, Tiffany's black veil lifts, rising right above her head, spinning

and spiraling, while each beam shoots down from the dark space above, hitting our foreheads. I am suspended, unable to move. My eyes roll up while my arms fall limp at my sides. I see from the corner of my eyes that the spiral of light has raised Elena from her slumped position. She is floating, suspended next to me, head rolled back and eyes closed. Her arms fall and splay open behind her. I reach over and grab one of her hands, releasing my unease in comforting another person, as the light continues to spiral into our foreheads. Like the night of the spades party, I feel a rush of words flood my brain. Too many words. More words than I can process. After it is over, the only words I remember are *Kill the imposter before the imposter kills you. Become what you are or suffer.*

The seventh lesson of wizard training is to kill the imposter, the person you became to survive, and embrace the original, the person you were before all the pain. The person you *are* at the core. The original, not the imposter, holds the true blueprint for what you are destined to become in this world. You will find no answers in imposters, but you will find everything at the source, in the soul of the original. The imposter cannot perform the highest level of miracles and rise in true power. Only a wizard, authentic and lifted, can be of the greatest service to the people around them.

The light retracts, and Elena and I both tumble to the floor. She looks around in fear. "What the hell is going on?!" I just stare at her in silence for several seconds, trying to process everything. I had never considered the fact that Elena might be a wizard, too. That wizards could exist on the other side of the world.

"I think," I begin slowly, "I think you're a wizard, too."

"A wizard?!" Elena exclaims, and recoils

before yelling at her friends to "Stop!"

Her friends spin around and stare at Tiffany in confusion. "But you said this stuck-up bitch think she betta than us," one of them yells back. Tiffany's black veil continues to whirl right above her, and I see that her eyes are slightly watery. She reaches down, grabs my hand, and pulls me up from the ground. Then we all just stand in the middle of the sidewalk, not looking at one another.

"Just go home," Tiffany says finally. "Just go home."

Remembering the Inextinguishable Light

A wizard?!" Elena asks again; this time her eyes are wide open and filled with doubt. "Come on, you can't believe that. There's no such thing as wizards. That's nuts. This isn't *really* the Matrix."

Elena gets up, fixes her clothes, and stands in the middle of her room with her hands on her hips. She looks bewildered and disheveled, as if she has just been released from a tornado. Her hijab, which fell off during the light spiraling, is bunched on the floor next to me.

"I'm scared, too," I respond. "I don't understand everything myself, but I know what kinds of things you've seen. I see them, too." I stop speaking. Elena and I sit in awkward silence. I want to say more. I want to talk about all of it: the time slowing down, the light spirals, the black veil. Everything. But I don't. I can't risk losing her as a friend, especially since she seems super freaked out.

"Hey, um, maybe you should just head home. It's been a

long day. I'll ask my mother to give you a ride. I think I'm just gonna finish some homework and go to sleep."

I stand up, grab my book bag, and begin walking toward the door. I am suddenly overcome by sadness. I have finally found another wizard, but she's too afraid to accept what we are and face what's happened. I'm terrified she's going to abandon me, just like Tiffany, and I can't bear it. I pause in front of her doorway, before turning around and looking at her one last time. "This is the red pill, Elena," I say, referencing the famous scene from *The Matrix* when Morpheus tells Neo he can either take the red pill and wake up or take the blue one and go back to sleep. "You said you don't want to pretend anymore. You said you wanted to be yourself. Well, you're a wizard just like me. Whether you choose to swallow the blue pill or the red one, you're still a wizard. Nothing can change that. And wouldn't it be better to try and figure out what's happening together instead of pretending it doesn't exist?" Elena softens and we stand looking at each other for several seconds.

"How far down does this rabbit hole go?" Elena asks, breaking the silence.

"I don't know," I respond, "but I guess we'll find out."

Elena grabs a notebook and pen from her book bag and sits on the edge of her bed. "All right, then," she says, "tell me everything."

Tiffany disappears after she and her friends jump me. I haven't seen her in weeks, but Davante insists on walking me home from the bus stop every day after I tell him what happened.

"Yo, that's fucked up," he says. "That's really fucked up. Black people need ta stick together."

I have started liking another boy named Prince Mack, who lives in the neighborhood and is very popular, but I still get excited when I see Davante waiting for me at the bus stop, since we usually hold hands on the way home. We still haven't talked about what the hand-holding means, but I think he likes me as more than a friend. He's even started bringing me stuff, like candy and the other half of his bologna sandwich from lunch, which he knows I love. On our walks, he always wants to talk about "the black struggle" and how black people need a new movement for equality in America "'cause ain't shit equal."

Today he is talking all about Malcolm X. "Ey, do y'all be reading like black stuff ova dere at dat white school?" Davante asks. "We readin' *The Autobiography of Malcolm X*, and it's really good. It show how Malcolm X wasn't just mad for no reason. How dem white people back in da day pushed him to da edge."

We haven't read anything about Malcolm X, but we are reading a book about Martin Luther King Jr., whom I know Davante doesn't like as much.

"Man, all dat peaceful shit he preached didn't work," Davante barks. "We shoulda done it Malcolm's way and put dem honkies outta dey misery like my parents say."

I look straight ahead and say only "Okay" in response to

Davante. He has become increasingly like his parents and goes on and on about the "problems wit' honkies" for most of the walk home. I don't disagree with much of what he is saying, but once he starts talking, he doesn't stop, and he gets mad if I interrupt. So I just walk and nod occasionally so he thinks I'm listening carefully, but I'm really thinking about Prince Mack.

Once we get to the back door of my apartment building, I start shuffling through my pockets searching for my keys.

"Ey, I wanted ta ask you a question," Davante says awkwardly.

Oh God, I think to myself, assuming he is going to ask me more questions about "honkies."

"Ey," he says again, in a much softer voice, while placing a hand on my arm. As soon as he touches my arm, I understand what's happening. "I wanted ta know . . . if it would be okay . . . you know . . . I think you so beautiful . . . a beautiful black queen . . . I don't know . . . I was jus' wonderin' if it would be okay to kiss you." I am so shocked by the desire that rises in my body when he asks, even though I thought for sure I would never want to kiss him, since he's like a brother to me. I nod yes in eager excitement. He takes a deep breath and then leans his head toward mine. When he kisses me, I am overwhelmed by how good it feels. The tingling sensations start, my heart is beating really fast, and it feels like eighty thousand firecrackers are going off all at once throughout my body.

"Wow," we both say simultaneously. Neither of us knows what to do next.

Davante starts walking down my driveway back out to the street while stumbling over his words. "Okay, well, awright.

I'll see you tomorrow I guess. Bye!" He waves and then starts running awkwardly away from me. I stand in front of my apartment door for almost an hour, smiling and staring straight ahead, and wondering when we will kiss again.

I don't have to wait very long, however, because we kiss again the next day, and the next day after that, and for many more days after that. I begin to look forward to leaving school and run excitedly toward the bus. It's always the same, him standing there awkwardly, me pretending to search for my keys, him placing one long, lingering peck on my lips, and then running away awkwardly down the driveway. I always glance around to make sure no one is looking out the window or turning into the driveway. Today, after he kisses me, he doesn't run right away. Instead, he asks if I'm going to the cookout tomorrow because he really wants to dance with me, especially during the slow songs. "Yeah," I say. "I'm going, but my mother will kill you if she sees me slow-dancing with you. We'll have to do it secretly somewhere in the park."

— — — ——o○o—— — — —

Cookouts are the only time we ever see all the people in the neighborhood come together: church folks, drug dealers, drug users, gangbangers, good students, bad students, sometimes even the pimps and hoes. People you otherwise never see suddenly show up at cookouts, which only happen two or three times every summer. Unlike amusement parks and trick-or-treating, I love cookouts. I love grilled hot dogs and cheeseburgers, fresh Kool-Aid, line dancing, and nice weather, all of which are present today. Everyone's here, except for Rone, who's still locked up in juvenile detention. My mother and I will go visit him sometime in the next few days. This makes me feel better about him not being here. We will do our best to bring the spirit of the cookout to him, or at least I will. My mother will likely be her normal, angry, strung-out self.

When I see Jessie, I run over to him and give him a big hug. As usual, he's smiling, and says, "Echo's at da party." He repeats this two more times before pulling a newly painted picture from his pocket. I unfold it and stare at it for several seconds before asking him who it is. It's a picture of a little black boy wearing a green shirt with a tilted gold crown on his head. Unlike the other pictures Jessie paints for me, this one has dark, heavy colors. There's a thick black halo around the little boy, who has a wicked smile, as if he's hiding something. The picture is weird and haunting.

"Who is this?" I ask again, but Jessie's parents roll him away toward the middle of the park, where everyone is starting to dance the Electric Slide. There is a rush of chaos and bodies as people run to form six or seven dance lines. Davante comes up behind me, grabs my hand, and pulls me into the dance.

I fold up Jessie's painting, put it in my pocket, and try to fall in line with everyone else who is already dancing. My parents, Dre, Ms. Patty, Ms. Jannie, Davante, Pastor Aily, and various people from around the neighborhood are doing the choreographed dance moves in perfect unison. I once saw a commentator on TV jokingly say, "Chapter nineteen, verse eleven of the Book of Black People Proverbs says: 'If thou art borneth blacketh, thou shalt knoweth how to doeth the Electric Slide.'" It's a joke, but also mostly true. Black people, as far as I can tell, all vibrate to the rhythm of the same beat. We, at least the black people in America, have been gone for four hundred years, but Africa still calls to us through the music. Our bodies and spirits remember. Except for my father. His spirit must have forgotten, because he has no rhythm at all. My father is so bad at dancing he looks like a burnt Gumby figurine bouncing awkwardly from side to side.

"Look at dis nigga," Ms. Patty says, referring to my father. "Lookin' like a damn black-ass scarecrow from da *Wizard of Oz*. Aprah, tell dat nigga to go sat down somewhere." As a testament to her own dancing ability, Ms. Patty never misses a beat while chastising my father's poor dancing. She remains in sync with the group the entire time. My mother laughs heartily before responding, "You know he ain't neva been able to dance. Let him go on and make a fool outta hisself, as usual."

The Electric Slide finishes, and the next song begins to play. Someone yells, "Ey, play dat again!" The DJ asks the crowd if they want to do the Electric Slide again. Without hesitation, almost everyone yells, "Yeah!" Davante, who has been dancing and smiling next to me the whole time, yells, "And turn dat shit up dis time!" My mother pops Davante on the shoulder and tells him to watch his mouth before we all start doing the Electric Slide for a second time. As I pivot to turn toward Lake Erie, which cradles the park, I see a little lighthouse just off the shore. I remember the day Tiffany and

I almost drowned and how, in this moment, I'm so glad we didn't. We would have missed it all. I wonder if the lighthouse is a promise for all the good things to come, if I've finally made it to the other side of all the pain and obstacles. I smile a wide toothy grin thinking about it, and a calm hopefulness descends upon me as I move freely and joyfully to the music. I pivot and turn one more time, suddenly catching a glimpse of Prince Mack smiling at me two rows back. Immediately, my own smile fades to terror as my body locks up with embarrassment. I begin dancing awkwardly offbeat. A million thoughts and feelings race through my mind as I try to think of a way to get away from Davante, who has not left my side since he got here. It's been nice kissing Davante, but Prince Mack is so tall, muscular, and good-looking.

When the Electric Slide finally ends, I pretend not to notice Prince Mack continuing to stare at me. I can't believe he's staring at *me*. He could have any girl he wants, so why would he be interested in me? I look around to see if any pretty girls are standing nearby—maybe he's really looking at someone else. But only old people, Davante, and my parents are around. I glance back one more time, and this time he smiles again and waves at me. I turn around excitedly and ask Davante if he could go and get me a hot dog; the grill is on the opposite side of the park. When he agrees, reluctantly, and only if I promise to go find a secret dancing spot when he comes back, I quickly make my way to the table that has all the drinks. I pour myself a cup of grape Kool-Aid, which is my least favorite, and gulp it down nervously. I feel someone tap me on the shoulder and I know it's Prince Mack. When I turn around he says, "Ey, ain't yo name Erika or Echo or some shit like dat? You one of dem smart kids dat go to da white school on the West Side, right?"

I am stunned that he knows anything about me. I'm unable to find words, so I just stand there with my mouth hanging open, but no sound comes out. I tell my brain to produce words, but there are too many signals coursing in every direction of my body for it to obey.

"I see you a little shy, huh? I like shy, quiet girls. But you don't gotta be shy around me . . . You like da cookout? It's a nice day today, huh?"

When I still don't say anything, Prince Mack takes a pen and a piece of paper out of his pocket. "Well, here, I'ma write down my number," he says. "You can call me anytime you want." He hands me his number and smiles before saying, "I'ma be waitin' to hear from you, a'ight?"

I nod and watch as he walks away. I fold the piece of paper carefully and put it in my pocket.

I pour another cup of grape Kool-Aid, which is the only kind of Kool-Aid they seem to have here, before someone else taps me on the shoulder. I spin around and see that it's Tiffany. I jump back in fear and confusion and tell her to leave me alone, that I don't have anything to talk to her about after what she did.

"Nah, nah, listen," she says. "I'm not on some bullying shit no more, not since dat day."

I switch views and see that Tiffany's black veil has still not descended again and covered her, but is hovering right above.

"I'm sorry . . . for what happn'd. I realize now dat shit wasn't right. When I seen dem hittin' you like dat, it flipped some kinda switch or somethin'. I jus' . . . It wasn't right. I tole all dem girls ta leave you alone. Dey ain't been messin' wit' you, right?"

I shake my head no.

"I jus' been feelin' . . . I'on' know . . . different since dat day. Like jus' better somehow. Like less bad about everything . . . my life . . . da way things is."

I stare blankly at Tiffany, suspicious of her motivations. I can tell she wants something from me, but I don't know what. I'm still angry about everything that happened. I don't trust her at all, so I respond coldly, "I don't really know what to say. Maybe you just realized dat what you was doin' was wrong. Maybe you feel better since you're no longer going after someone you've known since we were little. I would feel better about that, too."

Tiffany drops her head in dissatisfaction at my response. Maybe she didn't just want something from me; maybe she needed something. Forgiveness? A way to understand the black veil? An understanding I know I can't give her. I suddenly feel bad at my cold response and search for additional words to try to make her feel better.

"Look," I say, "I can't tell you why you feel different, but if it feels good not to beat people up, maybe keep not doing that and you'll continue to feel better."

Tiffany nods. "Yeah, a'ight. So we cool?" she asks while extending her hand.

I stare at it for a few seconds before finally shaking it and replying, "Yeah, we cool." I watch as Tiffany starts walking away, before stopping and abruptly turning around.

"Oh yeah," she says, "one more thing. I seen you talkin' to Prince Mack . . . and I just wanted to tell you, you should stay away from him. He ain't no good person."

I nod as if I agree, but I become very angry when she finally walks away. *Now I see what she wants*, I think to myself. *She wants Prince Mack and thinks I'm going to steal him away like what happened with Jessie. I knew she couldn't be trusted.* I take another sip of Kool-Aid and shake my head in disgust and satisfaction at having figured out what Tiffany was up to. I become even more determined to make Prince Mack my boyfriend.

I have been fantasizing about Prince Mack, who's four years older than me, since the day I first saw him last year outside the penny candy store. He is shouting into the pay phone, telling someone to "go pick my daughter up for me, 'cause I got somethin' I gotta do." It's a hot summer day, so he is wearing basketball shorts and a basketball jersey with no T-shirt underneath. I stand on the sidewalk, staring at the bulging muscles of his arms, and peek down at his calves, marveling at how perfectly sculpted they are. I have never seen a person in real life that looks as good as he does. After a few seconds, he slams the phone receiver back into the cradle before heading into the penny candy store. I timidly walk in after him, trying to stay invisible, and continue to observe him out of the corners of my eyes. He buys a bagful of candy before darting out of the store. I look around and see that I am not the only girl watching him. I race home, throw the bag of candy I bought myself on the kitchen table, and lock myself in my room.

I lie on my bed and imagine kissing and touching Prince Mack while rubbing myself down there. The urge to touch Prince Mack is so intense, I reach over, grab a pillow, place it between my legs, and pretend that it is Prince Mack. I touch the pillow all over while intensely rubbing myself on him. I rub desperately, trying to relieve myself of the tension flowing through my body. I start to feel sensations I have never felt before. I rub faster and press the pillow deeper into me. I start breathing harder and moaning uncontrollably. I don't know if anyone can hear me, but it feels so good, I don't care. Suddenly, I feel an intense rush of pleasure take over my entire body. Pleasure that releases the tension I have been building for so long. I hold the pillow in my arms, resting. I stare at the ceiling and smile while also sweating and breathing hard. I don't understand what has just happened, but I know I want to do it again, need to do it again. I feel guilty for rubbing myself in the same way the flesh man down the street did, but this feels different. I feel alive after doing this, not sunken, embarrassed, and dirty like with him.

Now, after the cookout, I think about Prince Mack even more while using the pillow over and over. I pull his phone number out of the top drawer of the nightstand and wonder what it would be like to talk to him on the phone. I'm too afraid to call, so I put the number back in the drawer and fall asleep. I frequently fall asleep after using the pillow, from the exhaustion of all the moving and grinding. I fall into a very deep sleep—so deep, I almost feel like I'm in a coma. In one dream, I'm back at the park where the cookout happened, but only Jessie and I are there. We are sitting by the lake looking at the gray lighthouse, which shines the brightest, most exuberant light I've ever seen. The sky is dark with clouds of various colors, just like I saw on the night of the spades party and at Elena's house. The clouds move slowly, meandering, seemingly not in a rush to get anywhere. Jessie calls out jokingly, "That's my cloud." We both laugh, and Jessie looks at me like he did the day in the shack. I bashfully

look away while the officer looks through my book bag and purse. My mother glares at the officer while handing over her jacket and purse and saying, "I hate comin' here. Don't do nothin' but brang back bad memories." My mother and I go through this every time we come to visit Rone here at the juvenile detention building, which is always so grimy and cold, with sad, angry people everywhere. I hate coming, but we can't leave Rone alone. He's always so happy to see us. As soon as we walk through the door into the visiting area, his face lights up and he smiles excitedly. The guard tells us we have fifteen minutes, and I instantly feel pressured to say everything I can think of before we have to leave. My mother has been spinning further and further into her own web of insanity, but she tries to be on her best behavior. Right now, her best is drinking coffee and staring

up at the sky in silence. I ask Jessie what he's thinking about. "I was just wondering when J is gonna get here," he says. I look at him in confusion until I see a figure dressed in all white start to descend from the sky. The figure is celestial, surrounded by a white halo around his entire body that shines so brightly, I have to shield my eyes from the glare. The halo disappears once the figure lands on the ground in front of us. Jessie stands up and slaps hands with the figure, who I now see is Jesus.

"J, I got yo Vienna sausages. Here, man."

Jesus grabs the can from Jessie and says, "Duuude!"

Jessie responds, "Duuuuuude."

They both laugh before hugging.

"Well, I gotta get going. You know I can never stay long, since this isn't my world anymore. Just came for the sausages." Jesus then looks directly at me and says, "By the way, I found out about these delectable treats from watching over you and your family all these years. I can't come back and intervene, but I try to send signals here and there. It's the least I can do as the Savior of the Universe." Jesus smacks his teeth and points his finger at me. "I mean, amirite?" he says while laughing and placing the can of Vienna sausages in the pocket of his white robe. Jesus puts his arms out, rolls his head up, and rises back into the sky while saying in a heavenly voice, "Remember, the light is always there. It never really goes out." His voice suddenly fades and he admits, "They make me say that. I don't really know if it's true." He laughs hysterically to himself until he ascends out of sight.

"He's just joking," Jessie says. "He can be a handful in whatever mystical world this is . . . But he's right, you know . . . It never goes out. You cain't never get rid of it. Sometimes you cain't see it if the clouds or something else covers it, but it's always there . . . the light."

I look at Jessie in total confusion and ask him what he eats in here.

"Boxed mashed potatoes and meatloaf," Rone says. "And yes, it's as nasty as it sounds. It tastes like food you'a get out of a dumpster . . . Ey, also, I was gon' ask if you can put twenty dollars on the commissary so I can get some chips and candy bars and stuff like that."

I say yes and watch as he lights up again, smiling chummily like he always does when he gets what he wants. He asks me how I'm doing in school.

"Made straight A's again," I say.

"That's real good, sis," he responds. "You always was da smart one . . . I was thinkin' 'bout goin' back to school when I get outta here in two years . . . Ey, I was also wonderin' . . . You think I can still be a pilot when I grow up? You think I can still do dat?"

His question overwhelms me, fills me with an irrepressible sadness, and I fall silent. *I don't know* is what I want to tell him. *I don't know if it's still possible.*

I roll my eyeballs all the way up to stop the tears that have started to collect in my eye sockets. I stare at the sullen faces of George Washington, Thomas Jefferson, and James Madison hanging on the walls of this unimaginable place. I think about the irony of these white men putting the words *liberty* and *justice* in the Constitution while owning slaves and creating a system that keeps my brother caged like an animal in here. I become enraged. I feel like I need to do something, need to change it or make it better somehow. Even though I don't really know what to do, I turn to my mother and tell her I need to stop the time. She is so empty and dead inside, she simply nods and says, "Go on 'head, den," while continuing to stare blankly out the window.

"What you mean stop da time?" Rone asks.

I don't respond and begin to wind the time down, watching as

Jessie grows cold and dark. Suddenly, all the lightheartedness of the previous moment filters out of his eyes and he speaks with urgency. "Listen to me. I wish I could explain it all to you, but I can't. You have to make a decision. You have to—"

Before he finishes his sentence, he starts stuttering like he does sometimes in real life.

"I don't understand," I respond.

"Listen, you have to—"

But he can't get his words out. I hear the distress in Jessie's voice and become frightened at what he is trying to tell me. Suddenly, he reaches into his back pocket and pulls out a folded piece of paper. I see that it's the same picture

of Jesus

that we have hanging above our stove at home. *Jesus and the three stooges of democracy*, I think to myself. The time has wound down to a halt, freezing Rone and everyone else in the detention hall except our mother, who still stares out the window in a daze. I look again at Rone. I start talking to him, pleading with him in his frozen state. "Please, Rone," I say. "Please, you have to change. You can't keep going like this. I hate seeing you like this." Tears start falling from my eyes. I grab his frozen hands and tell him how much I love him and how I remember who he was as a little boy before the black veil descended, before he lost himself in the madness of our environment. My mother watches me pleading with Rone, seemingly unaffected, and continues smoking her cigarette. A few minutes later, she mashes the butt into the ashtray, grabs one of my hands, and then rolls her eyes all the way up into their sockets, as far up as they will roll. She takes a deep breath, the deepest breath I've ever seen her take, like it will be the last one she ever takes. Her entire body inflates with air. She exhales and begins saying, "Ancestors of da past, present, and futa' come thru, speak thru. Come thru to dis time and place, here and now. Speak what is needed." I look up again at all the pictures

that Jessie has painted for me and ask him why he painted this sad-looking boy in a green shirt. "I don't need any sad pictures," I tell him. "Look where I live." Jessie doesn't respond and keeps looking at the lighthouse. The colorful clouds continue grazing across the sky like cows in a pasture. It's one of the most beautiful sights I've ever seen, but I feel deeply frustrated with Jessie. I start yelling at him. "I'm so mad at you! How could you leave me like this? Just tell me what it all means. Just tell me!" I start crying, and Jessie puts one of his hands gently on my back, which relaxes my entire body and stops my tears.

"Look," he says after sitting quietly, "I love you and I always have. I'm gonna be here for you no matter what happened to me. I just need you to remember that the light in there," he says while pointing at my chest, "never goes out. Remember that, okay?"

The eighth lesson of wizard training is that there is a light in the center of our souls that never goes out, even in the darkest, bleakest times, because we are keepers of strength and possibility in this world. If that can be internalized during tough times, a wizard can remain risen and transformed instead of sinking to the very bottom of the darkness. This lesson is hard to remember in the moment, though—very hard to remember.

I stand up and tell Jessie I have to get home and do my

homework and that I still don't know what he's talking about. I start walking home. When I've walked a few feet, I turn around to see Jessie one more time, but when I glance back, he has disappeared and the light in the lighthouse has gone out. The clouds in the sky turn dark gray and blue. The temperature dramatically drops below freezing, when moments ago it was warm and balmy. I zip up my jacket and suddenly feel myself being sucked through some kind of portal, until I wake up, gasping for air, back in my apartment, where

my brother's head begins to roll slowly up toward the pictures on the wall. So slow, it looks like he could be in *The Exorcist*. He looks hypnotized as he stares with glazed eyes at the wall. Suddenly, each of the pictures begins to uncurl and speak. They are old white men, but they don't sound like the white people I see on TV and in movies. Instead, they sound like people from my neighborhood, like my father and his friends. One by one, they speak directly to Rone:

> *Gotta wake up, Rone.*
> *Gotta see it all differently.*
> *Gotta wake up fast.*
> *Gotta find da light inside.*
> *Gotta do it soon, befo' it's too late.*

After each of them speaks, they return to their sullen, frozen positions. Time speeds up and everyone slowly starts moving again. Rone looks dazed and says, "Ey, I swear dem pictures was just talkin' to me, man. Sayin' how I gotta wake up and shit. You ain't see that? . . . Man, dis place drivin' me crazy!"

I wonder what it all means, how it will impact Rone. If it will help him change in some way. "I didn't see it, Rone," I say, "but it sounds like good advice to me." Before I can say anything else, the guard interrupts and tells us that our fifteen minutes have passed and we have to leave. We are not allowed to give Rone a hug for fear that some kind of contraband might be passed from visitors to inmates. So we all stand up in a circle looking at each other. My mother returns briefly from her blank state to acknowledge the sadness of the moment. We lock eyes. She and I nod warmly at Rone, giving everything in those nods, because they are all we have to give. We give our love, our hope that he can turn it around, our deep sadness at having to leave him there, alone in his orange jumpsuit. We would nod a thousand more times to show him how much we still love him.

So we all stand in a circle unable to touch, wanting to stay with each other for a little while longer because even in this madness, there is still safety in us being together. I nod again at Rone, and I see he understands. He knows what has been given. His eyes soften and he nods back. My mother says, "Be good, Rone," and I borrow her words, "Yeah, be good, Rone."

Planting a New Story

Do you think you'll ever get locked up?" Elena asks. "Like your brother? I visited my oldest cousin in prison before we left Iran. He was an oil smuggler and got caught, beaten, and arrested. He was always trying to get rich, like my grandfather, but never went about it in the right way. Always looking for quick ways to make a lot of money. He's still in that awful prison. I think about him all the time and about what I'd do if I ever had to go to prison. If I ever ended up there, I hope it's for something I believe in, to help other people. I'd be a woman warrior, a Muslim hero. We could use one of those in the world for sure."

I laugh and respond, "Well, I hope I never get locked up, for any reason, even justice. Maybe that makes me a coward. I don't know, but juvenile detention is the worst place I've ever been in my life. I imagine prison must be ten times worse. I never want to go, and I hope my brother gets it together when he gets out so he doesn't have to go to prison, either."

Elena and I are sitting in the field by the train tracks watching the clouds swirl and churn, brewing thunderstorms that will pour down any moment, which is what we have been waiting for. The clouds form a dark canopy right above us. It's the middle of the day, but it almost feels like nighttime. We love the moodiness of the whole scene and the way the air smells right before a storm. Jessie is with us and sits painting in his chair while Elena and I lie sprawled out on the jagged grass. Her hijab sits folded next to us.

"It's still part of me, but I don't need to have it on all the time," Elena says. "It's kind of like my cape, you know, a complement to the whole woman-warrior-hero persona. There are billions of Muslims in the world, and I'm one of them, right here under people's noses. When they look at me in my hijab, they can't escape the reality of diversity in the world. I like that, being the reminder. Plus, it makes me feel like I'm part of something bigger than myself—my family and the land I come from. Me and my people, united for all to see, demanding the world recognize who we are."

I glance over at her hijab, which she's taken off to feel the wind in her hair, and am inspired by my badass warrior best friend.

We are both fifteen now and go to different schools, but Elena still comes over sometimes on the weekends. Henry E. Tarver Public School, the black high school on the East Side, has honors classes, unlike the black middle school, so I transferred back over. Elena goes to a private high school on the West Side. Her mother drops her off on her way to the medical school, which is two or three miles from my apartment, and complains the whole drive over about how "dangerous and unsafe this neighborhood is." Elena's mother speaks about the East Side like it's another country, like it's not just right across the bridge. In many ways, she is right. I wish someone would do a documentary to show the rest of the world what America is really like for some of us. I wonder what people around the world would think if they saw how racially divided everything still is here. Elena never says anything about how poor and broken-down my apartment is, especially compared to where she lives, but I know she must be shocked at the difference, too.

We always pick up Jessie when we go to the field, which is still one of my favorite things to do. Now we are resting in the grass, staring up at the clouds, talking about wizard things. "Holy shit, I just had an epiphany," Elena says. "We are living in *The Matrix: Cleveland Edition*. We can stop time, like the actual ticking time. That's so rad." After the portal first opened in Elena's room, Elena eventually comes all the way around to accepting her wizardry and we start practicing miracles together. We have learned many things from our training: that saying *Show me the light* stops you from seeing other people's black veils, but not your own if it's covering you; that once it's wrapped around you, it merges totally with your energy field. We also learn that you can only stop time before a miracle. If a miracle is not performed while the time is stopped, it starts speeding up back to normal on its own, which means you can't take advantage and do bad things in the timeless space. As it turns out, the portal to the in-between opens on its own when someone is in distress or when a message needs to be transmitted to help a wizard grow.

There's still a lot we don't know, however. I wish we had someone else to teach us more things, but my mother has continued her descent and says she still doesn't want me to participate in "all dat wizard shit," even though she helped me reach Rone at the juvenile detention center two years ago. "It ain't gon' lead you nowhere productive. Only dat schoolin'a do dat," my mother says repeatedly. Rone will be getting out in a few days. It's been two years since the miracle my mother and I performed at the juvenile detention. Elena and I have been thinking about what miracles we can perform to help him stay out of trouble. I feel a surge of happiness thinking about Rone's upcoming release, which means all the people I love will be free soon. Maybe we can all come to the field again, like old times.

I gaze over at Jessie and remember the time before the accident. He looks so peaceful now, painting quietly in his wheelchair, occasionally looking up at the clouds as if he is waiting for something. My mother says you have to be grateful for the people you knew in childhood since the people you meet as an adult "is already ruined and no good, but you always 'member da innocence of peoples you knew as kids." I decide I will cherish every Jessie I've known—I know who he was as a child, who he was before the accident, and who he is now. I'm so happy he's here. Even though things have changed, I still feel safe and protected whenever I'm near him, like that day in the shack. "Since we live in the Matrix, maybe Jessie's like your Oracle, watching out for you. He knows when Agent Smith is nearby," Elena said earlier today. I don't know if that's true, but I know he's still my person.

Elena's my person now, too. I've learned you can have more than one person be your "person." It's such a relief to find people who are just like you. Elena is a quirky, resilient warrior who has managed to maintain an open heart. I suddenly have an overwhelming urge to reach out and grab her hand. My whole body starts buzzing with discomfort at the thought of it, but I force myself to do it anyway. I squeeze her hand, signaling my gratitude at having found her. When the tingling sensations start unexpectedly, I begin to pull my hand away in embarrassment, but Elena rolls her head toward me and kisses me on the lips. It's the softest, sweetest kiss I've ever received. Afterward, it feels like a thousand butterflies are fluttering through my body. We both stare at the sky, unsure what to do next. I peer over at Jessie with uneasiness, worried he might have seen us and remembering our unfulfilled kiss in the shack. I wonder if he remembers also.

The tension between Elena and me builds, until she takes her hand out of mine, and starts pointing at the sky. "Look!" she shouts. "The rain's starting." Elena grabs her hijab and wraps it around her head to protect her hair.

I look up and see a few raindrops break away from the clouds and land on our faces. We know more will follow, and we rise in anticipation of the downpour. I notice that the clouds seem to mold and stretch themselves as if they were stretching around some kind of round object, trying to poke through.

"Hey, look!" I say, pointing at the sky excitedly. A black

crow pokes its head through a hole in the cloud, but the hole seems to be too small so it struggles to pull the rest of its body through. After lots of wiggling, it finally manages to pass through the hole. It circles right above us and caws several times. Jessie is transfixed.

"That was weird," I say to them in confusion.

"Yeah, it was," Elena says, then asks, "Do you want to do it now? Looks like it's just about to pour."

I nod and say, "Yeah, let's do it now."

We quickly untie the six balloons tied to Jessie's wheelchair. I told Elena about how we released balloons with prayers and blessings at church when I was younger and suggested it would be cool to do the same thing now, only instead of prayers and blessings, we put folded copies of Jessie's art inside. We each take two balloons.

"All right, on the count of three," I say. "One, two—"

"Oh my God! Look at that!" Elena says while pointing frantically at the sky. We both crane our necks awkwardly up and see a ton of birds begin to pour through the same hole the first one came out of. There are at least a hundred birds, and they circle around and around right above of us, cawing shrilly. I grow fearful inside and ask Elena what it means. "I don't know," she says, staring up with her mouth wide open. We stand there watching the birds, with two balloons each in our hands and Jessie taking in the skyline to my side.

Jessie's two balloons float up. One of them drifts away, far beyond the train tracks, but the other one jolts right up into the cluster of birds. We hear a loud *pop!* and watch as the deflated balloon falls back to the earth. I run over and pick up the debris. A small gray lighthouse on a key chain lies beneath it. I stare down at the lighthouse in disbelief, chilled by the sight of it. Elena peers over my shoulder as big, fat raindrops begin to fall all around. "Where did that come from?" she asks, but I don't respond.

Miracle at *Titanic*" is what we call our plan to conduct a miracle for my brothers at the movies. We pick *Titanic* because it's our current favorite and we've already seen it five times. Even though Elena hates sappy movies, she loves the epic drama of a massive sinking boat. We decide if it works, if we're able to get the ancestors from the in-between to speak through Leo and Kate to influence my brothers, it will be our biggest miracle yet.

"Can you imagine if it actually works?!" Elena asks excitedly.

"Yeah, I know," I respond enthusiastically. "Then they'll have to call us something else. Not quantum wizards, but badass boss wizards."

Elena laughs cheerfully and says, "I *love* the sound of that!"

Elena's mother has agreed to join us for the movie at the second-run theater near my neighborhood. I don't have enough money for all of us, so the only way our plan will work is if Elena's parents give her the money. Initially, Elena's mom says no, again citing the sketchiness of the East Side. But Elena convinces her mom to "chaperone" (and pay) for the event by agreeing to come tour the medical school next month. "My mother is so stoked about me coming to her work. She thinks it means I've finally decided to become a doctor and all her wildest dreams are coming true." The thought of it fills Elena with boredom and disgust, but she's committed to helping me save my brothers.

We begin methodically planning all the details. The first part of our plot will be to convince my brothers and a few of their friends to go see *Titanic*. We convince them by promising to also buy them tickets to see *Blade* or *Rush Hour* next weekend. *Titanic* was the number one movie in the country last year, especially with young women (and anyone with a soul). My brothers and their friends eventually agree to come, but say they "ain't gon' cry at dat girly movie." We nod our heads, but already know they won't be able to resist. We know what's coming. Everyone leaves *Titanic* in tears: men, women, children, teachers, doctors, cops. Probably even cold-blooded killers. "Maybe that's how we solve crime epidemics," Elena says jokingly. "Take the criminals to several viewings of *Titanic*, and eventually they'll start singing like a canary." We both burst out laughing at jokes that we are sure are funny only to us. "If the miracle doesn't work, at least it will take down their shells," Elena says, "and make them feel something again deep inside." I haven't seen my brothers without their shells since Jessie's accident, so getting them to be a little vulnerable would be a miracle in and of itself. Rone, who is still adjusting to life outside of juvenile detention, seems to have grown an even thicker shell now that he's out.

At first my brothers are very hesitant, even after I offer to get them tickets to *Rush Hour*. Rone says, "Come on, Echo, you know I ain't goin' ta see dat soft shit. And my boys definitely ain't goin'. What you want me to see dat for anyways?" I ignore his question and remind him that he owes me for giving him my old Game Boy for his birthday. "A'ight, man. A'ight den, but you gotta get yo rich friend to buy me and all my boys tickets to *Rush Hour* next week."

"Deal," I say as we shake hands like gangsters in an old-fashioned mob movie. Only instead of mobsters, we are siblings, and the list of what is owed between siblings is probably just as long as what is owed between gangsters. Rone smiles chummily, like he always does when he thinks he's out-maneuvered me. *But it is I who has outmaneuvered you*, I think to myself. *And for your own benefit, fool*. I pat myself on the back for my obvious cleverness.

Once I convince Rone to go, he convinces all the others. Rone has turned into a natural leader, thanks to his stature and commanding personality. He is already as tall as my father, even though he's only fourteen years old, and he exudes confidence and charm. Dre looks up to him, like the rest of Rone's friends, and follows his lead on many things. Dre has already seen *Titanic* with Elena and me twice before, but he agrees to come again since his soft heart still craves connection. He has hardened for sure, but the core of who he has always been is still there. Unlike Rone, he hasn't lost that yet.

When we get to the theater on the day of the movie, Elena's mother buys Rone, Dre, and their friends whatever they want, including pop, hot dogs, nachos, and an assortment of candy. They hold the food tightly to their chests as if someone is going to steal it from them. "Relax," I say. "Ain't nobody gon' take nothin' from y'all." A lifetime of never having enough has convinced them otherwise, so they refuse to release their grip on the snacks and candy until it's all gone. My brothers and their friends are on their best behavior, as I've warned them they better be. They move quietly through the movie theater, not displaying their usual rowdiness. They attempt to call Elena's mother Ms. Farahmand out of respect, but they slightly mispronounce it calling her Ms. Far-med instead. Neither Elena nor her mother corrects them, both being charmed by their effort.

I wonder if Elena's mom is uncomfortable being around so many black people. The group of us must look strange to outside observers: five black boys, a black girl, and two Persian women in hijabs, casually bouncing through the theater. Elena's mother does not seem at all fazed by the whole scene; she's much more down-to-earth than she was at that first dinner. Elena said her mother was thrilled to chaperone us at the movie since she feels like Elena never wants to hang out with her anymore now that she's in high school. "She'd hang out with me in the bathroom if I invited her," Elena says jokingly. "I figured a movie would be much more pleasant." We both burst out laughing, but stop when we see Elena's mom glaring at us. "Have you already called the guy about Part Two of the plan?" Elena asks.

"Yes," I respond. "I scheduled it for Saturday afternoon. He lives not too far from you."

Miracle at *Titanic* is only the first part of our mission. Next step is to try to move my family out of the neighborhood we've been trapped in all my life. I've been applying for apartments on the West Side for months. I plan to use all the money I make working at the Cleveland Clinic after school on the first month's rent and deposit. I have already visited over ten apartments in white neighborhoods, with Elena joining me sometimes, and have been turned down for all of them.

Before we visit, I call and ask them if they accept Section 8, the government program that helps poor people pay their rent. If they say yes, I quickly hurry to the apartment and try to convince the landlords to rent to me and my family. I lie. I tell them that we are quiet people. That my brothers love school and are good students, like me. I tell them my parents are retired and live on Social Security disability, but they worked all their lives. My father was a welder and my mother a seamstress. I watch the faces of the white people twist as my brown flesh walks through the door. I see how quickly the decision is made. How quickly they see "people like me" as trouble, even when Elena and her almost-white body (without the hijab) is standing right next to me.

I hope this place on Saturday will finally be different. I have a good feeling about it since the man was so nice over the phone, even after I tell him where I currently live and that we are on Section 8.

The three-bedroom house is at the end of a tree-lined street. Elena and I walk up the stairs of the small porch and ring the doorbell. A middle-aged white man answers the door; he tells us he is an attorney, and this rental property is his. We follow him into the kitchen, a kitchen so luxurious, so sparkling, I'm afraid to touch anything. I can see that there is a fireplace in the living room. *I always wanted a fireplace,* I think to myself, *so I can snuggle up and read all the books in the world.* I see from the kitchen window that a freshly cut, beautifully manicured lawn wraps around the property. I imagine my brothers and me sitting out on the lawn smiling, drinking Kool-Aid, and talking about what it was like to live on the East Side all those years ago. The neighborhood is bursting with big weeping willows that invite reflection and deep thought, and also shield the houses and the people from the harshness of the sun. There is very little green where I live, which quietly hurts us. I know the importance of living near growing, thriving things, which is nature's way of reminding us of all that is flourishing and possible in this world. *My family can flourish in this house surrounded by majestic weeping willow trees.* I watch a squirrel scurry down one of the trunks before

turning and making a wide circle around the second concession stand, which has a long line of people waiting to buy snacks. I stop in front of the bathroom and ask Elena to save me a seat. When I come out of the bathroom, I bump into Prince Mack. He's here with two friends to see *Rush Hour.* "Ey! Echo, right?" he asks curiously. "Ey, why you ain't neva call a nigga? Usually I cain't stop dese girls from callin'. What, you really, really shy?" I am mesmerized by how good Prince Mack still looks. I notice the fullness of his lips as he licks them slightly with his tongue. His brown skin is so buttery and smooth he glistens, like he is always standing directly in the sun. And his skin stretches so perfectly over his toned muscles, I have to pull my eyes away to keep from staring. Prince Mack is right, I am shy, especially when it comes to boys. I just know I'm a beast and boys don't like beasts, except Davante and Jessie. Davante and I broke up the summer before we got to high school. The thrill of kissing him wore off, and I started to feel like I was kissing my brother. He was very disappointed, but he said he would find other girls in high school and I would be jealous. I smiled and wished him luck with all his other girls. He was very upset I wasn't mad, but I'm glad we are no longer seeing each other.

Being a shy beast isn't the reason I never called Prince Mack, however. I just got spooked after my dream with Jessie by the lighthouse, like I should stay away from him. Seeing Prince here at the movie theater, two years later, makes me feel like I made a mistake. We could have been together all that time if I hadn't let my fear get the best of me. I wonder if he will give me a second chance.

"I'on' know, I jus' be studyin' all da time," I say shyly. "I forgot. Dat's all."

Prince Mack smiles and says, "Oh yeah, you one a' dem smart girls. I like smart girls . . . Well, look, I'ma gi'u my numba again a'ight?" I nod my head yes as he starts writing down his phone number. "You betta call me dis time, a'ight?" he asks in a sultry voice while biting his lower lip.

"Okay, I'll call you tomorrow," I say decisively.

He hands me the piece of paper and then leans down and lingers in front of my face before kissing me softly on the lips. The tingling sensations start immediately and I feel like I'm going to explode. One of his friends leaves the bathroom, and as they walk away I hear his friend say, "Man, how many girls do you got, dude? Gimme one, man." I get a sinking feeling in my stomach when I hear them both laughing, but I push the fear and doubt out of my mind and decide I will still call him tomorrow. He may have had other girls before, but I'm going to be the best girlfriend he's ever had.

By the time I get to the theater, the movie is about to start. I search in the darkness for my brothers and Elena. When I finally spot them, I make my way to my seat. Elena asks what took so long. "Nothing," I whisper. "I just ran into somebody . . . an old friend . . . by the bathroom. We were just catching up." We both turn toward the movie screen and watch as

the middle-aged white man moves furtively around the kitchen. He offers us a glass of water or lemonade. We decline and continue to look around the house. "This is a very nice kitchen," I say, enamored. I can tell he is confused. He knows he and I are not equal, because of the racial difference, but he doesn't know what to make of Elena. He keeps looking over at her every time he asks a question.

"So which one of you applied for the house? Are you together or . . . are you related . . . what questions do you have about the house?" he asks while looking eagerly in Elena's direction. Elena and I both pause briefly, trying to determine if there is some angle we should play in this moment; if we should be dishonest and use Elena's perceived almost-whiteness to our advantage. I can tell Elena is thinking the same thing, but *what would happen when the time came to move in?* I think to myself. *And me and my whole black family showed up instead of Elena.*

"I applied," I say confidently after a few moments, realizing there's no way around telling him it was me. "It would be for me and my family. My mother and father and two brothers."

I watch disappointment roll over his face like clouds before a storm. "Oh," he says simply.

We are all quiet

as the first scene of *Titanic* unfolds. We are glued to the screen as it all happens: the greatest steamship of its time soars through the open ocean while one of the actors proclaims triumphantly, "Not even God himself could sink this ship." Elena, Dre, and I know he is wrong, but I'm not sure if Rone and his friends know what is going to happen. They just know it's a movie about "some people on a boat." We watch Rose and Jack—Kate and Leo—fall in love all over again: Jack's courageous attempt to save Rose from jumping off the back of the boat, their subsequent frolicking and dancing in the "lower-class" cabins, and their steamy hookup in the back of the 1912 Renault Type CB Coupe de Ville. My brothers giggle when Kate's hand pushes against the window. I can tell they are slightly embarrassed and

guilty, which he tries to hide by looking past me at the painting over the kitchen sink, but I can tell by the guilt in his eyes, he knows he should give me a chance. His face softens when I tell him I want to be a biomedical engineer and help create lifesaving technology for people around the world. I can see my words resonate and land on his soft parts. Elena acts as my wing woman, confirming everything I say. "Yeah, she's the smartest person I know. You probably won't find a better tenant."

Elena and I keep pressing into him with all the passion and hope in the world. I can see the ambivalence in his eyes. He wants to help. He believes the lies I tell him about my family. "My mother and father have doctors' appointments, so they couldn't come. I just got off work myself, but I had to come take a look. The place sounded so amazing and affordable in the ad." I use my proper, white-girl English, enunciating all my syllables just like I did on the phone. No one has taught me how to do this; I instinctively know this is what is needed to persuade this man—I need to speak to him in his native language and not like how my parents and the people in my neighborhood speak. I press further, trying to convince him, trying to work against his conditioning about "people like me." This house, this new neighborhood, will be a portal that helps change the trajectory of my brothers' lives. This will catapult them into orbit around the mantle of possibility instead of being stuck in the under-belly of American society. I just know it. I infuse my voice and eyes with sincerity and warmth. He keeps softening as

the boat starts to sink. When my brothers and their friends realize the reality of what is about to happen, I am surprised by their response. One of Rone's friends turns to him and says, "Nigga, dey all 'bout to die! Nigga, what da fuck?! Dis shit sad as fuck." We watch as the band decides to stay and continue playing while the ship sinks, which is a final effort to provide some grace and decency in such a barbaric moment.

Another one of my brother's friends whispers, "Aww shit, nigga, da band gon' stay on da boat. Nigga, dat's some gangsta shit. I wouldn't do dat shit, but I respect it." His voice cracks and Rone responds, "Nigga, you cryin'?!"

The friend recoils in terror, saying, "Nah! Nigga, I ain't cryin', but I ain't 'spect dis shit to be so sad."

Elena's mother leans over in shock and whispers, "Please stop using that word and no more talking or curse words during the movie!"

"Yes, ma'am," they all reply in unison.

The boat finally sinks, and Rose lies on a plank in the middle of the frigid ocean while Jack holds on to the edge of the plank, having decided there isn't enough room for both of them.

Dre says loudly, "Man, come on, why she don't let him on top of dat wood, man? You can fit a whole basketball team up dere!"

They are all very upset that Jack does not join Rose on top of the plank. They feel like it's some kind of inexcusable injustice that must be rectified before the movie ends. They are so upset, they can't stop talking about it, even after Elena's mother tells them again to be quiet.

Another friend blurts out, "Man, dat's foul! Both dey asses can definitely fit on dat piece of wood. Dat's a big piece of wood! Shit, nigga, you best believe I would have climbed right up on top of dat bitch and been chillin', waitin' fo dem lifeboats."

They all start laughing, but I can tell that their shells are lowered and they are all visibly shaken by how the story is unfolding. I look over at Elena and nod my head, indicating it's time for us to start the miracle. We wind the time down and follow my mother's instructions for calling the ancestors. We watch as Jack and Rose, as well as everyone in the theater, begin to move in slow motion. Elena and I check to make sure my brothers' eyes are wide open, looking straight ahead, locked

on the painting hanging over the kitchen sink, which is a picture of Martin Luther King Jr., "who inspired him to become a civil rights attorney and fight for justice in the world." He stares at the painting as if he's trying to reassure himself, remind himself of something. Then he turns and locks eyes with me. I transfix him in my gaze, which is no ordinary gaze, but the gaze of a thousand ancestors traveling across time and space to assist me. Elena watches alertly nearby while also projecting as much warm, focused energy as she can in the middle-aged white man's direction. We envelop him. We compel him to bend to our will. I see Elena nod her head from the corner of my eye, and we begin to freeze time. It winds down and down and down until the man stands frozen, gazing up at Martin. Suddenly, Martin begins to unfold from his position and looks directly at the man and begins speaking. I am overwhelmed hearing his famous voice pour out

of the movie screen. Leo and Kate both sit on top of the plank and stare in our direction. It feels like they are looking directly at us. It's amazing and creepy at the same time. They hold hands and then begin speaking, alternating after each sentence:

> *We have already said you have to wake up*
> *We are rooting for you*
> *We are always rooting for you*
> *We want to try a different approach*
> *We want to show you what you could become*
> *The highest version of yourself*

I assume they must be talking to Rone, because he is the only one we have tried this miracle on. The screen suddenly goes totally black. Elena grabs my hand as we both stare at the black screen in anticipation of what will come next. After a few seconds, a man in a white shirt begins to slowly materialize on the screen. The camera is zoomed all the way in on the man, from the chest up, and the image is blurry at first until it comes all the way into focus. We see that it's an older version of Rone in a pilot's uniform. He stares straight ahead and says, "Watch this." The screen switches to a view of older Rone soaring high above the earth in a Boeing 757. He looks so professional flying the plane through the clouds. When he lands, he announces proudly to the cabin, "Ladies and gentlemen, we have safely arrived back in Cleveland, Ohio, which happens to be my hometown. Some may call it the 'mistake by the lake,' but I call it one of the greatest cities in the country. On behalf of American Airlines and the entire crew, it's been our pleasure to serve you this evening. This was my very first flight, which I guess I can tell you now that we've landed safely. It's been my dream all my life to be a pilot, and so it's been an honor to fly with you today."

Me, my parents, and Dre are all onboard for his first flight. We race to the front of the plane and give him a big group hug and tell him how proud of him we are and how we all knew he could do it.

The camera zooms in on Rone's face and upper body again, and he looks straight ahead and says, "Tell yourself this story instead." The screen suddenly goes black again.

When it comes back on, a man at a podium begins to materialize. We see that it is Dre and he is preparing to read from his book of poems, *Lessons from the Rising*. Dre looks directly out into the theater and says, "It's not too late." Then we watch as Dre travels all over the world, sharing his poetry and the life experiences that inspired it. He is proud and compassionate. On the last night of his book tour, our parents, Rone, and I all show up to surprise him in the audience.

When he asks if anyone has any questions at the end of his talk, I raise my hand and say, "Dre, I have known you all your life. Since you were a little boy when we used to run around that open field together and spiral prayers for everything we wanted to be when we grew up. It has been the great honor of my life to watch you blossom into such a sweet, caring, compassionate, and intelligent young man and to watch you achieve your dreams. I am so deeply proud of you. Your words have not only inspired me, your big sister, but people all around the world. Can I come up and give you a hug?"

He drops his head bashfully, like he always does when put on the spot, and responds, "Yeaaah, sis, come on up."

I race up to the stage and give him the biggest hug any human has ever given another. I grab the mic and cheerfully shout to the audience, "And he's single, ladies! He's a thoughtful Aquarius who's got his shit together. What a catch! Don't be shy, come get 'im!"

Dre shakes his head while saying into the mic, "My sister is a little off, but I love her."

The audience laughs uproariously before unleashing gleeful applause at the whole scene. The camera then zooms back in on Dre as he stares straight ahead and speaks forcefully with conviction

like he always has. I am astounded by the power of Martin's words. He looks directly at the middle-aged white man and says,

> *And now, here is your opportunity to help,*
> *To open a portal where there was none before,*
> *To bend the arc forward, for the benefit of someone else.*

When he finishes, he turns his head back to its original position and freezes. The time begins to unwind, and the man starts rapidly blinking his eyes. "Oh my God," he says, "I feel like I just passed out." He then chugs an entire glass of water in front of us. I can see that the middle-aged white man is disarmed, that he is on the verge of saying yes. I know I have to say something to press further into him while he is soft and receptive. I wait for the words to come, the ones that will convince him to open this portal for me and my family.

I begin speaking. "I promise I won't let you down," I say. "If you just give us a chance. No one seems to want to rent to us over here, but my family and I would take real good care of your place. And you don't have to worry about us paying the rent every month since we have Section 8. They pay on time every month. I know people don't usually accept Section 8 in these kinds of houses, so I'm real grateful you do."

Something about the way I say "these kinds of houses" causes him to bristle and disconnect from me. He is reminded of the distance between us, of the gaping inequality. He is inspired by MLK, but only from a distance. He will fight for our rights, but he doesn't want us in his neighborhood, in his house. All the softness evaporates from his face, and I know I have lost him. He can't overcome the story he has been told about "people like me," even though he thought he had convinced himself he didn't believe those kinds of racial things. The seed has been planted too deep, all hope is lost. I look back out the window at the trees, not wanting to leave them. Stinging disappointment settles in my heart and Elena's eyes, which dart intensely at the man. I can tell she wants to say something, but I furtively shake my head no.

"Well, it was certainly nice to meet you ladies," the man says. "I'll give you a call if I need any further information." His eyes roll in

Elena's and my direction. We have just seen scenes for both my brothers' and all their friends' possible future lives. Now Leo and Kate are looking at Elena and me. They begin speaking, alternating their sentences again as if they are channeling all their words from an unknown place:

As for you two

Know that no miracle is guaranteed

Here, today, we have simply

planted seeds

What happens with those seeds is

up to them now

It can't be forced

It must be chosen

But the seed is important

The seed can grow into a different
story, if there is willingness

And nothing is more important
than the ability to tell yourself a
different story

A new story that goes against what
the world has told you

The ninth lesson of wizard training is learning to tell yourself a different story about who you think you are on the inside. People underestimate the power of telling a different inside story, but it's the only real power we have to create new lives for ourselves. Usually, all of us have some kind of bad story seeds that eventually sprout into a spoiled harvest. If you want a lush, bountiful harvest, you must replant yourself from the inside. You must uproot all those bad seeds planted by others and plant new ones that will grow different stories inside of you.

Leo and Kate turn toward Elena's mother. They both stare silently at her. Elena and I sit on the edge of our seats, holding our breath, wondering what they will say next. We both exhale when Leo and Kate finally begin speaking:

And so here you are

Sitting in the toxic soil of what you
know is a false story

You didn't want to see

    Took the blue pill

And now you seek to blind her, too

But she is awake

    Working in both realms

The force is in her

    And you, too

We hope you will plant

this new story seed

    So that you will not be

    the imposter you have taught

    your daughter not to be

Elena and I watch as Kate and Leo return to their original positions on the plank. When the movie finally ends, and all the other people have left, the eight of us sit there silently trying to process what just happened. Elena and I from a place of knowing, and everyone else from a place of not knowing but feeling that something unusual has happened from the deep-inside place, the seed place. After sitting in silence and heavy emotions while the theater workers eye us curiously and clean around us, Rone says, "Man, I take it all back. Dat was a life-changing movie. Like, dat was da best movie I eva seen in my entire life. I wanna see dis again next week instead of *Rush Hour*."

"Yeah," I say in a daze. "That was the best movie I've ever seen."

Reading the Signals

I'm gay," Elena says to me abruptly and without warning. We are sitting at her dining room table, studying and drinking tea. "I just wanted to say it out loud to you, to another living person. So if you are, too, you can just say it now."

I look up at Elena and smile. "Well, I kind of already figured you were, since you never talk about boys and, oh yeah, you kissed me."

Elena chuckles.

"I don't know for myself if I like girls," I say. "I'm confused about that. For now, I think I mostly like boys, but who knows in the future. Who knows."

Elena smiles and nods enthusiastically, but I can tell she's a little disappointed. "Well, you're the only person I've told," she says. "I still don't know if I can tell my mother, even after the Miracle at *Titanic*. I don't know if she's ready to accept me being a wizard and being gay. I think it would be too much for her right now, but she has been a lot more chill and isn't pressuring me as much since then. She was so impressed by how respectful and polite your brothers were, except for the cursing. She has totally dropped her daily PSA about the East Side. She's been more quiet than usual, and we still haven't actually talked about what happened at the theater; I don't know if we ever will. Maybe some people will never truly accept who they are even after a miracle like that . . . Regardless, I've decided I'm going to do what I want. I'm going to have a wife and live in Brooklyn with our seven cats, goddammit! Pussies galore!"

Elena slams her fist on the table in triumph. I stand up and start clapping. She laughs uproariously before sipping her tea. I walk around the table and give her a big hug, letting her know I support her dreams and she will always be my person.

We eat snacks and keep talking about everything: which colleges we're thinking about going to (I'm thinking of Dartmouth for the majestic wilderness and cute boys, which I've seen in the brochure, and she's thinking about Yale for its theater program); my upcoming date with Prince Mack; and whether the Miracle at *Titanic* worked. I have been observing my brothers carefully since that day. Some things are different, and some things are the same. They now study with me sometimes and ask for my help on their homework. I can see that they seem to be reaching for their education with a new vigor and hopefulness, but they are still struggling with the same addictions they had before the miracle. They drink less and smoke less weed. I know they are trying in a new way to overcome all the bad seeds that have been planted inside them.

The new seeds haven't taken root and broken ground yet.

I see their struggles and do my part to keep pushing, to keep watering, to keep reminding them of the futures they saw on the movie theater screen, even though they are not consciously aware of what they saw. Rone has been talking more and more about how to become a pilot, so I know deep down he was at least receptive to the miracle, which is the most important part. The other person's receptivity. "I'll just keep trying," I tell Elena. "I'll try forever if I have to."

Elena smiles warmly and squeezes my hand. "And what about that guy? The one I don't like. I mean, who calls themselves Prince Mack? Come on, I really feel like he's bad news. I like Davante! Go back to him. He's always yelling about black power, but he's got a gentle heart. I can tell . . . Oh, hey, I was thinking, why don't you let me come over there with you? I don't know, I just have a bad feeling about it. I promise I won't make a sound. You won't even know I'm there."

I laugh and tell Elena of course she can't come. "What are you going to do? Sit downstairs and do your homework while we make out upstairs? It'll be fine. I had doubts, too, but he was really sweet at the movie theater. I'm gonna go tomorrow, and of course I'll call you as soon as I get home."

"Thanks, kid," Elena says playfully. "I'll be waiting for the call."

— – — ——o○o—— — – –

On the day I go over to Prince Mack's, I stand outside on the sidewalk for several minutes just staring at his house, not believing I'm about to go into the house of the best-looking boy in the neighborhood. Me, the ugly beast. I stand on the sidewalk so long that one of the neighbors asks me if I'm lost. I snap out of my daze and shake my head no. I slowly walk up the stairs. I scan my outfit again to reassure myself I look the best I possibly could. I'm wearing a black shirt, earrings that hang down the side of my face, a green puffy coat, and a maroon skirt with no stockings, even though it's very chilly and almost winter. I'm also not wearing my glasses, which means I can't see anything far away. I squint my eyes repeatedly to try to see in front of me as I walk to his house. I feel ridiculous without my glasses and in this outfit, because it's so cold, but I push all those feelings away and ring the doorbell.

As soon as I press it, Prince Mack forcefully swings the door open, as if he's been waiting. He says, "Nice ta see you, gurl. You look cute."

He smiles like he did at the movie theater, but for some reason, in this moment, I feel weird about it. Today his smile feels crooked and deceptive somehow. I tell myself to snap out of it, but I can't seem to relax. Even after we go inside and sit on the couch in his living room. He is talking, commenting on how nice I look, and about how much he likes sweet, shy girls. I am watching his mouth move, but I barely hear what he's saying because my body won't stop locking up. I feel like a brick or a stone. All my muscles clench simultaneously. And I suddenly feel so heavy and sunken, like the black veil is near. I have an overwhelming urge to leave and start looking all around in confusion for the veil. I feel like it's hovering right above me, but I don't see anything.

I wonder why I feel this way after having fantasized about Prince Mack for so long. He notices my unease and says we should go up to his room and watch TV because "it's more comfortable and relaxing up there." He goes to the kitchen, grabs two cans of Pepsi from the refrigerator, hands me one, and motions for me to follow him upstairs. I carry the can of Pepsi awkwardly, looking for places to leave it or throw it out since I hate pop and can never bring myself to drink it. *I should ask him if he has Kool-Aid*, I consider, but I decide against asking since I don't want to disappoint him by turning down his offering.

I follow him meekly up the stairs, noticing all the pictures hanging on his wall along the way. Pictures of him and his family in various places: on vacation, in church, in front of the house. I pause when I see a school picture of his kindergarten class. I scan the picture trying to find him, trying to see what he looked like as a kid. I stop at a smiling little boy wearing a green collared shirt. I wonder if it's Prince Mack. The boy seems so familiar to me, but I can't quite place him. I shift my head to the side like my old third-grade teacher, Mrs. Samuels. I scan my memory, trying to figure it out. The more I stare at the picture, the more my body locks up. I feel frozen, like I can't move.

Prince Mack calls from the top of the stairs, "Yo, you all right? I know, I know, I was cute even in kindergarten. Dat's what all da girls say." Realizing it's a mistake to mention other girls in this moment, he quickly adds, "I mean, dat's what my momma always say, about how cute I was. Come on up. I got some otha pictures in my room if you wanna see more."

It takes all the strength I have in my body to turn and walk up to him. I have to shout at my brain to *Move!* over and over.

I keep walking slowly up the stairs until I get to his room. I look around and see that he has posters of Michael Jordan, Tupac, and Snoop Dogg hanging on his walls. I sit on a chair across from his bed, holding my back totally erect, careful not to slump my shoulders, and still holding the unopened can of Pepsi in my hand. I smile plastically like I do when I'm around white people. In this moment, I come to understand the purpose of smiling plastically. It's to hide how you really feel inside. Right now, I feel very weird and I want to hide the strange feelings that keep popping up. I suck all my feelings back in, swallowing them while watching Prince Mack move around the room. He picks up dirty clothes from the floor, puts them in a hamper, straightens the sheets on his bed. When he finally notices me sitting on the chair across the room, he says, "You don't like Pepsi or somethin'?"

Sensing the disappointment in his voice, I suddenly open the can, take several sips, and smile plastically again.

He sits on the bed and asks, "Why you sittin' all da way ova dere for? Come sit next to me."

Again, I have to muster every ounce of strength in my body to get up and walk toward him. I set the can of Pepsi on the dresser by the bed and sit down next to him. As soon as I sit, my mind starts flooding with words like what happens with the light spirals from the in-between: *This is not right. Leave. Get up. Leave. Move. Get up. Go downstairs. Move now.* I'm confused by these words because they do not match the desire I've had for Prince Mack for the past few years. Just like the weird feelings, I push them down and swallow them.

"You're so pretty and cute," Prince Mack says while moving one of my earrings to the side and kissing my neck. I try to make his kisses feel good, like they do in my fantasies, but this doesn't feel anything like that. Everything feels wrong. In my fantasy, I feel safe and at ease, not heavy and afraid like I do now. Here, in this moment, I feel like prey, like I'm about to be devoured by a hungry wolf. Prince Mack slides his hand up my thigh and under my skirt and then jabs his fingers inside me mercilessly. I wince, but try to hide the pain. When he keeps jabbing, I tell him it hurts, but he acts like he doesn't hear me and starts grabbing and rubbing me all over. I become paralyzed with fear and panic. I want him to stop. I plead for him to stop from the inside, but the words don't leave my mouth, so I shake my head no in terror, over and over, but Prince Mack ignores all my signals.

When he tries to kiss me on the lips, I turn my head away, which upsets him. "Come on, girl, what you think you came here to do? You know what's up. Now, just relax." He pushes my body backward, down toward the bed, but it won't bend because it's stiff like a board. He keeps pushing until I feel like I am moving in slow motion. My gaze follows the line of the ceiling all the way back until I hit the pillow. My eyes land squarely on the ceiling, and I know it is the only place I will find refuge from what is to come. So I go there, early, make a camp on the ceiling for the duration of the event.

He pushes my skirt up. My brain sends signals to my hands to push it back down, to please push it back down, but my hands don't move. They are terrorized also. All of me is terrorized. *I should have left*, I tell myself. *I'm so stupid for wearing a skirt, for coming here. God, I'm so stupid.*

As Prince Mack prepares to launch his full assault, I try one more time to lift myself up somehow, but I'm paralyzed, pinned under the weight of his massive body. He pulls down his basketball shorts. I watch from the ceiling. I want to scream, but no sound comes out. I pray for voices; that someone comes home now, right now. For voices coming from anywhere—downstairs, in the hallway, outside. But none come, not even my own.

Prince Mack pushes himself inside me, which causes waves of pain to shoot up the length of my body. He doesn't fit. He's too big, but he pushes and pushes until he finally breaks in. I shriek in pain. I whisper for him to stop, but he just tells me to "Shhh." I stare at the ceiling, at myself sitting up there. At the spirit that has left my body to survive this massacre. I think back to the Miracle at *Titanic*, about the flash forward of who I could become in the future. Rone would become a pilot, Dre would become a poet, Elena would become a famous actress who also advocates for human rights, and I would become a therapist. Not a biomedical engineer like I have been planning, but a therapist who helps other broken little girls. I see on the screen, all the broken little girls lining up outside my office, waiting to see me, waiting for me to teach them how to un-break. Each little girl comes carrying a thousand pounds of bad seeds that have been planted inside them. I look deep into their eyes to see for myself what has been done to them, to bear witness. They need a witness. And when I see the sadness, which looks exactly like mine, I tell them what must be done, about the journey that must be taken to survive it. Their eyes swell with tears at hearing that it can be survived. They have come to me for hope that it can be survived.

But that hope is being ripped from me now by this monster on top of me. He is a monster. *How did I not see this before?* Prince Mack starts moving faster and faster, moaning and breathing louder and louder until he finally releases himself inside me. He thrusts as far and deep inside me as he can before rolling over and also staring at the ceiling. I wonder if he can see me up there. If he can see all my hopes and dreams up there bursting and popping like the balloon that day in the thunderstorm. He thinks he has taken my body, but really he has taken my soul and the souls of all those little girls I was supposed to help. Now it will not be me who helps them. It will not be me, because there is no more hope inside me. Jessie and Jesus are wrong—the light can go out. The line of my entire life collapses to a single point, to this single moment. This unthinkable, unmovable moment. I know that who I was to become is no longer possible. I dissolve myself into the reality that my life is now over.

"Did you like it?" he asks with such ease and comfort, I wonder if he's joking. When I don't say anything while my exposed, lifeless body remains motionless next to him, he starts laughing and says, "I know you did. They always do. When you wanna come back over?" He stands up and fixes his clothes while telling me I have to leave because his mother will be home soon, and he's not allowed to have girls over anymore, "so I'on' make no more babies wit' dem lil fass tail girls." I watch as he brushes his hair in amusement in front of the mirror.

I push my skirt down and stand up, but I am still on the ceiling. I tell my legs to move, and they comply. My body moves lifelessly through space. I walk down the stairs and look at the pictures of his family again. I wonder how such nice, smiling people managed to raise a rapist. I wonder if they know they have raised a rapist. I pause again in front of the kindergarten class picture. I find the little boy in the green collared shirt, trying again to remember. I stare until it finally clicks. This was the picture Jessie painted for me. This was what he was trying to warn me against. Suddenly, my mind fills up with all the warnings, there were so many: Tiffany telling me to stay away from him, Elena's bad feeling, the popped balloon with the lighthouse underneath, and the dream with Jessie and Jesus. There were so many signs, and I missed them all.

The tenth lesson of wizard training is to pay attention to warning signals that appear in your life. Become alert to what the universe is trying to point you away from. If you can wake up fast enough, certain tragedies (though not all) can be avoided. And for those times when you don't manage to wake up fast enough, be kind to yourself in the storm that will follow.

I continue walking down the stairs, without mercy or

Embracing the Ancient

The black veil has a voice. No one told me about that, about how much it talks, constantly, nonstop, pumping my brain full of angry words. It repeats the same things over and over, *This is your fault. You caused this. You are a beast. Only beasts get raped. You should just end it. End yourself. No one would care anyway.* The voice hypnotizes me. I watch its words circle around and around in my mind until I am compelled to agree: Yes, I should end it. Yes, I caused this. Yes, no one would miss me. Yes, I repeat again and again.

Not only does the black veil have a voice, but it also has a screen on which it replays the most terrible scenes from my life: The flesh man. The thrusting. The can of Pepsi sitting on the dresser. Jessie's accident. The flesh man. My mother on the bathroom floor. The thrusting. The accident. The juvenile detention hall. Thrusting. Pounding. Ripping. Tiffany and her friends chasing me. Thrusting. Pounding. Ripping. I watch the scenes in agony, but I don't try to stop them. I lie in my bed watching them play out in my mind over and over.

I have been horizontal for three days. Horizontal with no urge to eat. Horizontal with a bladder full of pee. I went to the bathroom once, but now I just pee in the bed when I can't hold it anymore. I pull the covers over my body so nobody can see my soiled sheets, but they probably smell it anyways. My eyes are also closed. They have been closed for three days while the black veil plays out its carnival of dark memories and thoughts.

My mother sits on the side of my bed wondering what is wrong with me. At some point, I ask her if she sees the black tar dripping down the walls, or if it's another trick of the black veil. I don't ask her this out loud. Instead I try to send a message to her telepathically, because I can't make my jaws open to release words. She doesn't answer me, so I assume she didn't get my message, but she keeps coming to my room every few minutes to check on me.

She doesn't understand.

She can't find me.

She sees my body lying on the bed in front of her, but she knows I am not there. She knows some part of me is gone, but she doesn't know why. She doesn't think to check the ceiling because she doesn't think *that* happened to me . . . again. "Ecka, baby, what's wrong? Are you sick? Did somethin' happen? Ain't like you ta miss so much school." I open my eyes and stare blankly up at my mother. She waits for my mouth to move, but no words come. She keeps talking to me, telling me things she thinks will make me rise, make me speak again. "Davante called. Said he takin' notes and collectin' all yo have been an anchor for them all their lives, a North Star for how they should move through the world. I have conducted miracles on their behalf to try to alter the trajectory of their lives. Now I am no more, and they don't know how to process it. My father comes. In his drunkenness, he is unable to show up fully for me, even now. He looks at my lifeless body and sees that I am dead, which prompts him to speak the sweetest words he's ever spoken to me. "I know I ain't yo biological fatha, but I luvs ya like my own. Always have since da first day I set eyes on ya . . . Hell, may even luv ya more'n dem hard-headed-ass brothas of yourn. I'on' know what's wrong wit' ya, but I hope ya come back to us. We cain't lose you, too. We done lost so many. We cain't lose you, too." The sincerity and love in his words is almost enough to raise me from the dead. I come down from the ceiling briefly to be close to him and listen. I see the softness that I had forgotten was in him. I almost smile, but I roll over and close my eyes again instead.

On day six, Ms. Jannie comes. I hear her loud voice bellowing from the driveway. "Let me talk to da girl. The power of da Lawd will get her up out dat bed. Believes me 'bout dat," I hear her tell my mother. Ms. Jannie thinks she can save me with her God. She thinks her hollow biblical verses will move life back into me. She is wrong. She doesn't know that I have been shattered and no longer believe in her God, which I haven't believed in since Jessie's accident. What God would allow these kinds of things to happen to good people? I may be a beast, but I know deep down I'm a good person. *So what?* I think to myself. It doesn't matter anymore. None of it matters. I am beyond saving now. I return to the ceiling when I hear her stomping up the stairs. I know I will have to be strong to resist her loud voice and compelling presence. I put up my shell, and watch and wait patiently.

I expect Ms. Jannie to come busting into my room shouting Bible verses and dousing me with holy water that smells suspiciously like vodka. She doesn't do that, however. As soon as she walks into my room and sees my lifeless body, something inside her changes. She takes off her coyote coat and tosses it on the chair across the room; then she stands totally still. She looks different and not like her normal boisterous, larger-than-life self. She looks like a tree, a large redwood tree planted right in the middle of the room. She is quiet. More quiet than I have ever seen her in my entire life. Her large body bristles and grows even stiller. She is solid and unmoving. Quiet and ancient. And seemingly without her Jesus. I don't understand. She just stands there quietly, observing me on the bed.

Then from her place of stillness, stark in the middle of the room, her eyeballs begin to roll up toward the ceiling in the direction of my camp. I am overcome with anxiety and want to hide, but there is nowhere else to go. The ceiling *is* my hiding place. She keeps rolling her eyeballs upward, unnaturally so, until she sees me, camped and hiding. Her eyes pierce through me. I feel as if she can see everything, not just where I am hiding, but all the way to the beginning of me and all the way to the end. It is not a regular gaze, but the gaze of one who has known and seen things outside of what her "Lawd" would allow.

In this moment I come to understand who Ms. Jannie really is. No one tells me, but I know that she must have sat on the ceiling before at some point—how else would she know where I'm hiding? She locates me so easily and knows exactly what is happening. I begin to wonder if her Bible-thumping Jesus-loving is an act to provide her with the illusion of certainty and stability in the world. Deep down, if she has sat on the ceiling before, she must know there are other ways, other truths, other powers. My mother runs from this power and these truths with the alcohol and the white rocks. Ms. Jannie runs with her Jesus and a religion she knows is not always the answer. Right now, she knows it is not the answer.

The eleventh lesson of wizard training is that a time always comes, a crucial moment of knowing, when all illusions must be dropped, all masks must be removed, and the power buried deep inside must be embraced and wielded. Ms. Jannie stands there, square in the center of the room, knowing that this time has arrived.

"Ms. Jannie, you awright?" my mother says as she comes rushing back into the room. "You don't look like yo'self. You look strange. What's wrong wit' ya?"

Ms. Jannie unrolls her eyeballs from the ceiling and stares again at my lifeless body on the bed. Without looking in my mother's direction, Ms. Jannie tells her to go down the street and get Mary Jacobs and tell her to "prepare fo a cer'mony."

"Now, now, Ms. Jannie, you know I cain't do dat!" My

mother waves her hand at Ms. Jannie in terror. "We not gon' put my baby thru dat, you heah! Not afta what happn'd to me. No, Ms. Jannie! I says no!"

Ms. Jannie turns her head slowly in the direction of my mother and speaks crisply and decisively. "Dis ain't 'bout you, Aprah. Listen to me carefully—we don't got much time left. Go get Mary Jacobs and tell her we need da cer'mony right now."

The seriousness and authority in Ms. Jannie's tone overpowers my mother, who immediately rushes out of the apartment. It's below freezing outside and the snow is just starting to fall, but my mother rushes out with no coat and a single purpose. That purpose propels her forward with an urgency that prevents her from feeling the cold. She could have been shot in the chest at that very moment and it would not have stopped her from achieving this purpose—she would have held the bullet in suspension, would have stopped the time, and died after she achieved her mission. Such is her love for me, her only daughter.

- - — —––o0o–—— — – -

This is how my mother killed her own mother, in a cer'mony to raise my mother from the dead after what her uncle did to her. This is why my mother prayed her entire life that such a cer'mony would never be needed for me. But cycles, experiences, and patterns often repeat themselves, moving from one generation to the next. Daughter becomes mother so quickly.

I have already decided I don't want any kids. So at least it will end with me. At least there will be no more daughters in our family to go through this, unless my brothers have daughters. I spiral prayers that they don't, that this never comes to pass in our family again.

The cer'mony, short for ceremony, is designed to help heal someone and call her spirit back from the above plane in the in-between. Life can become so difficult that the spirit actually leaves the body and says "No more" before the body has died. The ceremony must be administered within seven days, or the person will stay permanently stuck there. It can only be conducted by a quantum wizard who has been trained in the ancient healing ways, who can help the person fix what has been broken and guide them back. Mary Jacobs is that person.

Everyone in the neighborhood knows about Mary Jacobs, about her magic, but no one really *knows* her. She was married once, but her abusive husband died mysteriously in his sleep even though he was otherwise robust and full of life. People only go to Mary Jacobs when they need spiritual healing and miracles that can't be provided by a regular doctor or a pastor and his white Jesus. Otherwise everyone stays away from her and knows she is not quite of this world. She never goes to church or cookouts, and she barely speaks. She often sits on her porch in a rocking chair late at night. She drinks from a white mug and is always looking north, singing quietly to herself. There are always birds around her house. On the porch or circling above. I saw her out there once, around ten o'clock, all by herself, with a pigeon sitting in her lap, staring into the night sky as if she were waiting for someone to come. I walked quickly past her, pretending not to see her sitting there, chilled by the power she exuded.

Everyone also knows that Mary Jacobs "ain't all black." They say Mary Jacobs is a quarter Cherokee on her mother's side, a quarter black on her daddy's side, and a quarter magical on both sides. Say her mother's mother belonged to a tribe just north of Georgia and west of North Carolina. Say she learned all her magic stuff from her grandmother. Say her grandmother was well traveled and studied the ancient ways from coast to coast, absorbing as much wisdom and knowledge as she could. Say her momma and her daddy wasn't nothing but alcoholics, so her grandmother took her in and shepherded her through the madness of her upbringing. Say if it wasn't for her grandmother, she might have turned out just like her parents, but her Cherokee grandmother lit the way for her, planting seeds that might not have otherwise sprouted.

Lots of black people like to brag about their mixed Native American heritage: "Oh, you know, I'm part Indian, too. No, for real! On my daddy side." Mixing between black Americans and Native Americans grew out of slavery when runaway slaves sought refuge with Native American tribes. As I get older, I realize that many black people don't want to be "just black," because they don't want all the negative consequences that come with being only black. If you can claim Native American heritage, you might be able to claim lighter skin or "good hair," symbols that elevate your status in society ever so slightly. And when you are at the bottom, *slightly* means a lot, a whole lot. I wish I were slightly something else so that I could have some relief from the consequences of blackness also, but I know I'm probably "just black." The life I am living is what happens to "just black" girls.

- - — ——o◇o—— — - -

When my mother reaches Mary Jacobs's apartment, the only one with a beet-red door, she bangs so fiercely and agonizingly that Mary Jacobs swings open the door and screams, "Well, who is it, then? Knocking like a goddamn fool!" Once Mary Jacobs recognizes my mother, her tone and body language soften immediately and she proclaims, "Lord, Aprah, you gon' freeze ta def out heah. Is you high on dat stuff again? What's wrong wit' ya? What you want?"

My mother starts pleading and tells her that she has to come quick. That "something is wrong wit' Ecka." That Ms. Jannie is there and said to "tell you we need a cer'mony." That we don't have much time left. The words pour out of my mother's mouth, each racing to be quicker than the last. Mary Jacobs observes my mother in total silence and then suddenly begins laughing hysterically.

"Ms. Jannie? Bible-thumpin', Jesus-lovin' Ms. Jannie sent you ova here in da middle of winta?" Mary Jacobs continues laughing. Her whole body shakes with spasms of a glee only she understands. She slaps her knees and clenches her belly while proclaiming, "Is hell done froze ova? Is dese da end of days? Ms. Jannie done come back to da ways of da cer'mony. Aaaand you, Ms. Aprah? You done come back, too?! Lawd, I knows dese must be da end of times. All da fools is finally coming home to roost!" She continues laughing until my mother interrupts and tells her now is not the time for this and it's urgent and could she please come right now, but Mary Jacobs continues laughing. "I tole her big ol' country, coyote-fur-wearing ass dat she'd be back. I tole her. She done damn near married dat blue-eyed Jesus. And you know womens don't like to get no divorces. Lawd, dey stay wit' dese niggas till da end of time. Well, it look like Ms. Jannie done finally got rid a' dat nigga dey call Jesus. Ain't nobody eva seen da nigga in da flesh, and yet he done hypnotized da whole world. A wizard if I eva seen one." Mary Jacobs continues laughing hysterically as tears run down her cheeks.

My mother stares in disbelief. Everyone also knows that Mary Jacobs is a little scattered. At seventy, she is allowed to be whatever she wants, to present herself as she pleases, and take up as much space as she deems necessary. The wisdom radiating from her glassy gray eyes and gray hair grant her a candor and freedom no one else in the neighborhood has. "Hol' on, Aprah. Let me put ma coat on. I ain't gon' freeze out dere like you. I'm an ol' woman now . . . And jus' so you know, I done already seen ev'rythang. Yo gurl is trapped way up. Now dat she done stop salivating ova Jesus, Ms. Jannie finally right about somethin'. I done read da field. We don't got much time. She done been brutally raped. Got her trapped way down. Far down. Got to go and get huh. I ain't gon' tell you who done raped huh, 'cause I know you'a kill 'im if ya knows. And ain't no sense in huh losin' you, too. She already done lost you in so many ways. So I ain't gon' tell ya who done it. Come on in here and hep me get ready. We can brang her back to you, and we'a make sho don't nothin' happ'n like what happn'd to yo momma. I always been sorry 'bout dat. But it was a mistake, Aprah. You gon' have ta fo'give yo'self 'ventually."

- - — ——o○o—— — - -

The women have always been my saving grace. I don't realize it until this moment, watching from the ceiling, as they prepare to do something to reach me. I don't know what they are doing, but I know it is all for me. I watch my mother closely. She sets the candles on the table next to my bed and lights each one methodically. Her mouth doesn't move at all. In fact, her jaw is clenched. I can tell she knows what has happened to me by the newfound deftness of her movements. Her body no longer moves in confusion around the room—asking *What happened?*—but strides with the certainty of knowing. I know Mary Jacobs, mysterious healer-wizard, has told her. Though she moves with the certainty of knowing, inside she prays to the quantum field for my resurrection. "She has to survive it," she repeats to herself over and over. She spirals her prayers and thoughts with such concentration and force, I can see them rising off her, like mist on a river.

Those prayers alone are not enough this time, however. A

whole community of women wizards is needed. And tonight there are three, including Ms. Jannie, who is also a wizard, and always has been despite her love affair with Mr. Jesus Christ.

— – — ——o○o—— — – –

In the beginning, my mother was also drawn to Christianity, with its certainty and clear-cut answers. It allowed her to mask her growing fears of what might happen to her in the world, of who she might become, and of what she might do. Church was her only refuge from the things her uncle did to her. My mother would sit, alert, in the pews of Pastor Wallace's old church on 105th and Euclid as he talked about angels, heaven, and demons that walked the earth. "A demon steals the body of the innocent, scars the mind and soul of the meek, and desecrates the temple of the sacred. He can find you anywhere. You can't hide. He might sneak into your room at night while you sleep and find you when you least expect it," Pastor Wallace proclaimed passionately in church. "And the only way to get rid of a demon is to remove him from darkness and restore his soul to the light."

My mother became convinced that Pastor Wallace was talking about her uncle and that he had to be killed, so she started hiding a knife under her pillow every night, trying to work up the courage to restore him to the light so that he would finally leave her alone. She saw a story on TV one night about two siblings who murdered their parents while they slept by stabbing them in the heart. *Their parents were probably demons also*, my mother thought. *If they could do it, so can I*, she repeated to herself over and over until she gathered the courage to do what she knew she must to end it.

— — —— ——o○o—— —— — -

Right now, my mother is both far away and very close to a past she has spent her whole life running from. Somehow, she is sitting here again with all the ghosts she tried to bury, singing the same song they sang at her ceremony, a song I never heard before. Mary Jacobs and Ms. Jannie join, while continuing to prepare the room. They sound like dark angels, singing the saddest, most beautiful music I've ever heard. My mother grabs an assortment of towels and sheets, handing them to Mary Jacobs, who builds some kind of makeshift mat in the middle of the room. I initially watch their preparations with excitement and confusion, but terror rolls over me when Ms. Jannie suddenly turns off the lights and begins walking toward me. She grabs me from the bed and lays me on the makeshift mat. I am still watching from the ceiling, but even if I were in my body, I wouldn't resist. The power of their coordinated actions makes it clear that resistance is futile. After Ms. Jannie gently lays me on the mat, my mother, Ms. Jannie, and Mary Jacobs sit in a circle around me as candles burn on the nightstand in the background and the darkness envelops everything else. They have stopped their dark-angel singing now and are all silent.

They sit with their eyes closed until Mary Jacobs breaks the silence and begins chanting the same chant my mother chanted that Saturday night in the purple dress: "Habercito nyucatana sumacsinchi machainini . . . Cielo, cielo." She later tells me the chant activates a higher spiritual consciousness and sends a signal to the in-between to open the portal in preparation for a miracle. Her voice is haunting, and it pierces every part of me. Mary Jacobs's voice alone releases me. Penetrates the thick shell I have built around myself. The power of her voice totally disarms me. Somehow, her voice is both hollow and full, far and near. At once, the black veil lifts and I am undone. I begin to cry.

Mary Jacobs instructs me to "Swallow the darkness. Cultivate it. Then restore the light. You came from the light. The light is your center, your beginning and your end. The light is your ancestor, but first you must know darkness." She reaches into a small bowl sitting next to her. It looks like it is full of dirt or sand. She grabs a handful and throws it on the candles in front of us until they all flicker out, except the large white candle right next to me. The room is almost totally dark now. "Swallow the darkness," she says again. I don't know what she means, but I feel myself sliding down, down, down, losing my grip on the ceiling. I fight to hold on, but I know she will have me soon and I wonder what she is going to do to me.

LESSON 12

Anchoring the Singular Purpose

It all happened in a flash. Nobody could believe it. There she was, my mother, plunging a knife deep into her mother's chest. Then a series of traumatic scenes. Mary Jacobs smacking both of her cheeks and screaming, "Aprah, Aprah! Wake up, girl! Oh my God! Wake up, girl!" My mother writhing and struggling to reach for the knife again, to plunge it farther all while shouting, "He was a demon! I sent him back to da light like da pastor said!" Ms. Corrine Turner jumping up to call 911 and trying to think of a story, any story but this one, to explain what had happened. She would tell them that it was an accident. That the girl had woken up from a bad dream about demons and just happened to have a knife under her pillow, which she plunged deep into the corridors of her mother's chest. And they would believe her because she's only a child.

Then the wails would start. A chorus of wails. Wails from sirens, ambulances, police cars, investigators, morgue hearses. Wails from people: friends, family, neighbors, church members.

Then eventually wails from my mother herself, when she realized what was happening, what she had done. The authorities didn't believe her, of course, because she wasn't a child in their eyes. She was a black child. And a black child is just as guilty as a black adult in the eyes of the law. So they dragged her away in handcuffs while she screamed, "Noooo! It was an accident! I didn't mean to! No, please! Noooo!" She screamed with the intensity and high pitch of a child who has just lost everything. She was only ten years old, but she knew her life was over from that point on. She decided right then that there could be no redemption for her and that she must be irreversibly broken. When the police officers finally got her outside and were about to put her in the back of the car, her eyes rolled up to the sky

which has transformed into the in-between. I have returned to my body and the ceiling has totally dissolved. I am lying on the makeshift mat of towels and sheets. I stare up and watch specks of dazzling light rain down while colorful clouds move slowly against a dense, dark black space. Ms. Jannie and my mother chant with low-pitched, throaty voices. Mary Jacobs begins speaking to someone who is not in the room. It's like she's speaking to God or some presence beyond her. "Who among us was not born in darkness? Who among us was not made by the light? Dark and light, two sides of the same coin. Two parts of existence. And now she is trapped in darkness, far, far away from the light. We know she must learn to cultivate the darkness.

And to do that, she must go back to the beginning. I am ready to come to the above plane to help her. We know that rising from the dead can only happen in the above plane. We humbly ask permission to rise." Mary Jacobs then gently places her hand over my eyes and says "sleep." I cannot resist her. As soon as I close my eyes, I hear

someone singing "What a Friend We Have in Jesus." My mother looks around at all the girls in the Warriors for Jesus prayer group, which meets every Sunday afternoon at two in the chapel room. My mother has been coming since she was first placed in juvenile detention three years ago. She initially started coming under the instructions of her caseworker, who told her turning her life over to Jesus would be part of her rehabilitation and would increase her chances for an early release. So my mother drags her lifeless body to the meetings and sits half singing and half listening while everyone talks about their love of Jesus. My mother is always slumped and scowling, trying to find some reason to stay alive. She knows Jesus is not enough reason, not after what happened, but she plays along in hopes of getting an early release.

The first thing they do after singing is list all the sins for which they need forgiveness, past and present. My mother always lists one sin, the same sin every week: "I killed my momma. Dat's my sin."

Then the group falls silent until someone else begins listing her own sins. "Well, I wish I had listened more to my grandmamma," one short, light-skinned girl with a big fore-head begins saying. "Like she was right about everything. Like how she told me not to steal or drink or smoke. Dem my sins, but if I had listened to her, I prolly wouldn't be here. Now she not here no more." She done gone on

to a place that seems to be totally abandoned. I was sucked up through some kind of portal and I woke up here in this giant warehouse place that doesn't have any walls or ceilings. The floor looks like black marble but doesn't make a sound when you walk on it. It's just a wide open space that extends out infinitely in all directions. There are beams of light that flood the space from an unknown source above. The last thing I remember before waking up here is Mary Jacobs placing her hand over my eyes. I don't know where I am—I don't see Mary Jacobs, Ms. Jannie, or my mother anywhere. I stand up and look around. I pick a direction and start walking, hoping I will see someone, anyone. I see a form start to materialize just on the horizon in front of me. I start running toward the figure screaming, "Hey! Hey! Where am I?" I run faster and faster until I finally reach the figure, who is sitting in the middle of the floor fac-ing away from me. "Hey! Do you know where we are?"

As I get closer, I discern that the figure is a little girl. When she turns around, I see that there are tears in her eyes. I ask her what's wrong, but she just looks at me with the saddest eyes I've ever seen in my life. I sit down in front of her and try to cheer her up by telling her jokes and making funny faces. None of it works. She pulls out a pink box that has a black ballerina in it, just like the one my mother gave me. She hands it to me and says, "It doesn't work anymore." I open it and see that she is right. The light has gone out and the ballerina doesn't spin. "It's broken," the little girl says. "We're all broken and you have to help us." As soon as she says that, I see that there is a circle of young girls sitting around us. They all look so beaten down,

"like I don't have anything to live for," my mother says to the white lady missionary at the prayer group when it's time to share how they are feeling. "I don't feel nothin' no mo, inside. Do that make me crazy? Dat I don't feel nothin' about killin' my own momma?"

The white lady missionary smiles softly at my mother and says, "No. That's actually a very normal response to something like what you've been through. The mind can't process the magnitude of what happened. Can't make sense of it, so you shut down completely . . . I hear what you're saying about feeling like Jesus isn't your purpose here on earth. I understand and respect that. But what I can tell you is that you have to choose a purpose, something you believe in deep down. You can't make it in this world without anchoring yourself."

The twelfth lesson of wizard training is this: You must choose a singular purpose, one story that will drive your life forward. Without one, you will crumble into insanity or apathy; both are unbearable. Your purpose is the most important seed planted inside of you, because it is the tree from which all the other branches grow. It's the most important story you tell yourself about why you exist. It must be chosen carefully and thoughtfully.

"So I want to ask you right here and now, April, what do you want your purpose to be?" the white lady missionary asks my mother. "What do you want your reason for staying on this earth to be?" All the other girls in the prayer circle

                                                                      stare at me
in anticipation. "I don't know," I tell them. "I don't know what my purpose is. Not since the rape. It's nothing but suffering down there. I don't want to go back. I can't go back."

The little girl who gave me the ballerina box stands up, grabs my hand, and walks me over to an area to my right, but still inside the circle. I see a magic carpet just like the one from kindergarten. We stand on the magic carpet, and the little girl takes both my hands and says, "Let's twirl!" We twirl around and around each other until we are both smiling and laughing gleefully. "Make a wish!" she says.

I close my eyes and try to think of something, but nothing comes. I open my eyes and smile plastically to mask the fact that I haven't made a wish; I don't want to disappoint her. "Wanna know what my wish is?" she asks excitedly. I nod. "I want to help all the other little girls in the world figure out how to un-break." As soon as she says this, I know who she is. She is me, but the beginning me before it all happened. She has the same braids I used to wear before I relaxed my hair.

She is wearing the same T-shirt from the night of the fire. Her total innocence buckles me. I fall to my knees and grab her hands. I tell her how sorry I am. How I never wanted any of this to happen. How this is all my fault. How I didn't pay attention to the signals. "I'm sorry I let you down," I say to her with my head hung in front of me.

One by one each of the other little girls, who have been sitting in a circle watching this whole scene play out, gets up and brings me a gift. One little girl brings me a rose, another brings me a crystal, another a small stuffed dove, and on and on. When they have laid all their gifts on the magic carpet in front of me, younger me says, "Those gifts are all new seeds. You can use them to regrow the light. The rose will help you regrow your open heart, the crystal will help you regrow your ability to hope, especially in times of despair, and the dove will help you regrow your innocence. We are both still luminous, you know, even after what he did."

Suddenly, I see a woman stand up from the circle. I hadn't noticed her before, so I wonder if she has been sitting there the whole time. When she starts walking toward me, I see that it's Mary Jacobs. She hands me a shovel and tells me I can dig anywhere in the space to bury the gifts. I grab the shovel and begin digging furiously, breaking the black marble floor, and then digging into the dirt below. As I dig, memories start to flood my mind. So many memories

"about who I was in the beginning, befo' all dis happn'd. Back den, I thought my purpose was to be a seamstress. Thought I was gonna be a big fashion designer, but I watched dem dreams dissolve befo' my eyes . . . And now . . . Well, now I just want my future chi'run to have a betta life dan I did. I always wanted kids, to show 'em dat thangs could be diff'rnt. So I guess I want dat to be my purpose. Fo my chi'run, my future chi'run to not hafta live like I did."

The white lady missionary smiles warmly and places her hand on my mother's shoulder. A guard, who has been standing by the door the entire time, barks, "Hey! No touching!"

The missionary removes her hand reluctantly and says to my mother in the most compassionate voice she can muster, "Ms. April, that's a fine purpose if I ever heard one, and it shows you still got some light left in you. You still got some hope left in you. That's all you need to survive. Light, hope, and a purpose you believe in." My mother turns her head toward her, eyes welling up. The first time she has cried since the night she killed her mother. She dissolves into tears and buries her head in the white lady missionary's arms. The guard doesn't bark again. His own humanity leaps forward in this moment. My mother cries and cries as the white lady missionary reaches for the box of tissues. She plunges her hand

frantically into the dirt. I throw the shovel to my side and dig until my fingers hurt. Every emotion I have ever felt bubbles up in my body as I dig. Suddenly, I start screaming at the top of my lungs: "I hate everything! I hate everybody!! Why did they do this to me?!

They took everything from me! They beat me and my brothers in the middle of the living room! She let us burn in the fire! The flesh man put his hands in me, even though I told him to stop! That monster raped me!" I stop digging and sit on my knees, crying. "He took everything from me. I just wanted him to like me."

Mary Jacobs walks over and puts her hand on my back and then kisses me on the forehead. "I know, dear one," she says. "I know what has been done to you. And I'm so sorry. Bury all of it, put it in the ground and cover it with eternal dirt." I start throwing the gifts into the freshly dug holes and covering them up. Before I finish, one of the little girls brings me another gift. She hands me two double-A batteries and says it's to turn the ballerina box back on. I toss the batteries in one of the holes and keep burying. After all the gifts are buried, I lie exhausted on the ground and stare into the dark space above. I lie there for what feels like an eternity. Mary Jacobs and the little girls all sit quietly in a circle around me, having witnessed the whole scene play out.

Suddenly, I hear a rumbling deep beneath the ground. I sit up and place my right ear to the ground as the noise grows louder and louder. It sounds like a car driving up through the dirt. The sound gets more intense until several geysers of light begin to shoot up out of the ground. It's so much light, I can barely look at it without being blinded. The geysers of light hit the dark space above—which isn't a solid ceiling, but somehow still causes the beams to bend and shower all of us in bright light. I shield my eyes with my arm, the light is so bright. All the little girls start twirling and clapping while screaming, "Yay! Now she can rise! Now she can return!"

Little me celebrates and twirls with the other girls before bringing me the pink ballerina box. When I open it, the black ballerina starts to spin and her light turns back on. The sight of it overwhelms me. I place my hands on the sides of her arms. "Thank you," I say. "Thank you for not giving up on me." I kiss her on the forehead and release her arms.

Mary Jacobs, who has been watching this entire time, grabs my hand and tells me that we have to return now. I start to follow her, then look back at the little girls one last time. I remember again the future vision for myself, all the broken little girls coming to me for help, to figure out how to un-break. *May it be so. May it be so.*

I hear Mary Jacobs yelling, "Come back! Come back!" while smacking me on the cheeks. I feel myself being sucked through some kind of portal or tunnel at light speed again. I hear my mother and Ms. Jannie also urge me to "Come back, come back!" I want to tell them I'm on my way. *I'm coming.* Suddenly, my eyes splatter open and I start gasping for my breath. I tussle and writhe frantically while Ms. Jannie and my mother hold me down.

Mary Jacobs says, "Nah, nah, dere, dere, baby gurl. Relax. You done made it back. You done da hardest work of all. You done turn dat light back on. Nah, nah, dere, dere, baby gurl. Dere dere." Her voice relaxes me. I stop struggling and lie still.

When I finally catch my breath, I sit up and see my mother and Ms. Jannie looking at me with warmth and compassion. They are holding hands, just like Elena and I did after the miracle in her room. Mary Jacobs cradles me in her lap, rocking me like a newborn baby. Ms. Jannie and my mother both hum with deep throaty voices that sound like old Negro spirituals.

They all look so transcendent and powerful. I try to absorb as much of this moment as I can because I know the biggest miracle of my life has been performed. I bask in all of it, marinating in the endless compassion and grace of these three ancient wizards. I remind myself again of my purpose so I don't forget: to uplift the others, the broken. I look around one last time at my mother, Ms. Jannie, and Mary Jacobs. I thank them again silently with my eyes.

And on the seventh day, I rise from the dead.

Uncovering Optimal Potential

But still, like air, I'll rise . . ." Mrs. Marleen Delaney, my eleventh-grade English teacher, is reading a poem by Maya Angelou to the class. I have never heard of Maya Angelou before she reads this text, but the poem speaks to me. Reminds me of that night, of my own rising, several months ago, of all the little girls. At the end of the semester, we will have to choose a poem from a famous poet and recite it in front of the entire class. When Mrs. Delaney tells us we'll have to do this, I feel like throwing up. No part of me wants to stand in front of the judging eyes of my peers and perform. Why do teachers always make you do stuff like this? They forget so quickly how brutal high school can be. I try to think of ways to get out of reciting the poem. I already know she's not gonna go for it, but I'm determined to convince her. *I'll have to do something extraordinary.*

In addition to Maya Angelou's poems, we are also reading her memoir, *I Know Why the Caged Bird Sings*, and learn that Maya didn't talk for five years after she was raped. I wonder if she was a wizard also and got trapped in the above plane. Did

she have to regrow the light? I don't think men really understand the full impact of rape and what it takes from us, how
it cauterizes the light of our souls. My mother says the day of
reckoning is coming for them. I hope it comes soon.

        — — — —○○○— — — — —

So *nothing* will happen to Prince Mack?!" Elena asks me when
I finally tell her what went down. "He doesn't go to jail? He
doesn't get questioned? He just gets to rape freely with no
consequences?!" I don't know how to answer Elena. How to
tell her most of the women in my family and neighborhood
have been raped or assaulted in some way, and almost none
of the perpetrators, including my mother's uncle, face consequences because nobody cares about black women. I think
again about all the little girls in the above plane. *I care. And
I'll be there waiting when they are ready to regrow their light.* I
recommit to my singular purpose.

    "Well, my mother still doesn't know who it was. I can't tell
her or she'll kill him. I know she would. And even if we did go
to the police, are they really gonna believe me? I mean, I went
over there in a short skirt in the middle of winter, while no one
was home, and followed him up to his room. Nobody's gonna
believe me. Besides, I just want to move on and graduate next
year and go to college. That's enough for me. I don't need justice.
I've learned how to live without it."

    Elena looks deeply saddened and disturbed by my words,
but she knows that what I'm saying is true. "I'm just so angry,"

she yells. "I wish we could do, like, a reverse miracle or something, like a dark miracle to make him pay."

My mother says that not all wizards are helpers and that some carry out dark miracles. If a wizard remains submerged in the darkness of the black veil, or fails to give their power specific meaning and direction, she can end up using her abilities to do harm. My mother tells me that even though she's been trapped under the black veil for most of her life, the singular purpose she chose in juvenile detention has kept her going all this time and stopped her from turning to dark miracles. "It's hard ta turn against da light and use dat kinda power ta do harm. You have ta be really lost in da worl' ta go in dat direction. But you ain't got ta worry 'bout all dat, 'cause you done did what you needed ta do ta come back. I'm grateful fo dat. Lawd knows I'm grateful."

Henry E. Tarver Public School here on the East Side has far fewer resources than the middle school I went to on the West Side. But even though we have less money, I'm convinced we have better teachers. Teachers like Mrs. Delaney who assign us books written by people who look like us, and who can truly see our potential and encourage us to go to college. I've been thinking about college for years, but it's only now becoming a real possibility. If I get in, I'll be the first in my family to go. Mrs. Delaney knows this and says she's going to do everything in her power to make sure I get in somewhere, which is why she's my favorite teacher. Many students claim she's their favorite.

Every time I walk into her classroom, she smiles at me like she can see inside of me, like she knows who I am at the core. She asks me every day, "How are you, honey?" She asks with such compassion and softness, I want to pour out my soul and tell her about all my problems—the rape, the poverty, the rising from the dead, the miracles, the drug addictions—but I just say, "I'm fine," so she doesn't think I'm unhinged. Only other wizards can understand the journey I've taken.

Still, there aren't enough teachers at Tarver, so some classes here are mixed with both regular students and students in the Gifted and Talented Program. That means Tiffany is in a few of my classes, like Mrs. Delaney's, but I keep my distance from her.

I have five close friends at the black high school on the East Side. They call us the "Tarver Six" because we have the highest GPAs. No one remembers who first started calling us that, but it stuck and makes me feel like I'm part of something important.

There are three boys and three girls in the Tarver Six, including Davante, who is now in honors classes after finally having tested into the program for high school. Rodman is a jock who loves sports but doesn't play because of a collarbone injury that never healed properly. He also flirts with any girl with a pulse. Jin is the self-proclaimed "Asian Queen of the Ghetto," known for being one of the only out LGBTQ kids at school. Karen is light-skinned, shy, and very pretty (but doesn't know it yet). And Alexis is our resident type A overachiever who wants to be valedictorian. She's always

cheering, "To science and beyond! Just science it! Science is more than good, it's gr-r-r-reat!" All our corny cheers come from popular slogans that Dr. Craven has "reimagined and retrofitted for the young generation of scientists." They're pretty ridiculous, but the cheers put the biggest smile on Dr. Craven's face. Before we go off to work in real science labs throughout the clinic, Dr. Craven gives us a lecture on the latest scientific developments and concepts, so we, too, "can be on the cutting edge of science and technology." We listen, take notes, and then sprint off to our individual labs, which are staffed by some of the best researchers in the country.

I stay in the lab for as long as I can, even after I have finished my work, to avoid going home. I sit at a desk in the corner, working on homework, or stenciling if I am bored. I stay until nine o'clock sometimes. When the cleaning staff finally arrives and it's time to leave, I begrudgingly close my notebook, pack my things, and head home, where the windmill of chaos is probably underway. I never know what I will find when I get home: a fight between my father and mother; someone passed out on the floor; or my brothers' friends, most of whom are dope boys on the corner now, scattered around the apartment smoking weed. That's why people like Mrs. Delaney and Dr. Craven are critical to me and the Tarver Six. They push us to carry on.

So when I hear that another one of my brothers' friends has been shot or locked up, I carry on. When the electricity or gas gets turned off, I pay what I can and carry on. When my parents fight, screaming at the top of their lungs and throwing things at each other from across the room, I carry on. And when I get home late at night after work and find my mother strung out on the bathroom floor again, I drag her to bed, tuck her in, and carry on. I carry on even stronger after my rising.

Right after the cer'mony, my mother tried, cold turkey, to quit smoking crack and drinking. She wanted to do it for me since she could never do it for herself, but she only lasted a month and then she relapsed again, becoming even worse than she was before. I think her substance abuse increased because of how angry and disappointed she was in herself that she wasn't able to stop her addictions, even for me. That and the fact that she's still carrying a graveyard of ghosts inside. I've never been addicted to anything, so I can only imagine how hard it is to stop.

Dre and Rone are still struggling to take a different path while also trying to survive as best they can in this toxic environment. I begin to understand why it's so hard for new seeds to grow, no matter how epic the miracle that planted them. The seed alone is not enough. New conditions are needed to support the growth of the seed, which is why a new apartment in a new neighborhood was so important. I wonder if this is why white people have worked so hard to live separately from us? To keep all their money and resources to themselves in their nice houses and neighborhoods, so our seeds can't grow? I am enraged thinking about it, but I force myself to refocus on my homework. I press my pencil on the paper and continue.

The next day after class, as soon as everyone leaves, I hang around while Mrs. Delaney packs her things and cleans the classroom. I make small talk, like I have learned to do from going over to Elena's house. "How about the weather," I say to Mrs. Delaney nervously. "It's been so cold lately even though it's supposed to be spring."

Mrs. Delaney eyes me suspiciously while continuing to tidy things around the classroom. "Is there something you want, Ms. Brown?"

I pull a folded piece of paper from my pocket and hand it to her. "It's the first part of my poem," I say. "I wrote it last night. You didn't tell us to make up our own, but I wanted to do something unique and fresh. I just want you to know I went above and beyond for the assignment, but I can't under any circumstances perform it for the class. I just can't. I'll die if I have to stand up there in front of everyone." Mrs. Delaney continues reading my poem, seemingly ignoring what I'm saying. I keep pleading my case anyway. "I mean, I think sometimes adults forget what it's like to be insecure. And the other thing about it, I mean the most important thing, is if I do it, then they might see . . ." My voice trails off. I'm thinking about the beast that I know is still in me somewhere, buried. I know if I perform my poem in front of the class, everyone will finally see it and mock me for being so hideous.

Mrs. Delaney finishes reading and refolds the paper. "I get it," she says. "I understand now why you're afraid. This poem is brilliant. You are brilliant, and you're afraid to let everyone see because it's a scary thing to be vulnerable." Mrs. Delaney silently shakes her head, grabs her bag, and puts on her coat. My stomach sinks as I watch subtle disappointment roll across her face. I hate disappointing people, especially people who believe in me. I regret telling her. Maybe I should have just skipped school that day instead and said I was sick. Mrs. Delaney walks toward the door and turns off the lights. She pauses before exiting, turning to look at me. Her gaze is piercing as she says, "Echo, you'll never know what you are truly made of if you keep yourself hidden. And what's sad is that then we all lose, too. The world won't have you and all the incredible gifts you possess. The choice is yours, honey. The choice of whether you rise and meet your full potential is yours. The choice is always yours. See you tomorrow, honey."

The thirteenth lesson of wizard training is to choose to uncover your true potential, regardless of the obstacles in front of you. It will not be easy, but you will be very disappointed if you don't do it. I'm realizing that one of the most difficult things about life is figuring out what you are really made of, rather than living down to the negative expectations of others.

I stand in the dark classroom all alone after Mrs. Delaney leaves, her words still slicing through me like a sword. I came back after my rising, but I have remained hidden. I have tried to make myself invisible for protection. I understand now there is a huge loss in hiding like I have been doing. Something about it feels so tragic. I repeat Mrs. Delaney's words in my mind: *The world won't have you.* I hate the way it sounds. I well up with regret at all that has been lost already, at all that has not been revealed. And I vow to become visible, to be witnessed, no matter the consequences.

Performing Miracles of Unity

I sit at the kitchen table, flipping through the book of poems by black writers Mrs. Delaney passed out at the beginning of the semester. Even though I have already written the first part of my poem, I have been stuck trying to finish it. I hope some of the poems in the book will help me to find new words. I read every verse carefully and come to understand what Mrs. Delaney meant. So much has been given and uncovered in each poem. What if these writers had all stayed hidden? I shudder at the thought of everything that would be lost. At what the rest of us would have missed. I continue flipping through the book, pausing at Langston Hughes's "A Dream Deferred." The poem reminds me of my dad and my brothers and all the boys struggling in my neighborhood. *So much lost potential, so many dreams deferred.*

I soak in Langston's words, let them wash over me. The poem sparks something deep inside me, inspiring me to rework and reimagine what I've already written. The next lines of my poem suddenly begin to come forward. I press my pencil into the page as the words pour out like molten lava bursting out of a volcano. I write and rewrite. I erase and find new words until I feel like the poem is finally finished. I wince at the thought of having to recite publicly what I have written, especially in front of Tiffany and Alexis, but I'm determined.

I reach down into my soul again for courage and remind myself, *If you can, you must*, which is something Mrs. Delaney always says to us. I realize that I'm probably going to have to reach for courage for the rest of my life, so I may as well practice now. *I can do this.*

Jin and Davante come running into Mrs. Delaney's class one week before we have to recite our poems, screaming at the top of their lungs. "Oh my God! Oh my God!" School is over for the day, and Karen, Rodman, and I have been sitting in the classroom thumbing through homework and SAT books, waiting for the rest of the Tarver Six to arrive so we can walk to the Cleveland Clinic together. Alexis, who is usually the first one to arrive, is not here, and no one knows where she is.

Jin and Davante won't stop screaming and yelling "gurl!" Rodman tells them to spit it out or shut up and sit down. They are acting as if a bomb just went off. Jin is fanning himself and pretending to faint. Jin's parents are first-generation immigrants from South Korea who "never wanted a gay son, but are proud he makes good grades and is planning to go to college." Jin wants to go to New York University so he can study theater and "further enrage his unreasonable parents." His parents don't yet know he plans to study theater. Jin says he will tell them after they get his rich uncle in South Korea to pay his tuition in full. They want him to be a doctor or engineer so he doesn't end up like them, managing a local grocery store in a poor black neighborhood.

Jin is one of the bravest people I know. He paints his nails and wears colorful vintage clothing that reveals his eclectic personality. He refuses to change or hide himself even though our school is super homophobic and queer kids are constantly getting picked on. "They beat my ass if I'm hiding," he says. "They beat my ass if I'm not hiding. So I may as well not hide all this fabulousness, gurl."

He always has to add "gurl" to his sentences when he has something important to say: "Guuurl, did you see that new episode of *Fresh Prince* last night?" "Let me tell you where I went yesterday, gurl!" "Gurl, did you hear about what's going to be on the test?"

So when we hear Jin scream, "Gurl! Oh my God! Guuuurl!" we know something major has happened.

Davante just keeps repeating "Oh my God" over and over.

"What is it?!" I ask in agitation. "If you're not going to tell us, at least stop torturing us with the yelling."

Jin takes an exaggerated deep breath and says, "Okay, so you know how Alexis has been basically writing her valedictorian speech since ninth grade? How it's her goal in life to be, like, number one at ev'rrrrythang? Well, she ain't number one no more!"

Rodman and Karen scream, "What?"

"Who's number one, then?!" I ask.

Jin and Davante look at each other, smile, and then shout simultaneously, "You!"

"It's you, gurl!" Jin continues. "The chemistry teacher told Alexis she's getting a B at the end of the semester because she didn't do well on not one, but two tests." He holds up two fingers dramatically. "Ya'll not tied anymore. That means there is only one person"—he drops down to one finger—"in this entire school who has made straight A's for three straight years, and that's *you*! Unless you're planning on gettin' a B when you're a senior next year? Then it might be a tie. Ohmygod, if it's a tie, you guys should lip-sync for your life to determine who gets to give the valedictorian speech. Ohmygod, can you please just get a B so that can happen? It would truly satisfy every part of my queer Asian soul."

I stare at them in shock, too shocked even to laugh at Jin's hilarity. When no words come out of my mouth, Jin says, "Well, don't just sit there, guurrl. Give us a speech! We demand a speech." They all begin to clap and shout: "Speech! Speech! Speech!"

I laugh along to their clapping before clearing my throat and reciting one of the most famous segments from *The Color Purple*: "'All my life I had to fight. I had to fight my daddy. I had to fight my brothers. I had to fight my cousins and my uncles.' Nah, I'm just playing! Wahoooo!" I scream as everyone else cheers.

I know this will create a wedge between Alexis and me. I

know that's why she didn't come to Mrs. Delaney's class after school today like she always does when we have to work at the Cleveland Clinic. Like Elena's parents, Alexis's parents put a lot of pressure on her. Her father is an aircraft marshal, helping direct planes during takeoff and landing, and her mother cleans and cooks for rich white people on the West Side. They are always telling her she has to be the best at everything and get into the best college, especially since they've sacrificed so much for her. They have been diligently adding money to her college fund since she was a baby. I rarely meet black people like Alexis's parents; they are not on drugs, they have regular jobs, and they seem so well-adjusted. I wonder how they were able to avoid the white rocks and the Colt 45s. I really want to ask them one day.

Alexis doesn't talk to any of us for the next several days. She comes to class and sits on the other side of the room far away from us. Anytime we try to talk to her, she pretends like she doesn't hear and ignores us. Alexis is very stubborn, especially when she wants something, so I assume she will never talk to me again. But I am surprised when she approaches me one day after school. She briskly walks up to stand right in front of me. I prepare myself for some kind of fight, clenching my fists at my sides. As soon as I look into her eyes, I see desperation, not anger like I thought. "Hey, Echo," she says. "Look, I'm sorry about how I've been acting. It's unfair to you and the rest of the group. I just . . . I've had my mind set on being valedictorian since I was little and to have that snatched from me has really affected me. I haven't even told my parents yet because I know how disappointed they will be. My father had already started coaching me on what to say in my speech." Alexis hugs a book to her chest and looks down with such deep sadness, I wonder if something else is going on with her. *Show me the darkness*, I think to myself, and almost jump back when I see that Ms. Perfect Alexis is covered in the black veil.

After my rising, I can not only see the black veil but also hear what it is saying to others. I hear Alexis's black veil telling her how worthless she is, how stupid she is, how much of a failure she is. My eyes flood with compassion when I see and hear this. I suddenly feel very bad for Alexis and try to think of kind words to say. Before I open my mouth, she starts speaking again. "I just really need this. More than anyone . . . And, umm, I wanted to ask you . . . I mean, it's a lot to ask . . . but I wanted to see . . ." Alexis's voice trails off before she finishes and she looks down at the ground.

"Alexis," I say, "I'm so sorry about all this. You can ask me anything. I think you're amazing, and I want to be supportive."

Alexis smiles meekly, perks up, and says, "Well, I wanted to know if maybe you could . . . I don't know if you'd be willing to, like, . . . get a B in something so we can be co-valedictorians?" I stand there in silence, staring at Alexis, not knowing how to respond to such a selfish request. She sees my hesitation and storms off while shouting down the hallway, "I knew you weren't a true friend!"

Tiffany, who always seems to be around when there

is conflict, walks up to me and asks what that was about. "Nothing," I say. "Nothing." Tiffany lingers next to me as if she wants to ask me something else, but she doesn't. "I'll see you later," she says eventually before walking off.

Tiffany's mother died of a drug overdose a few months ago. Her mother had overdosed a few times in the past but always managed to come back somehow. So when Tiffany initially saw her mother passed out on the floor, she thought she would wake up eventually. Or that she would be taken to the hospital and the doctors would wake her up like they always did. Except this time was different. Tiffany's mother's face was a deep blue color and her entire body was stiff like a board. Lil Man was sitting right next to her dead body, watching TV. Lil Man and Tiffany had both been living with Tiffany's uncle, per court order, but they stayed with their mother on the weekends. Everyone in the neighborhood knew something was very wrong when Tiffany ran out of the apartment screaming at the top of her lungs, "Noooo! God! Noooo!" As the ambulance was carrying her mother out, Tiffany refused to let go of her dead body and clung to her until her uncle finally managed to pull her away. I can't imagine what it's like to lose your mother, so I feel bad for Tiffany. Ever since it happened, Tiffany just keeps her head down on her desk. Mrs. Delaney doesn't bother her. No one bothers her.

When I get home later, while thumbing through all the college brochures I have collected from my guidance counselor—who has hundreds of them in his office—I think about what

Alexis asked me. I imagine introducing myself to people at college by saying, *Hi, my name is Echo Brown and I was co-valedictorian of my high school.* I hate the way it sounds, but I understand the pain Alexis must feel at having lost the number one spot. I flip through the brochure from Dartmouth—my first choice—and wonder if I'll get in. I imagine how many other students must be flipping through this same brochure and wondering the same. *Why would Dartmouth take me over them?* When I tell the guidance counselor I want to go to Dartmouth, he tells me to "be more realistic and aim for a third- or fourth-tier school, because it's better to do well at those schools than to flunk out of an Ivy League school."

He doesn't know what I can do. He's wrong, I try to convince myself while looking one more time at all the pictures in Dartmouth's brochure. The beautiful trees with different-colored leaves of brown, purple, orange, and red, once again promising a new, better life. The majestic snow that looks like it's been imported from a winter wonderland. And the cute boys who all seem to have dimples and take perfect pictures. One, with curly black hair, looks like Romeo from Immature. Another looks like my favorite Backstreet Boy, Kevin, and has dreamy eyes and perfect teeth. I stare at Dartmouth Kevin, wondering what it would be like to date a white boy. Wondering if white men would date a black girl who looks like me. Wondering what dating at Dartmouth will be like in general. I think about all the white men I see on TV and in movies and how they all seem to be so amazing. How they are always thoughtful and sensitive like Uncle Jesse

Ms. Green's class, who will be joining and also performing. One by one, all fifty of us will make our way to the front of the class and recite our poems. Everyone looks nervous and sweaty, just like me. Jin sits by the door and has his eyes closed while mouthing the words to his poem. In true thespian fashion, he tells us he will surprise the class with his creation. Not even Mrs. Delaney knows what he will do. Davante doesn't choose a poem, but instead picks an excerpt from Malcolm X's speech "The Ballot or the Bullet."

When it's Davante's turn to go, he easily performs a powerful, moving rendition of the speech. "I'm not . . . an American . . . I'm one of the 22 million black victims . . . of Americanism . . . We don't see any American dream; we've experienced only the American nightmare." He is wearing glasses similar to Malcolm X's and has also taken on Malcolm's cadence and speaking pattern. Several people are so moved by Davante's performance, they give him a standing ovation. He bows with pride, and I suddenly feel a renewed attraction to him, watching him deliver such a confident performance. He has a girlfriend now, so we can't be together, but I feel electrified watching him.

Alexis chooses Maya Angelou's "Still I Rise," which Mrs. Delaney introduced to us at the beginning of the semester. I knew Alexis was going to pick a Maya Angelou poem, since she always talks about how much she loves *I Know Why the Caged Bird Sings*. "It's such a simple, yet profound, portrait of black womanhood in America. Maya's wisdom, insight, and poetic rigor are truly something to behold," Alexis says one day in class while we are discussing the book. Alexis doesn't look in my direction while she performs her poem. I know she is waiting for an answer to her question. I have already decided, but I haven't told her yet, which means she glares at me in the hallway. The rest of the Tarver Six all think it's ridiculous she would make such a request, but they are not surprised, given her personality and the pressures from her parents. After she finishes her poem, I am annoyed and clap unenthusiastically while smiling sarcastically at Jin.

When it's Jin's turn, he stands, pulls a small stereo from his bag, and walks up to the front of the classroom. I hear people snickering and giggling all around the classroom, so I'm nervous for him, but he looks so confident in front of the room. He presses play on the speaker and proceeds to lip-sync "It's Raining Men" by the Weather Girls. Everyone's jaws drop simultaneously, including Mrs. Delaney's. We are all too stunned to laugh because he fully embodies his performance. He makes it through about half of the song before dramatically stopping the music and saying, "Now that I have your full attention, I'll be reciting a few lines from a speech by Harvey Milk, who was an advocate for the rights of gay and lesbian people and a man whom you all should know. He is one of the Martin Luther Kings of the movement for rights for people like me." Jin pauses nervously and continues, "You do not realize the impact your words have on me. When you call me things like 'faggot-ass Jackie Chan,' it dehumanizes and diminishes something inside me, leaves part of me wilted like a rose left indoors for too long. Like Harvey said,

'All young people, regardless of sexual orientation or identity, deserve a safe and supportive environment in which to achieve their full potential.' I will never be safe out there, but, dammit, I want to be safe in here, in Mrs. Delaney's magical classroom." He reads his statement with such conviction and passion, tears begin to well up in his eyes. He closes by saying, "My name is Jin and I am not a caricature. I am a human being just like you, and I deserve to be safe somewhere in this world just like you." The class gives him a raucous round of applause as he sashays back to his seat.

I am surprised at how supportive the class is, not just during Jin's performance, but during everyone's. There are a few snickers here and there, but everyone is mostly respectful and attentive. Maybe it's the gravity of the words. Maybe the passion in the performances. Maybe it's Mrs. Delaney's warning: "Anyone who is disrespectful during someone else's performance will receive one month of detention and fifteen percent off their final grade." Maybe it's a combination of all of these. Whatever it is, the class listens and seems to absorb the words from each performance. I have heard so many renditions of Maya Angelou's "Still I Rise," I nearly know the poem by heart myself. Each performer, including Alexis, especially likes to emphasize the line "Does my sassiness upset you?" One girl even snaps her fingers and rolls her neck while saying it and the class bursts out in laughter and applause.

When I hear Mrs. Delaney call my name, I stand and walk timidly toward the front of the room. I feel everyone's eyes burning a hole through me. I face them and tell them I chose "A Dream Deferred" by Langston Hughes, but I rewrote it a little. "Oh wonderful," Mrs. Delaney exclaims. "Another remix. You are all very creative and innovative. I applaud you." I smile at Mrs. Delaney, and take a deep breath.

> *What dreams have they forced you to defer?*
> *Did you want to be a pilot and fly planes?*
> *Did they say you wouldn't make it in the Ivy*
> *League?*
> *Did you want to be a poet and write your poems in*
> *the stars*
> *like the ones that came before?*

Immediately after I speak the first lines of my poem, the class grows quiet. No one moves, and I watch as every set of eyeballs in the room rolls forward, simultaneously, landing directly on me, as if compelled by some unknown force. I feel energy and electricity in the room that I've never felt before, but I'm not quite sure what's happening. I am not trying to stop the time, but it begins to wind down, just like when I am deliberately performing a miracle.

> *Maybe the darkness inside stole your dreams?*
> *Left you broken and buried*
> *In a womb of despair*
> *Did you have to rise up out of the dirt, too,*
> *Learn to cultivate the light again, too?*

Everyone in the class starts to move in slow motion. I watch as one girl lifts her hand to scratch her face, but her hand freezes in midair, hanging in suspension right beneath her chin. I glance over at Tiffany and Alexis, who are not freezing but appear to be in a hypnotic state. They both stand up and begin repeating the lines of my poem. The rest of the girls in the class, also seemingly hypnotized, stand up and join hands, all repeating after me. They don't repeat the words in unison; instead, they each repeat them at their own pace and tempo so that their voices sound like a chorus rising and falling, like waves in the ocean. I continue:

> *Did you ever think you would watch your parents*
> *crawling around on the floor,*
> *chasing the white ghost?*
> *Did you ever think you would be next?*

The girls all echo the word *next* one after the other.

Next   *Next*

     Next   *Next*

       Next   *Next*

        Next

My father said he remembered the time before he knew he was next. Said he remembered when he was nine years old, how he would run barefoot on dusty dirt roads lined with fields of cotton before he knew about the white rocks and

Colt 45s. Said he remembered when the white wizards would gallop through his small town after midnight screaming, "White power! No place for niggers!" They were not really wizards, but sheep with guns and all the power of the world. When my father's family and the rest of his little town heard them galloping through, they would jump out of their beds and spiral prayers to the good Lord for assistance.

The next day, when the sun was shining again, Big Momma, my father's grandmother, would tell my father not to let those cowards in white bedsheets steal his courage or his dreams. She would tell him that he was "gon' leave the South and become a big man in the North." She had already prophesied it, seen it written in the fabric of the universe. She would then tell my father to get on his knees and pray to the good Lord for all that had been provided, all that will be provided, and for the strength to continue on. And he would obey. He would clasp his hands together so tightly, imagining himself as a big man in the North, and with so much conviction, the palms of his hands would turn totally white from the pressure of his clasping.

> *What kind of dreams you got festering,*
> *burning inside you?*
> *How many nights you had to sit on the ceiling*
> *Waiting for dem dreams*
> *Chasing dem dreams*
> *Hoping they wouldn't steal dem dreams?*
> *Tell me 'bout dem dreams*
> *Tell me what dey was*

The girls, who are still holding hands, begin speaking. It doesn't sound like their regular voices, though. They sound like their inner little-girl selves, like the children in the above plane, innocent and ethereal, remembering what they wanted to be when they were young:

"I wanted to be an astronaut and fly way above the earth, but how can I soar with no money and no hope?"

"I wanted to be a doctor and help save people, but then my momma died of a crack overdose."

"I wanted to be a designer and make clothes, but my teacher told me to be more realistic about what's possible for me."

After all the girls finish speaking their dreams, all the boys in the class begin sharing all the things they wanted to be and all the reasons they couldn't do it. I am astounded at all the dreams that are being lost. The tragedy of it propels me to speak louder, more forcefully. I begin calling for the wisdom of the time past. A portal to the in-between opens. The ancestors hear us and transmit all the knowledge and experience they gathered on this earth. Their energy teaches us how to overcome and unifies the entire classroom. I am astounded when many of the black veils in the classroom begin to lift and hover, rather than suffocating their victims. For a brief moment, with the veils lifted, I see everyone for the first time, as they truly are, beneath all the shit.

The fourteenth lesson of wizard training is that miracles of unity have the power to lift many black veils at once. The power of connecting and uniting many souls creates such a rush of hope, goodwill, and light that it's impossible for the black veil to hold its grip. Miracles of unity, more than any other kind of miracle, can lead to the total transformation of a person at the seed place because individual power multiplies in community.

After all the miracles and messages stop, I stare out at the class and finish my poem:

> *What dreams have they forced you to defer?*
> *And what do you plan to do about it?*

No one says anything when I finish, so I stand there in silence, waiting for Mrs. Delaney to tell me to sit down since no one is clapping. When I glance back at Mrs. Delaney, she has a strange new look in her eyes. "Here she is," she suddenly says cryptically. "And so she has risen." Mrs. Delaney claps vigorously, and the rest of the class follows. They clap with such enthusiasm and respect, I am overwhelmed by the authenticity of their witnessing and by the gratitude with which they receive my accidental miracle. I feel proud and connected to everyone here for the first time ever.

Burning the Nest

Mrs. Delaney doesn't say anything to me for the next three days. She barely even makes eye contact. When I try to talk to her after class, she rushes out and says she can't talk. I start to wonder if something's wrong, if she's mad at me for some reason. If maybe she didn't like my remixed poem after all. Everyone else besides Mrs. Delaney seems nicer, more radiant, and more connected. Some black veils have returned, but many are still lifted days later. Every morning feels like summer camp, with people smiling and talking to each other. I don't know how long it will last, but our class finally feels how I've always wanted it to. I wish the rest of the school could feel like this, but I am glad to at least have one supportive space for now.

Alexis even apologizes for asking me to get a B. "I shouldn't have asked you that," she blurts out one day after school. "I really did let my ego get to me, but I'm sure you'll be a great valedictorian. I'll do my best as your salutatorian wing woman. And I'm happy for you. I hope we can all be friends again." She smiles plastically and gives me a hug. I can sense the strain in her smile, but I accept her apology since I always knew she was compassionate deep down. "Hey, have you noticed anything different about Mrs. Delaney?" I say to Alexis. She shakes her head no at first, but then says, "Actually, she seems even nicer after the recital. I swear she's constantly giving me an intense, encouraging smile. It's like Mrs. Delaney on compassion steroids." Shocked by Alexis's response, now I'm the one smiling plastically, trying to hide my concern about why Mrs. Delaney seems to have turned so cold to me. "Oh, well, cool," I say. "Never mind. I'll see you around!"

After Alexis leaves, I open my locker and watch as a small piece of folded paper falls to the ground in front of me. I open the note and read it. All that's written inside is one word, "Prom?" There are little black spades drawn all around the word. I wonder who it could be from and am surprised that someone is asking me. I'm still not sure if I'm going, although the Tarver Six has discussed attending as a group—that is, all of us except Davante, since he has a girlfriend. It's not the big senior prom, which will be next year, but the junior prom. I run down the list of all the nerdy boys in the eleventh grade who might have asked me. Kendrick? Tony? Rodman? Derrick? Stephen? I fold the piece of paper up and put it in my pocket. I close my locker, walk down the hallway toward the door, and decide I will turn down whoever it is if they ever reveal themselves. I'd rather focus on my college applications instead of some stupid school dance.

I am shaking my head at the thought of prom when Mrs. Delaney suddenly emerges from her classroom and walks toward me. School has ended and the hallway is mostly empty, except for Davante, who is waving from the other end of the hall so we can walk home together.

"Echo, can I talk to you for a minute?" Mrs. Delaney says. The seriousness in her tone concerns me, and I again wonder what I could have done wrong.

I yell down to Davante and tell him I'll see him tomorrow. He looks disappointed, but I don't have time to explain before following Mrs. Delaney into her classroom. Mrs. Delaney takes off her coat and sets her bag on the desk. I clench the straps of my backpack, waiting for her to tell me what I've done.

Mrs. Delaney stares out the window before finally beginning to speak. "I can't stop thinking about your poem and how brilliant it was. How much promise and potential you have," she says. "I've been thinking about how to say this without offending or alarming you." She turns around and looks directly at me and continues. "I'm concerned about you. I know everything you have been through and are dealing with at home. I think you need a safe space to really focus on the college application process, which can be quite daunting, to ensure that we don't miss anything, that you get to go to the best school possible, where you can continue to thrive. And there are things you'll need to know about the world . . . about life, important things that can't be taught in books, in a classroom. I know you must be wondering what I'm talking about. And I don't know how to say this." Mrs. Delaney pauses for several seconds before continuing. "I think you should move in with me and my husband until you go off to college. I know how it must sound. I don't know what your parents will think, if they will allow it. But I want to support you in the best way I know how."

I stare at Mrs. Delaney in disbelief, mouth wide open, while still clenching the straps of my book bag.

"Yes, I thought that might be your reaction," Mrs. Delaney says when I don't respond. "But I'd love for you and your parents to consider—"

"Okay," I say, cutting her off midsentence. "I'll move in with you." I am surprised when the words fall out of my mouth. I sense the gravity and truth of what she is saying, and the importance of what she needs to teach me.

Mrs. Delaney is shocked at my quick response. She starts speaking a mile a minute, stumbling over her words. "Okay, I mean, all right, then. Well, when do you want to come? I haven't even told my husband yet. We will convert our library upstairs into a bedroom for you . . . And I'll talk to your mother, make sure she's okay with it . . . And I think it's best if we didn't tell people here at school since they won't understand . . . Maybe we can have you move in at the end of this week, before the school year is over. That way we have the summer also . . . . I mean, it doesn't have to be this week if that doesn't work for you. It can also be in the fall. I imagine a teenager might want to spend the summer before their senior year relaxing and having fun."

I listen carefully to everything Mrs. Delaney outlines before saying, "I can move in this week . . . I'm not a normal teenager." Mrs. Delaney smiles and asks if she should schedule a call with my mother or drop by my apartment in the next few days. I think for a second about the best approach for telling my mother, who will be very upset about all this. "I'll tell my mom," I say to Mrs. Delaney. "And I'll let you know what she says and which day you should pick me up." Mrs. Delaney nods her head in excitement and says, "All right, then, very good. Let me know if you need anything at all in the meantime."

"I will," I say before walking out of the classroom.

When I get to the hallway, I am surprised to see Davante waiting for me right outside the door. I'm still processing what just happened and don't really feel like talking to him right now. "I thought you went home." I say.

"Oh, yeah," he says. "I started walking home, but then came back to wait for you so we could walk home togetha . . . What you was talkin' to her about? You ain't in trouble, is you?"

I shake my head no as we head toward the front door. I pull the folded piece of paper from my pocket and hand it to Davante, changing the subject. "Look what somebody left in my locker today. Who do you think it could be? I already ran through the list of every nerd in our grade, but still don't know. You think it was an underclassman? Maybe Daniel or Cordoby? I bet it was one of them. They always smiling at me in the hallway and congratulating me on being the new top of our class."

Davante holds the note in his hands while remaining

awkwardly silent. I wonder why he's so quiet. His forehead is sweating and he looks like he's seen a ghost.

"What's wrong with you?" I ask. "You of all people don't have any theories about who it could be? . . . What? You want to talk about the usual? How the government is conspiring against black people?" I shake my head teasingly, but he still doesn't say anything. "Is everything all right?" I ask. "What are you and Kimberly wearing to prom?"

Davante stops in the middle of the sidewalk and says sadly, "We broke up."

"Oh no!" I respond in surprise. "I'm so sorry to hear that. Let's stop at the penny candy store. I'll buy you all the candy you want. The sugar rush will make you feel better. Come on, let's go." I tug at his arm, but he remains pinned to the sidewalk.

He looks down shyly before finally beginning to speak. "I was wonderin' . . . I mean . . . I know it hasn't been nothin' between me and you for a while . . . But I think about dem afta-school kisses we use'ta do in middle school all da time . . . I know you said you don't want to go to prom and all dat, but I mean, I'on' know. I was thinkin' dat maybe we can go together?"

A wave of sadness comes over me. Both for the disappointment it will cause him when I say no and for the trauma from Prince Mack that makes me very hesitant to get close to a boy again. I stand there not saying anything, wanting to avoid it all somehow.

"Okay, then. It's cool," Davante says, quickly walking away. "I undastand. Don't worry about it. I'a see you around."

I watch Davante move farther and farther up the side-walk. I open my mouth to call after him, but when no words come out, I walk the rest of the way alone to my apartment.

- - — ——∘∘∘—— — - -

When I get home, Dre and Rone are sitting at the kitchen table drinking out of plastic Kool-Aid cups.

"What y'all talking about?" I ask.

"Dis grown-folk's business," Rone says jokingly.

Dre chimes in and says, "Yeah, dis a A and B conversation, so C yo way out." They both start laughing hysterically as if they have made the funniest joke in the world.

"Ha ha ha," I say while grabbing a cup of water.

Dre looks up at the picture of Jesus over the stove and says to Rone, "I swear dat nigga be moving ta different positions. Man, wasn't his hands in front of his chest before? I'm tellin' you, dat nigga be movin'."

Rone laughs and replies, "Nigga, you high. How a picture on da wall gon' move?" Rone opens a can of Vienna sausages and bag of plain potato chips. "Want some?" he asks while pour-ing everything on a plate. Something about the way he gener-ously offers fills me with a different sadness. I look into both my brothers' eyes as a flood of memories comes racing back: us playing in the field, me trying to help them with their homework, the miracles at the juvenile detention center and *Titanic*.

I think about the earlier conversation with Mrs. Delaney

and become even sadder. What will happen to Dre and Rone if I leave?

"Hey," I say solemnly. "What y'all think about me going to live somewhere else before I leave for college next year?"

They both stop laughing and eating and look at me in silence. "What you talkin' 'bout, Echo?" Rone says. "Where else would you go?"

I see the look of sadness in Rone's eyes and decide in that moment I can't leave them.

"I'on' want you ta go, Echo," Dre says. "I mean, I know you gotta leave when you go to college next year, but I'on' want you ta leave befo' then." Dre gets up and gives me a hug. "Don't leave us, sis."

I tell Dre I'm not going anywhere and he doesn't have to worry. Dre smiles, reassured, before both of them get up, put their dishes in the sink, and say they have to go do something important.

"But I don't want y'all on the corner," I say. "Y'all don't want me to leave, and I don't want y'all on the corner. I know that's where y'all goin'."

Rone turns around from the kitchen sink and says, "What else we supposed ta do, Echo? We ain't like you wit' all dat studyin'. We ain't goin' to no college. I know dat now . . . But you don't gotta worry. We jus' doin' a lil bit ta get by. We gon' apply fo some jobs at Walmart and McDonald's so we can get off da corner. Don't worry, sis."

I watch them both start walking toward the door. I yell,

"Wait! Can I read you dis poem I wrote for my English class? I wrote it for both of y'all and Dad."

Rone reluctantly says, "Yeah, go ahead, but we only got five minutes."

I pull the poem out of my book bag, stand up, and read it to them. I wonder if the ancestors will come this time. If their black veils will lift and transform. I make it halfway through the poem before I hear a car pull into the driveway.

They both walk quickly out the door. "That's a good poem, sis," Dre says while leaving. "That's nice. Love you, sis."

Every time they leave, they always say the same thing, "Love you, sis," and then give me a hug before bolting out the door. And every time, I try to think of words, any words, to make them stay. This time, I call out frantically, "Hey! Dre! Rone! I know you gotta go, but I just want y'all both to know I love you so much. And I tried everything I could to change the path and make things better for you, but all I could do was help plant new seeds . . . You have to grow the seeds, though. I can't do that for you. You have to realize there's another way."

Rone looks at me in confusion before also giving me a hug. They both say, "Okay, sis," before disappearing into the darkness of the hallway.

"Be safe," I say while standing in the empty kitchen by myself. I stand there looking at the door for . . . several minutes? Maybe an hour? Several hours? Waiting for them to come back. When my knees begin to buckle and the bottoms of my feet hurt, I finally sit down. I am all alone in the apartment and wonder if I will be this lonely my entire life. I force myself to start my homework. I force myself to carry on.

- - — ——o○o—— — - -

I have been sitting at the kitchen table studying for two hours when my mother finally comes stumbling home. "Hey, baby," she says before walking past me into the living room, where she starts moving and shuffling things around. I know what she's looking for. I close my textbook and sit panicked at the table, trying to think of what I will say when she asks what happened to the little white baggies she had hidden in the floorboards by the couch. I sit there frozen, waiting for her to come storming into the kitchen. When she finally does, she's not storming, she's smiling and asks me in the sweetest voice possible, "Ecka, baby, anybody been in da house today? Anybody come ova here today while I was gone? 'Cause I cain't find my stuff." I tell my mother no one has been over and ask her what stuff she's talking about. "Baby, now, come on. You far from a dummy. You know what stuff I'm talkin' 'bout."

She returns to the living room and begins frantically searching around the entire house. She pulls all the cushions off the couch. She pulls up several floorboards in the kitchen. She flips over all the mattresses and pulls the clothes out of all the dressers. When she's done, it looks like a tornado has torn through the apartment. She stands in the middle of the living room, scratching her face and shaking. Her voice, full of rage and frustration, shoots directly at me like a gun. "Ecka, you sho you ain't seen my stuff?! Don't play games wit' me, baby, you heah? I gotta have it. Come on now."

I instantly regret what I did only hours earlier. I wish that I could un-flush the toilet or that I had just thrown everything in the garbage so I could simply go and retrieve it all. There is no way to reverse it, so I stand silently across from my mother, looking down at the floor. "I'm sorry, Mom. I just don't like to see you like this. You don't seem like yourself anymore . . . You high all the time. And when you ain't high, you sleepin' all the time. It's like you tryna kill yo'self. Is you tryna kill yo'self? 'Cause I don't want to be in the world without you, after all we've been through."

For a brief second, a glimmer of who my mother used to be comes back and she softens. She recognizes how insane she must appear right now. The moment passes quickly as her rage returns, causing her to raise her combat shell. My mother has never raised her combat shell toward me, so my body fills with terror at the sight of it. The light in her eyes disappears entirely and she starts screaming, "You fucking bitch! You thank jus' 'cause you goin' ta college you betta than us?! You thank jus' 'cause you don't drank nothin', don't smoke nothin', you can touch my shit?! *My* shit?" She grabs a glass candle from the table and throws it at me, narrowly missing my head.

I run to my room and lock the door. I yell from behind the door, "Mom, please calm down! Please, this is not you! That stuff makes you like this. That veil makes you like this!"

My mother starts throwing an assortment of items at the door while screaming at the top of her lungs, "After all I done for you! You stuck-up lil bitch! Betta rememba where you came from!" After she runs out of things to throw, she starts banging on the door with all her strength, throwing her entire body into it.

I start crying and pleading, "Please, Ma! Please stop!"

But she continues, "You lil bitch! I wish I neva had no kids! I wish I neva had you and yo brothas so I coulda gone on and took myself out dis crazy-ass worl'! Afta ev'rythang I done done for y'all!" She releases a guttural, rage-infused scream before storming off.

I hear the apartment door swing open, hitting the wall, and I hear her stomping down the stairs. I sit on the floor of my room, cradling my head in my lap, as tears fall from my eyes. Her words slice through me, stinging all my soft parts, reducing the light that returned after my rising. A hurricane of emotion rages through: anger, sadness, grief, despair. *Fuck her*, I think to myself. *Fuck this place.*

I jump up off the floor with tears streaming down my face and begin packing a duffel bag full of clothes. I stuff as many clothes as I can into the bag. I run to the bathroom and grab my toothbrush before returning to the kitchen and stuffing my homework into my book bag. I remember the conversation I had with my brothers earlier, promising them I wouldn't leave. *I don't care*, I think to myself. *I am leaving this awful place.* I know that moving in with Mrs. Delaney will be both a gift and a curse. A gift because I know I will need whatever she will teach me for the journey ahead. And a curse because I will never forgive myself for leaving my brothers here alone in the chaos. I will bear the weight of that until I go to my grave. Jesus and I will have that in common.

The fifteenth lesson of wizard training is that every wizard must eventually leave the place that makes her. At first, home is a nest. But every nest must ultimately burn so that wizards can fly far, far away, into the horizon of new possibilities where their full potential is waiting to be developed and unleashed.

I wonder what Dre and Rone will think when they come home to find I am gone. I leave a note for Dre that has Mrs. Delaney's phone number on it and tell him he can call me anytime. I hope they forgive me. I hope they forget this and instead remember all the ways I tried to help. I hope they still think I'm "the best sister in the world."

Cultivating Receptivity

I stand frozen outside Mrs. Delaney's big white house on the West Side, too afraid to walk up and ring the doorbell. It's pitch-black outside, but somehow Mrs. Delaney senses I'm here, looks out the window, and sees me standing there.

She swings the door open and says confusedly, "Echo? Come in!" She grabs my duffel bag and tells me to have a seat on the couch, and that her husband, Mr. Delaney, is sleeping. "Is everything all right?" she asks with concern. "Obviously, I'm excited you're here. I just wasn't imagining you'd come tonight." I sit, smiling plastically, but don't answer her question. Seeing the deep sadness in my eyes, she puts a hand on my shoulder, smiles warmly, but doesn't press further. "Well, it's okay regardless. Welcome to my home. Come on, follow me up to your room."

The next day Mrs. Delaney drives me to and from school with her. When we get back after school, she sets all her bags down and offers me an assortment of drinks and snacks. (She doesn't have Kool-Aid, so I drink lemonade.) Mrs. Delaney tells me all about her life. I learn that she has one adult daughter, from a previous marriage, who lives in Philadelphia. I learn that her husband will be home from work in another hour or so and that he never had kids. "I told him last night you were here," she adds. "He was a bit surprised, but he's excited to meet you." I look around at all the expensive furniture, paintings, and objects in Mrs. Delaney's house. I imagine breaking something accidentally and then being asked to leave. I picture Mrs. Delaney throwing my duffel bag out onto the street while all her white neighbors stand on their lawns with crossed arms, shaking their heads and yelling for me to go back where I came from. *I hope that never happens.*

After Mrs. Delaney and I talk for a while, I go up to my room and sit on the edge of the bed with my back perfectly straight, afraid to touch anything. I've never had my own room before and can't believe how big and nice this room is, even though Mrs. Delaney says it needs to be cleaned. I look around at all the nice furniture and suddenly feel a surge of conflicting emotions. At once I feel excited, afraid, euphoric, unsettled, and deeply out of place. I am so uncomfortable, I have an overwhelming urge to go back to the nest I burned. I'm sitting there trying to talk myself out of leaving when I hear Mrs. Delaney calling for me to come down because Mr. Delaney is home.

I stand up and walk quietly down the stairs. I'm nervous to meet Mr. Delaney and wonder what he will be like. I walk down four or five steps and then stop cold in my tracks when I see him standing in the living room. My mouth falls open and I don't move or say a word. "Oh, now, don't be shy, honey,"

Coat Factory back when me, Rone, and Dre used to shoplift. We began shoplifting frequently, wanting better clothes than the ones our mother bought us from Goodwill, which look old and worn-out. We stole hundreds of dollars' worth of clothes until we were eventually caught by a black female cop, who took mercy on us. She collected all our stolen merchandise and told us not to come back or she would arrest us. "So don't come back. Y'all hear me?" That was the end of shoplifting for me, but not for my brothers. In fact, that was the end of all police contact for me except when the neighbors called the police on my parents during one of their chaotic fights.

I wonder if Mrs. and Mr. Delaney fight like my parents as I return downstairs in my stolen shirt. "Well, shall we head out, then?" Mr. Delaney says. "We're just going down the street, but the restaurant can be crowded sometimes, so we should get going." I follow them obediently to the car. I turn around and stare one more time at the Delaneys' massive house. I know that this place will be a portal, in the way I wanted that three-bedroom house to be two years ago. But this one is a portal just for me. Not for my brothers or my parents. I drop my head at the thought of it. My eyes well up with both sorrow and gratitude.

— — — ——o○o—— — — -

I stare down at the menu, totally disoriented. There are all these words I've never heard of before, like *cannelloni* and *tiramisu*. We are at a fancy Italian restaurant five minutes away. I try to scan the menu for something I'll like while Mr. Delaney tells me all about himself. How he's an executive at Morgan Stanley and knew from an early age he "wanted to work in a bank next to all the money." He asks me questions about school and where I'm thinking of going to college while I look over the menu in confusion. I smile plastically to hide the anxiety bubbling up in my chest. I've never been around an educated black man who talks like Mr. Delaney. There are a few black male teachers at my school, but none of them are like him. And anyway, I only know how to relate to broken black men. Mr. Delaney seems so calm, smart, and put together. It confuses me. I respond with short, curt answers to most of his questions, willing him to stop asking me things so the attention can shift focus.

Even Davante, who is one of the smartest boys I know at school, does not act or talk like Mr. Delaney. I wonder if Davante will become like this after he gets out of college. Davante says he wants to go to a black college like Howard or Morehouse, which is what his parents always hoped for. Davante is disappointed when I tell him I'm aiming to go to Dartmouth. "Black people, especially black people of the diaspora, can only be truly educated and supported at black colleges and universities," he says. "You have to know that you will never be able to fully integrate into historically oppressive institutions founded on the pillars of white supremacy. We have to always be aware of the plight of the black man in this country and seek ways to overcome our circumstances." I roll my eyes at Davante, annoyed by his newfound Malcolm X–modeled speeches, which he occasionally switches into when he wants to make an important point ever since the poem recital.

I try to justify my decision by arguing that an Ivy League degree might open doors that otherwise would be closed. I also tell him I'm tired of talking about race with him because he never listens and only wants me to see things from his perspective. "What about the plight of the black woman?" I ask him. "What about all the rape, sexism, abuse we suffer at the hands of black men in addition to having to deal with racism in larger society just like you? You talk about the plight of the black man all the time, but you never mention the black woman."

Davante always gets upset when I bring up the specific struggles black women face and tells me I should focus on supporting black men and that once black men are liberated, they will liberate black women. "Besides, talking about sexism and patriarchy is just a tool the white man uses to divide the community," Davante says decisively. I want to tell him about my rape. I want him to teach me how not to focus on it. I want to ask him why almost all the women I know have been raped and what he plans to do about that. And don't we have to fight that, too, the rape of women, which happens many times at the hands of black men? I want to tell him that either we address all the oppression within the community wherever it rears its ugly head, or we are not allies. I want to tell him all these things, but he is busy rattling off statistics about the number of black men killed by the police in the last five years. His eyes glaze over and he erases me like he always does when we discuss these issues.

As I'm thinking about Davante, the waiter arrives to take our order. Mr. Delaney motions for me to order first, but I tell him I want to take one more quick glance at the choices.

Really, I want to observe how he and Mrs. Delaney order so I can mimic them. I watch carefully how they interact with the waiter. When the waiter comes back to me, I order a cheeseburger and French fries. It's the one thing on the menu I know I'll really like. I tell him to please add extra cheese and extra ketchup. He asks me how I'd like my burger cooked and I say, "Not pink on the inside. All the way cooked." He smirks at my response and I know I haven't chosen properly somehow. "Well done, then," he says while grabbing the menus and shuffling off. Neither Mrs. Delaney nor Mr. Delaney says anything at my choice of the cheeseburger, but I can read the subtle energy shifts in their bodies. They wanted me to order something else. A fancy dish to better represent my first fine-dining experience. I feel like I have already disappointed them.

The restaurant is only the first upscale place they will take me. They bring me to orchestra concerts, lectures, plays, and more fancy restaurants—all places I have never been before. All places where I feel deeply isolated. I observe everything. How people walk, talk, and hold their bodies, even how they use their utensils. It's still foreign to me, but I force myself to mimic them and always make sure to use my white-girl English when speaking.

I have high hopes for Mr. Delaney, for who he will be in my life with his big education and fancy way of acting and speaking. Because he is black, I expect him to wrap me into his fold and usher me safely into the world of highfalutin customs and procedures. I expect to grow closer to him as time passes and maybe come to see him as a father figure. Instead, I grow away from him. It's like he is judging and carefully observing everything I do. I can see it in the way he cuts his eyes sharply at me when I make a mistake. I understand that just because someone is also black does not automatically mean they have the capacity to nurture you or even truly see who you are. I keep waiting for an understanding from Mr. Delaney that never comes. Not because he doesn't want to, but because he doesn't know how to nurture a dark-skinned black girl.

His assault on my being begins slowly, with little comments dropped here and there. To me, it feels like a full-blown attack. To him, it probably feels like he's playfully batting a kitten—a poor lost kitten that he has taken in, fed, and given shelter to—with his large paw, totally unaware of the force and impact of that paw.

I am not fooled by his professional demeanor and credentials. I know he cannot see me. I can tell by how he glosses over and minimizes some of the things I say. When I tell him I have been through some very hard things, he tells me about how "the young generation doesn't know how good they have it these days." He then gives a detailed account of all the obstacles he has overcome in his life, including the racism he faced in his youth and career. Every time I mention a struggle or a challenge I face personally, he trumps it with another obstacle he personally overcame, invalidating everything I say.

It won't stop there, however. He will also attack my intelligence. He will repeatedly call me "dummy" and "stupid" when I make a mistake or don't know something. The worst will be when he calls me these things in front of his family, all of whom are black, at family dinners and gatherings. When others laugh at his comments, I will laugh along, trying to appear okay. I mask the deep well of pain his words stir up inside me. After dinner, when no one is looking, I hide in the bathroom trying to choke back my tears and the sense of alienation from being around "proper" black people who laugh at my degradation. He calls others in his family "dummy" also, but it doesn't seem to impact them in the same way.

And there are so many other comments. He will tell me how some of the people in his family told him not to "bring no dark woman home," to preserve his proper status. When we watch TV in the living room after dinner, he will comment on the appearance of the women on the screen, light-skinned and whites being "fine and attractive," not knowing that I am waiting for him to say that a woman who looks like me is fine or attractive also. He never does. He will assert himself on subjects he knows nothing about, like suicide. Saying things like, "Suicide is never the answer. I don't care how bad life gets, there's always a way out," not knowing how many times I thought about killing myself in the past. Not knowing that both of my brothers have attempted suicide. He will marvel at the fact that I "speak so well and don't sound ghetto at all." Not knowing that I understand the subtle judgments he is making. Even though I don't talk "ghetto," the rest of my family does, so I wonder what he would think of them.

He will call me ugly on the day of my senior prom after I return from getting a face full of makeup at the mall. I have married to him and so she must justify his behavior some-how. I am constantly afraid they will ask me to leave, so I accept her justifications and do my best to live inside of them.

I try to focus on all the good things Mr. Delaney does. Like when he drives me to my old neighborhood, "the ghetto," to get my favorite ice cream or sausages, which they only sell in poor areas. Or when he teaches me how to drive in the parking lot of Safeway on a Sunday afternoon after they have closed and how he takes such care to make sure I get everything just right. He stays out there with me all day until I understand blind spots in the side mirrors and I can reverse and accelerate like a pro. Or how he spends so much time trying to prepare me for the "real world" by teaching me important life skills like setting a table, properly using a knife and fork, opening a bank account, and balancing a checkbook. He says I'll have to know how to "blend in" to certain environments because some people will be watching and waiting to judge me just because I'm black. When he tells me these things, I can feel his deep concern and care for my well-being, and I can see him like how Mrs. Delaney must see him as a warm and compassionate person.

I will try to suckle nectar from the fruit of his actions and make it mean something to my heart. I will try to make these things feel like love, but I can't. All I feel are wounds. And I need a target, a place to aim my resentment for how badly I have been treated by the men in my life. Not only for the wounds he has given me, but the wounds from all the rest of them as well: my biological father, my stepfather, the flesh man, and Prince Mack. This is what Davante doesn't understand. He doesn't see all the wounds I have from black men also. His wounds are from "the man," and mine are from men, all the men, including black men. And I want Mr. Delaney to pay for all of their sins. Because he, out of all of them, should know better. I want him to be available to me in a real way. I need him to be what I hoped he would be, but people rarely turn out the way you hope they will. I am only seventeen, but I have learned this lesson many times already.

When we return home, after that first dinner, I again sit on the edge of my bed, with a belly full of cheeseburger and fries. I try to identify all the new feelings stirring inside. Something between giddy enthusiasm and deep fear, like standing on the edge of a mountain you just climbed. I wonder how many more things won't turn out like I want, even after I have climbed to the top. How much more disappointment will there be? I turn the lights out and lay my head on my pillow, which has a fresh new case that smells like lavender and peppermint. None of the pillows at our apartment have pillowcases, or if they do, they are old with holes in them. I take another deep breath and then close my eyes, waiting for sleep to wash over me.

Elena comes over to Mrs. Delaney's house two days after the restaurant dinner. "Do you like it here?" she asks when we get upstairs to my room. I shrug my shoulders and say it's quiet and peaceful, but I'm nervous about how things will go with Mr. Delaney. "And you didn't tell your parents?" Elena asks. "They don't know where you are?" I shake my head no and say they are probably too drunk or strung out to notice anyway. "Wow," she says. "My mom would have put out a missing persons alert." Elena keeps looking around the room while I lie on the bed thumbing through one of my textbooks. When we hear a knock at the door suddenly, we both sit up and stare. "Come in," I say finally while clearing my throat. I'm not used to people knocking. In my apartment, everyone just barges in when they want something.

Mrs. Delaney walks in carrying a tray of snacks and two glasses of fresh lemonade. "I thought you might be a little hungry, so I wanted to bring you something to munch on until dinner." Elena and I watch her in silence as she sets the tray on the dresser. She lingers for a little while and looks like she wants to stay and talk. I ask her if she wants to sit down. She sits in the armchair next to the bed. At first she sits quietly, listening to Elena and me talk all about classes at our different schools, crushes, school dances, and college applications. Eventually, Mrs. Delaney starts telling us all about her life, about what it was like when she was in high school. How she knew she was going to be a teacher since she was in first grade. "I just knew there was nothing else I wanted to do in the world," she says. Elena and I both listen and marvel at the life experience of someone almost triple our age. "I wonder what I'll be like when I'm that old," Elena says before catching herself. "I mean, when I get older. You're not that old, Mrs. Delaney."

Mrs. Delaney smiles amusedly, fixes the hemline of her dress, and says, "It took me a long time to learn wizardry. To understand what it was and how to wield it." Elena and I both look at each other in shock when she says this. I had wondered how Mrs. Delaney had remained unfrozen during the poem, how she'd seemed to be able to see and understand me on deeper levels, what she'd meant by "important things that can't be taught in books," but I hadn't been certain until now. Elena and I sit excitedly on the edge of our seats as she continues. "I was resistant for a long time because I was afraid of the responsibility that comes with this kind of power, but now I know in my old age it's better to be powerful and integrated than fearful and internally split." I briefly wonder about all the things Mrs. Delaney knows. I try to imagine what she might have seen over the course of her life, what miracles she's conducted, what she's learned about how to navigate all this. After Elena and I share with Mrs. Delaney all our miracles, she begins explaining many of the things we have been confused about. She explains why time stops right before a miracle, what the in-between is, and why it's so hard to permanently get rid of the black veil.

"Well," Mrs. Delaney begins, "to me, a miracle is an occurrence that bends the normal laws of reality. The possibility for a miracle at any given time is always there, but only a wizard can seize that possibility to execute a miracle by connecting to a different realm, which is why the time stops. The miracle happens outside of normal time and space.

"As far as the in-between goes, it's a portal between this world and the next. It contains all the energy of the universe, including past spirits that have moved on. The in-between can assist us in conducting our miracles by spiraling messages to us when we're ready to receive them and grow. Sometimes the messages are transmitted through little details in nature.

"The above plane is where we go to conduct miracles of understanding, like rising from darkness, regrowing light, or changing the trajectory of someone's life."

Mrs. Delaney says she has one more very important thing to tell us about receptivity, which is also the sixteenth lesson of wizard training. "All of this magic depends on you," Mrs. Delaney says. "The most important thing I want you to remember from all I've shared is that everything unfolds in its own time. You can't force your development as a wizard, or come to know things before you are ready. The miracles and revelations emerge based on your own progress and eagerness, which is why some wizards don't even realize what they are until late in life. So the key to growing and expanding is to remain in an open state of receptivity. You must carefully cultivate receptivity in the same way you cultivate light. Then you will become quickly aware of what's happening around you and what to do next."

Elena and I glance at each other in astonishment before saying, "Wowww."

"Boy, am I glad I didn't take the blue pill," Elena says enthusiastically while looking at me. "Everyone says the rabbit hole is scary, but I literally never want to leave. Don't try and beam me back up, Scotty, because this is a-ma-zing. How long did it take you to learn all that stuff, Mrs. Delaney?" Elena asks.

"A very long time, but it won't take you as long because I'm going to keep teaching you everything I know, just not today." Mrs. Delaney stands up and walks toward the door while saying, "I've got to start dinner before Dennis gets home. Just holler if you need anything else."

When it's finally time for dinner, Elena and I wash up (I now know that means to wash your hands and maybe fix your hair). We sit at the dinner table staring at the feast of macaroni and cheese, baked chicken, roasted brussels sprouts, and mashed potatoes. The apple pie with vanilla ice cream will come later. Mr. Delaney is more relaxed tonight than he was at the restaurant. I wonder if dinner will be like this every night. We eat and talk for an hour until the phone rings. Mrs. Delaney gets up to answer it and when she returns to the table, we see by the look on her face that something is wrong. "Echo," she says cautiously. "Um, it's your brother Dre, and he says your mom . . . well, she's in a coma at the hospital. She had an overdose."

I listen to the words coming out of Mrs. Delaney's mouth in slow motion. I wonder if a miracle is about to happen, because it feels like the time winds down. But the time isn't winding down; my mind is just unable to process the words. "An overdose?" I cry in disbelief. Mrs. Delaney asks if I want her to drive me to the hospital, but I shake my head no. I don't want my mother to see the person I moved in with without telling her. "Okay, how about a taxi?" I nod yes. "I'll come with you," Elena says, but I tell her no also. Mr. Delaney tries one last plea to come with me. "No one should have to deal with this kind of thing alone. Let us come with you." I look into all three of their sympathetic faces and shake my head no again. The guilt at having left my family and now this happening is unbearable. I'm also used to handling all my problems by myself. I don't know how to allow others to help me. Inside, I wish they could just ignore what I say and come with me, but they don't. They believe my charade of not wanting them to come.

I bolt out of the Delaneys' house into the taxi all by myself. I stare out the window in a daze as the scenery outside the car changes from statuesque West Side houses to broken-down East Side apartment buildings. Watching the transformation between worlds further adds to my sadness. When I finally arrive at the hospital, I race inside to find my mother's room. Dre is sitting in a chair next to her bed by himself. He was home when she overdosed and he doesn't know where Rone and Dad are. He's slumped over and I see tears falling from his eyes.

"Hi, Dre," I say while walking into the room.

He runs over, gives me a hug, and starts pleading, "Is she gon' die, Echo?! I don't want her to die, Echo! Please come back home, Echo. Please come home! It ain't da same witout you."

I try to hold myself together. Try to be strong for the both of us. "She's going to be all right, Dre," I say. "She always pulls through." The words fall out of my mouth, but I don't know if they are true.

The doctor walks into the room and introduces herself. She is a white lady with red hair and freckles. She motions for Dre and me to sit in the chairs across the room from my mother's bed. "Do you have a guardian here with you? Your father or another family member?" the white lady doctor asks.

"No, but I'm eighteen," I lie, in case she says she can only release patient information to adults.

She looks skeptical momentarily but takes a deep breath and says, "Your mom suffered an overdose and a psychotic break."

Dre interrupts her, yelling in a shaky voice, "Is our mother gonna die? Is she?!"

The doctor smiles warmly at him and shakes her head no. "Don't worry, she's not going to die. We were able to pump her stomach and give her fluids to help restore her body to balance, but she is still in a fragile psychological state. We had to restrain her and put her on a high dose of Haldol, which is an antipsychotic drug, but it takes a week or two to kick in. We are going to transfer her to the psychiatric ward after her physical condition improves. It would only be for seventy-two hours to monitor her progress. We just want to make sure she doesn't harm herself or someone else." I stare at the doctor in disbelief. My mother, despite her addiction, has been my rock. Has helped sustain me and my brothers through all of it. Seeing the looks of sadness in Dre's and my eyes, the white lady doctor begins speaking again. "I don't know what's going to happen with your mother, but what I can tell you is for her to still be here fighting after everything she's gone through, I imagine she must be one strong woman. A lot of people don't make it back from something like this."

Many people have called my mother strong—relatives, neighbors, friends, teachers. Those same people have called me strong, too. They have said wizards are unbreakable, but I'm not sure anymore. They call us warriors because we survive it and they call us strong because it doesn't topple us. They call us magic because we manage to make miracles out of it. "Wow! Look at her take it all! She's so strong!" But for us, it's not a victory. It's a bloodbath. What happens after the bloodbath, when we finally fall?

When I walk over to my mother's bed and gaze down at her, unconscious and hooked up to several machines, she looks like dust to me, beaten down and shattered. Finally, shattered. I have never seen my mother like this, without her strength. The sight of it frightens and confuses me. If the rock of our family can fall, then where does that leave the rest of us? Immediately, I feel a bigger surge of guilt at having left and begin reevaluating my plans and reimagining my life. *I'll move back home. I won't go to college. I'll try to get a permanent job as a lab assistant at the Cleveland Clinic and stay home and take care of everything.* I think of all the ways I will have to become the rock of our family if this is the end of my mother. She is so young, only thirty-nine, so I hope this is not the end of her.

Forgiving Yourself

The next few days are a blur, an endless loop of going back and forth to the hospital. An endless loop of various people from around the neighborhood visiting and saying they "cain't believe Ms. Aprah done fallen. Not Ms. Aprah wit' all dat strength." And an endless loop of my mother remaining unresponsive in a coma in her hospital bed throughout all the visits. I've moved back into my apartment indefinitely until she rises from the dead, like she always does. Every time I walk into the hospital, I pray her eyes are open, but they never are.

On the fourth day after her overdose, I am waiting at the bus stop to go to the hospital when I see Tiffany running toward me. "I'm coming wit' you," she says. "I heard what happened to yo momma. I been meanin' to go up dere and see her." I don't want Tiffany to come with me, but I can tell by the look in her eyes she is determined to join. Maybe she feels sympathy for me after what happened with her own mother. Maybe she still feels bad for jumping me with her friends. Whatever it is, she stands at my side now like we are sisters about to face a storm together. We are finally sisters after everything that's happened.

The bus comes and we ride together in silence, not knowing what to say to each other. She asks me how I feel.

"Numb."

"I know da feelin'," she responds.

"How's Lil Man?" I ask.

"Oh, he okay. I'm takin' care a' him. He ain't so lil no mo. He already out on da corna slangin'."

I tell her my brothers are also out there on the block with the rest of the dope boys.

"I'm thinkin' 'bout applyin' to community college. Maybe gettin' an associate's degree or somethin' like dat to take care a' Lil Man while he still in school."

I look over toward Tiffany for the first time on the bus ride and tell her that sounds like a good idea.

When the bus finally pulls up outside the hospital, I take a deep breath to try to stop the emotion already bubbling up in my throat. It starts every time I get here, but I don't want Tiffany to see. "Hey, it's something else I wanted to ask you," she says as we walk through the hallways of the hospital. "Two weeks ago, when you was up dere doin' dat poem—I really like how you redid dat poem, by the way. You was up dere and I thought I seen somethin'. I'on' want you ta think I'm crazy or nothin' like dat, but I thought . . . I mean, I felt like everything was moving in slow motion or somethin', and den I seen dese black things up by the ceiling. I know it sound crazy. I wasn't high or nothin', but dat's what I saw during your poem." I turn and stare at Tiffany in disbelief. How could she know all these things . . . unless *she is a wizard, too?*

I don't have time to respond before we get to the room and I notice my mother is not there. I run to the nurses' station down the hall to ask where she is.

I assume the worst. "Is my mother dead?!" I scream. "Did she die?! Why didn't anyone call me?!"

The nurse tells me to calm down. "Your mom woke up last night out of her coma. We moved her to the psychiatric ward for further observation. She's in room 410, on the fourth floor. You can go on up."

Tiffany and I race up the stairs. When we finally reach room 410, I am relieved to see my mother lying there, asleep in her bed. I walk over and grab her hand. I am overcome by the sensation of her warm, living hand, which means she is still alive, still here. I suddenly feel an immense wave of compassion for Tiffany. What must it be like to be in this world without your mother? How is she functioning and going about her daily life? How is she even standing? My mother is still here, and I am already on my knees.

I stay there by my mother's side until I hear someone talking behind me.

"I asked y'all to leave me alone today. Tell 'em I got to keep cleanin' up."

I turn around to ask Tiffany what's she talking about, but there is someone else in the room. It's a black woman in a hospital gown sweeping the floor.

"What did you say?" I ask in confusion. "I think you have the wrong room."

The woman continues sweeping and talking to herself without any acknowledgment of me and Tiffany. I realize she's mentally somewhere else. Tiffany and I both watch her silently for a few seconds as she sweeps all around the room. I wonder why they would have a patient cleaning the rooms. I dismiss the whole scene and turn back to my mother, bowing my head and spiraling more prayers on her behalf.

The woman stays a few more minutes before walking toward the door, continuing to sweep while talking to herself. I am relieved to hear her leaving. Her presence disturbs me. Suddenly, the woman whips her head around in my direction, makes direct eye contact with me, and says, "Hey! Yo momma says meet her in the above plane. She up there waiting for you. Might be the last time, so betta head up dere fo it's too late. If she get stuck up dere, she'a turn out like me or worse. So betta gone on up." The woman walks quickly toward the door while repeating, "In the above plane, betta gone on up," and switching off the lights. As soon as she turns off the lights, the time starts to rapidly wind down.

Tiffany jumps up and yells, "What's happening?! What's going on?!" The ceiling disappears, and two light beams begin to form in the dark space above. They point in our direction before spiraling down and shooting directly into our foreheads. We are both compelled to close our eyes.

Initially, I assume the lights are spiraling some kind of message to us, like all the times before, but when the room begins to shake, I know something else is happening. We are both transfixed, suspended in the middle of the room while the light spirals into our foreheads. I try to reach for Tiffany's hand, like I always do with Elena. I can feel the fear pouring out of her body. As soon as our hands touch, a stream of memories is transmitted from me to Tiffany: Miracle at *Titanic*, the juvenile detention miracle, Elena's miracle, and the poem in Mrs. Delaney's class all flash before my eyes and are sent to Tiffany. I also receive an upload from her: I see Tiffany fearfully sitting on the ceiling when one of her mother's friends came into her room late at night and not understanding how she got up there. I see birds circling above her on the day of her mother's death, trying to warn her of what is to come.

When the upload is complete, the room stops shaking, but our eyes are still closed. My eyelids feel heavy, like they weigh a thousand pounds. I tell Tiffany we should count to three and try to open them. We both take a deep breath, count to three, and force them open. We are stunned by what we see. We are no longer in the hospital room, but at a beach. A vast beach with no beginning and no end. The sun shines and the sand seems to stretch for miles. There's nothing around but three white beach chairs to our left and a red bucket right next to the shoreline.

"Where are we?" Tiffany asks. "This is weird as fuck! Yo, how do we get back home?! What the fuck is going on?! And look!" Tiffany points to the lighthouse across the water in front of us. "Don't dat look jus' like da lighthouse up at Lake Erie? Yo, remember when we almost drowned up dere?! What da fuck is happening right now?!"

Tiffany starts freaking out, but I grab both of her shoulders and tell her to breathe. "We are in the above plane, I think, which is part of the in-between. I'll teach you about all that stuff later, I promise. Right now, we need to figure out what's going on."

Just as I finish telling her that, I see a form far in the distance, all the way down the beach, walking toward us. I point, and Tiffany spins around and screams, "Oh shit! Oh shit! Now, who is that?" I tell her to relax and that everything is going to be okay, even though I am terrified. "It's gonna be fine," I say more for myself than for her.

The form moves slowly, without apparent awareness that we have been waiting here patiently, in the middle of nowhere. I become increasingly concerned about where my mother is and how we will get back to the hospital room. Mary Jacobs is not here to guide us this time, so I don't know what is going to happen. The form draws closer and closer, and I see that it's a woman dressed in all white. I can't see her face yet, but the way she walks feels familiar to me. The closer she gets, the more familiar she seems. When she is only a few feet away and I recognize her, I stumble backward in shock. Tiffany grabs my arm, catching me before I fall.

"Mom?" I say when she is standing right in front of me.

"Hi, baby," she says before giving me a hug.

She looks so different here, ethereal and angelic. I have never seen my mother like this, so peaceful. I ask her how it is possible she is here and if it means she has died. I start shaking my head, "No, no, no, no, Mom, please tell me you aren't dead! Please, Mom, please!" She places a hand on my shoulder and I instantly feel a wave of deep, penetrating calm.

"I'm not dead, baby. Jus' got somethin' important to do

here and I know I cain't go back down dere unless I do it." Tiffany doesn't say a word and just stares like she's looking at a ghost. My mother places a hand on Tiffany's shoulder and tells her, "Everything will be explained in due time. You gon' be awright, sweetie, even without your mother down there. I promise, you gon' survive it."

My mother starts walking toward the white beach chairs. Tiffany and I follow her and ask what happens next. "I'on' know," my mother says. "We just have ta wait." We sprawl out on the beach chairs and marvel at the ocean in front of us. "Wowww, I neva been to da ocean befo'," Tiffany says. "I wish I could swim. I'd go see if I can find me some dolphins." My mother tells Tiffany she can swim here and that she should go give it a try. "Nah, dat's okay," Tiffany says with trepidation. "Maybe next time." My mother begins sharing memories from her life. "My momma use'ta brang me to a beach just like this when I was a real lil girl. She gimme a lil red bucket and I'a go and fill it up wit' sand, den pour it out and make lil sand castles. She be lookin' at me makin' dem sand castles and ask, 'Guess how much I love you?' I'd say, I'on' know, Momma, how much? She'd point down and say mo dan all da grains of sand on dis beach. And I'a look up at huh in confusion and say, 'But it's infinity sand out here.' She'a look down at me, smile, and say, 'Exactly, baby. Dat's exactly how much.'" My mother stops speaking and I notice she is crying. I try to think of something to say to make her feel better, but I decide to leave her be in the harmony of our surroundings.

I suddenly notice there are sand castles right next to the

water. "Hey, did the sand castles you used to build look like those over there? They just appeared."

My mother looks over and nods her head. "Yes, my God, yes." She stands up and walks toward the sand castles. She kneels down in front of them, touching them before starting to weep like I've never seen her weep before. "I'm so sorry, Momma. I wish I could take it all back. I'm so sorry." She sits there on her knees, sobbing. Tiffany asks if we should do something, but I don't know what to do, so we just sit while she cries and cries.

All the way down the beach, I see another form start to materialize. I point and yell, "Look!" "What should we do?" Tiffany asks. "Should we tell your mother?" My mother is still sitting solemnly on her knees, staring at the sand castles. I don't want to disturb her, so we just watch as the form gets closer and closer.

Eventually, we see that it's another woman who is also dressed in white. She looks much older and has silver hair that sits in a bun on top of her head. She walks over to my mother and touches her on the shoulder. My mother spins around and starts yelling, "Momma?! Momma?! It cain't be you. Momma, is dat you?!" The woman gives my mother a hug and then sits down next to her. "Hi, baby," she says, just like my mother said to me. "I know it's been a rough road for you down there. I know how hard it's been. It wasn't your fault, baby. You didn't know. And I want you to know I forgive you, my sweet girl. I forgive you a million times over in this life and the next." Hearing these words causes my mother to start weeping again. "I'm so sorry, Momma. I'm so sorry," she cries out. "I wished every day dat I could take it all back. Dat it could'a been me instead'a you. I just cain't live wit' it anymore, Momma. I just cain't live." My mother's mother places a hand on her shoulder and says, "I know, baby. That's why I've come to tell you that you have to forgive yourself. The time has come to forgive yourself. You can't go back down there until you do." My mother starts shaking her head no repeatedly. "I cain't do dat, Momma. What I did is unforgivable. What kind a' person 'cept a monster would do dat kind of thing? I cain't do it, Momma. I'd rather stay here wit' you. I don't wanna leave, Momma. I cain't lose you again. I wanna stay here wit' you." My mother's mother looks at her with such compassion and love, I understand why my mother doesn't want to leave.

"I can't stay here forever, baby. In fact, I don't have much time left. And I don't want you to be trapped in this place all alone. So you have to find the courage to forgive yourself." My mother shakes her head again and says, "I cain't, Momma." Suddenly, the clouds darken and grow in volume. They become rounded and puffy. The ocean water starts to churn and ripple. Tiffany and I both run over to my mother and grandmother and ask what's happening. My grandmother doesn't acknowledge us and instead urges my mother again and again, "Forgive yourself, baby. Do it now, baby. We're running out of time."

Way out in the middle of the ocean, I see a small boat rowing toward us. Just as I notice the boat, the clouds dissolve entirely and the space above turns black. A scene starts playing like it's a movie screen. "Yo, dis shit is wild as fuck," Tiffany says as we both stare up at the sky above.

In the projected scene, I see my mother in the hospital room below. The one we just came from. My mother is going into cardiac arrest. Her heart has stopped. The doctors attempt to save her as Tiffany and I wait in the hospital lobby. I see them attaching a defibrillator as one of the doctors yells, "Clear!" I scream, "What's happening? Is my mother dying down there?! What's happening?!" No one responds. The scene continues to unfold. Tiffany and I watch as they shock my mother's chest again and again, but her heart won't start. One of the doctors says, "Let's call the time of death at seven thirty-eight p.m." Another doctor pleads with him to keep trying. He is hesitant initially but agrees to continue. We watch as they reattach the defibrillator and once again shock my mother's chest, which heaves upward with unnatural force and momentum.

"You have to do it now!" my grandmother yells. "Do it now, baby!" The boat that was initially way out in the middle of the ocean now docks a few feet away from us. A third woman, also dressed in white, comes running toward us at lightning speed. Tiffany stands up and suddenly shouts, "Mom?! Mom!" The woman grabs Tiffany into her arms with such intensity, I think she might squeeze her to death. "Mom! I miss you so much. I miss you every day. I think about you as soon as I wake up and before I go to bed." Tiffany's mother holds Tiffany's face in her hands. "Listen, baby, I'm so sorry. I'm so sorry I couldn't fix it before it was too late. Before I came here. I want you to know I love you. I always did. More than you can ever know. And when you get back down there, you gon' have to make a choice, awright. I want you to choose the light, okay, baby? Can you do that for me?" Tiffany responds frantically, "I don't know what you're talking about, Mom. I don't know what you mean." Tiffany's mother gives her another hug before running back to the boat. She pauses in front of my mother and says, "Forgive yourself, Aprah. Not for you, but for your baby. You can still go back to her. I'd give anything to go back to mine." Tiffany starts to run after her mother, but her mother forcefully stops her. "You cain't come wit' me. I'a see you again," she promises. "I love you, baby." We watch as she gets back in the boat and rows into the churning ocean water.

The Code Blue in the hospital scene continues. The doctor says, "I think we've lost her, but let's try one last time."

My mother lifts herself up off the sand and announces into the ocean, "Okay! Okay! You win. I forgive myself! For killing my momma. For all the ways I failed my babies. April Marie Brown, you are forgiven." She sinks back into the ground, released.

The seventeenth lesson of wizard training is that forgiveness is inescapable. We are all destined for mistakes, transgressions, and impossible circumstances beyond our control. You can either choose to forgive yourself and be free, or suffocate under the weight of ghosts and graveyards.

The doctor yells, "Clear!" We watch as my mother's chest heaves upward one last time and her heartbeat forcefully returns. "She's back!" the doctor screams. "Incredible." The medical staff is cheering in delight and disbelief. The doctor who suggested they keep trying beams with joy.

* * *

My mother's mother hugs her after she forgives herself, wrapping her totally in her arms. "You did it, baby. You did it. When you go back everything will be different. You aren't carrying that big, heavy weight anymore. I'm so proud of you. I'll see you next time, okay?" My grandmother then looks over at Tiffany and me, who have been watching in shock nearby, while continuing to cradle my mother's body in her arms. "Go home," she says suddenly, and Tiffany and I both collapse onto the sand.

When we wake up, there is music blaring from the speakers. We are in prom dresses as people dance and twirl around us. We stand there in the middle of the dance floor motionless, like we've just seen the afterlife—because maybe we did? Jin runs up to us and says, "What's wrong wit' y'all? Let's dance!" He grabs my hand and starts to swing me around and around. I try to keep up while also struggling to process what just happened. Tiffany goes and sits on the bleachers by herself. I can see she is shaken and disturbed, and so am I. I'm spinning, but I'm not smiling or laughing. I keep thinking about the above plane, about my mother and her miraculous recovery. *She's still here*, I remind myself softly. *I'm so grateful she's still here.* Tears start to form in my eyes.

Jin whips me around and says, "Gurl, why you in the sunken place right now? You betta cheer up! We almost seniors! Eyyy, we only got one more year of high school left!"

Jin starts chanting, "One more year! One more year!" Several students hear and join in his excitement until there is a chorus of chants across the room.

Even Jessie, who attends special ed classes at Tarver and brought Elena as his date, is chanting. He won't graduate for another two years, but can't resist a good cheer. He claps glee-fully until Elena grabs the back of his wheelchair and spins him around. Once Jin releases me, Davante steps in and asks if he can have the next dance. I hesitate, teasing him, like I always do. The Tarver Six, including Davante, all came as a group, but I can see in Davante's eyes he still wishes I was his date. I want to slow dance with Davante, but I'm still trauma-tized by what happened with Prince Mack. My body sends so many confusing signals, I feel like I'm going to pass out. I look over at him and ask why he likes me, out of all the other girls.

"'Cause you smart, and you beautiful," he says, "and I think you really special. Like different from all da other girls. I can just tell."

We stand there awkwardly in silence for a few more seconds before he grabs my pinky finger and holds on to it. I smile and then turn toward him, curling into his chest. He wraps his arms around me and the fragrance of his cologne hypnotizes me, drawing me closer and closer to him. Then the music goes off abruptly. The DJ announces that was the last song.

Davante yells in disappointment, "Aww, come on, man! Just play one more. I finally got her."

The DJ ignores Davante's protests and starts packing up his equipment.

"You don't *have* me," I whisper playfully in Davante's ear while untucking myself out of his arms.

He smiles and says, "A'ight, y'all girls always playin' hard ta get."

The Tarver Six, Elena, Tiffany, and Jessie all head outside and sit on the curb in front of the school. We suck on grape Popsicles that were passed out earlier at the dance. Tiffany and I are mostly silent while everyone else talks jovially among themselves. We stare up at the full moon in the sky. Elena says she wishes her girlfriend (whom her parents don't know about) were here, but she's out of town with her family.

Rodman, who apparently has been trying to hit on Elena all night, shouts, "You gay?! Man, who knew." After noticing that Elena has taken offense to his comments, he backs off and says, "I mean, dat's cool. Nothin' wrong wit' dat. Jin gay, too. We don't discriminate in the Tarver Six." Still, disappointment stains his voice and mires his forced smile.

Davante asks how many planets we think are up there in the sky and if they have racism in their worlds, too. "I don't know," I say. "But I bet some pretty amazing stuff happens way up there in the sky." Tiffany glances over at me while Elena knowingly smiles. We all sit in silence for a few seconds, staring up until Jin blurts out, "Gurl, you know where I wanna go? I wanna go to Iceland." Everyone shouts at the same time in surprise, "Iceland?!" "It ain't cold enough in Cleveland for you?" Rodman asks. "I wanna see da Northern Lights," Jin explains. "It's at da top of da world, and you can see all dese colorful beams in da sky. You know I would fit right in wit' all dat color. I think maybe dat's my true home."

Surrendering to the Beyond

Junior prom fades into senior year at warp speed. Suddenly, there is so much to get done before it's almost over: college applications, senior pictures, and final projects. I try to keep up with everything that's happening, but suddenly the last four months of my senior year roll in like a slow mist over Lake Erie. Initially, I am wary of the mist, wondering what havoc it will wreak, what changes it will bring. If I will survive it. I know that by the time the mist rolls out, everything will be different. Everything is already different.

After my mother's miracle in the above plane, Tiffany and I somehow time-jumped right into the middle of our junior prom. I moved back in with Mrs. Delaney after helping my mother recover over the summer and the first part of senior year. Dre and Rone have slowed down their chaos-making for now, alarmed at the experience of almost losing our mother, and Dad, too, is on his best behavior, but I know it is only a matter of time before they start hitting the block again. My mother, who seems to be standing right side up for the first time in her life, says she is determined not to spin more webs of chaos.

I don't believe it until I see her at one of the Saturday-night spades parties. Instead of participating in the usual procession in and out of the bathroom, she has transformed into the caregiver at the parties, tending to those who pass out on the floor, are too drunk or high to go home, or are cloaked in the black veil. She moves around the room with a new radiance, gently looking after everyone, whispering all around the room in a calm and compassionate voice, "That's enough, now. That's enough." Everyone seems to understand and welcome her new role, even though they don't know about the instigating miracle in the above plane. Some ask her questions: "So you done gone straight and narrow now, Ms. Aprah? Well, good fo you. Pass me dem baggies, will you?" It's interesting to me how a person can change so much on the inside while their environment remains the same—and then how different that same environment looks after the change. I wonder how different this place will look when I come back from college. If the place that made me will eventually feel like Mars.

Not only is my mother different at her spades parties, but she also sits with Mary Jacobs late at night, drinking from a white mug, "absorbin' and learnin' ev'rythang she got ta teach me." Sometimes, even Ms. Jannie, who is still a fervent Christian, at least on the surface, comes and sits with them during their late-night talks. "I knew y'all would get here 'ventually. We all get dere 'ventually," Mary Jacobs says while laughing quietly to herself. I wonder if they will conduct any more miracles together. If they will use their newfound power of three to help any more young girls. I also wonder what it would be like to join them out there, three ancient wizards on a porch at midnight, but I'm still too intimidated by Mary Jacobs to find out.

Everything hasn't turned out perfectly, however. My mother is now diabetic, which contributed to her overdose being so bad. The doctors discovered that her blood sugar had severely spiked while she was at the hospital. Her kidneys are also functioning poorly, probably from years of drinking pop and alcohol over water, which means she has to go for dialysis twice a month. "I don't mind one bit," my mother says. "I'm jus' happy ta still be here. Lawd, I'm so happy to still be here wit' all of y'all down here on da good earth." Not long after her first dialysis treatment, my mother tells me she knows I have to go back and live with Mrs. Delaney. She knows there are things I still need to learn and she won't interfere. I am astounded at my mother's clarity and newly developed insight. *She has risen*, I think to myself, echoing Mrs. Delaney's words from the day of the poem recitals. *Here she is*, finally.

Everything seems to have mostly fallen into place going into senior spring. And now there are only four months left. I know they will fly by in a flash, so I start running, trying to keep up, barely stopping to eat, sleep, or breathe. I rise, run to school, run to class, run to the Cleveland Clinic, study for final exams, wait on pins and needles for college acceptance letters, order my cap and gown, write articles for the school newspaper, and search for inspiration for my valedictory speech, which I have been struggling to write for weeks. The pressure of trying to say something that captures the essence of 122 graduating seniors' high school experience is over-whelming, and also thrilling. I wonder what Alexis would do, but then I shake my head and remind myself that it's my speech and all I have to do is "be authentic and honest and give my best testimony," as Pastor Duneberry always says.

Pastor Duneberry is Mr. Delaney's pastor at St. John's African Methodist Episcopal, the oldest black church in Cleveland. Mr. Delaney said he and his family have been going there since World War II. On the night before gradua-tion, they will be having a special program called the Heart of the Black Man with a visiting preacher from Ghana. Mrs. and Mr. Delaney want us all to go together, including my father and brothers, but I'm hesitant given the fact that I still have so much rage toward black men and the fact that I now feel uncomfortable in churches. I still don't know if there is a God, one that made the in-between and all the world we live in, but I know I'm not a Christian. That said, I have been eager to have Mrs. and Mr. Delaney spend time with the rest of my family—they have only met my mother so far—so I tell them I'll think about coming.

Even though Mr. Delaney has softened toward me under his wife's influence, I still don't feel entirely safe or seen around him. I mainly hide in my room and smile plastically to conceal my unease with our relationship. One night when they think I am sleeping, I overhear a heated conversation between them in the living room. I sit at the top of the staircase, careful not to creak any of the wooden floorboards, craning my neck over the banister to catch every word. They are talking very quietly, but I can still hear, thanks to the enhanced acoustics in the stairwell.

"Look at how much I've already helped her, Marleen. I mean, I taught her how to drive, I bought her school clothes for this year, I've been driving her to college visits wherever she wants to go. Honestly, what more can I do, honey?" I become enraged listening to Mr. Delaney's words. Why do men always think material things can make up for what they don't give emotionally?

"Yes, you have done everything I've asked and have agreed to open our home to her," Mrs. Delaney answers. "But, Dennis, you haven't shown her your heart. You have shown her generosity, but I promise you she needs your heart more than she needs your money. Don't you remember what it was like to be young and confused in the world? Don't you remember how much you complained about your mom and dad not being there for you even though they gave you everything you needed? She has to see who you are at the core, or you will never find a way to really meet each other, and how sad that would be. You didn't sign up for any of this, I know that. You never wanted kids, and now I've pushed one on you. All I'm saying is, try to put yourself in her shoes. Her biological father abandoned her before she was even born, her stepfather drinks, and her brothers are slowly self-destructing. You have a real chance to make a positive impact, and not just with material things."

I am surprised that Mrs. Delaney understands my biggest issue with her husband. I return to my room and decide I'm not going to the Heart of the Black Man sermon. I don't want to hear more black men talking about how hard it is for them while not listening to the struggles of black women. I don't want to keep fighting for the liberation of black men when they don't seem to be equally concerned about fighting for me.

The turmoil of it tears me apart inside, but I don't know how to heal my wounds and mend the gap. I wonder if black men at college will be different. If all that education will help them understand the plight of the black woman, or if they will just find new ways to justify their blind spot like Mr. Delaney. *I hope college will be different.*

- - —— ——o○o—— —— - -

When my first college response letter arrives, I just stare blankly at it. Mrs. Delaney has placed it unopened in the middle of my bed. It is from Kenyon College, which is not my first choice, but this letter will set the tone and my expectations for all the other letters to come. I decide to wait and open it when I get to the dialysis clinic later that day. I know my mother will be thrilled to have me open the letter in front of her.

I try to meet my mother at the clinic every time she has to

go, even though I hate seeing her in any kind of hospital-like facility with tubes running out of her. But I know it means a lot to her for me to be there, so I've gone to almost every appointment. By the time I arrive at the dialysis center after school, the nurses have already hooked her up. She is lying on the bed with various tubes running out of her, staring at the ceiling.

"What you thinking about?" I ask while walking in.

"Oh, hey, girl. You know, I was just lyin' here thankin' about maybe takin' me one a' dem cookin' classes up at dat recreation center. I mean, I already knows how to cook soul food, but maybe I can learn how to make some of dem fancy white dishes. What you thank 'bout dat?"

I lean down and give her a kiss on the forehead and say, "I think that's a great idea. And you can add your own soul-food twist. Oh, and maybe you can start selling plates to make some money on the side or something like that."

I watch as a bird flies past the window outside and am suddenly stricken with unease. I just can't believe and trust that my mother has changed so dramatically. "Mom, what if it all comes back? The temptation. The black veil. What if it comes back?" My voice trails off from the sadness of thinking about it.

"It already done come back, baby. I don't thank it ever really go away. It's always somewhere nearby. Both da temptation and dat veil. But da difference is, now I got me some tools to stop it befo' it come down on me all da way. Dem pills da doctor gave me heps me a lot, too. I feel like I got real strength inside a' me for da first time. And I want you to know again, I know I done tole you a thousand times, but I'm so sorry, baby. I'm so sorry for who I was. Fo not protecting you. I'm sorry, baby."

I hold back tears while listening to her talk. "I forgive you, Mom," I say. "I forgive you."

"Lawd," she cries out to no one in particular. "Lawd, now dat's a miracle in and of itself."

I stand up and pull the unopened letter from Kenyon College from my book bag. "Guess what this is?" I say while holding the letter out to my mother.

"I already know dat's one a' dem college letters. Gone 'head and open it, girl!"

I smile at my mother, take a deep breath, and begin to peel the letter open. My hands are shaking, and I have to remind myself to keep breathing. I pull the folded paper from the envelope and keep it clasped in my hands. I look up at my mother, who's staring eagerly with all the hope in the world, with dialysis tubes draped down over her bed and an IV protruding from her arm. I feel her projecting the entirety of her soul into calling good fortune on my behalf. I wonder if anyone else in the universe wants good fortune for you as much as your mother does.

I unfold the letter and begin reading, "Dear Ms. Echo Brown, On behalf of the admissions committee of Kenyon College, we are pleased to offer you a spot in our incoming class. We hope—" I stop reading and start screaming.

My mother covers her mouth with both hands and starts

saying, "Lawd, Lawd, Lawd, I just knew. I just knew you was gon' make it, gurl."

Then she opens her arms and hugs me, unconcerned about the IV and all the cords hanging from her bed or the emergency call button protruding to the side. We squeal and cry with such joy, we don't realize we have pressed the button. We don't hear the emergency announcement ring out across the floor, "Code Blue in room 222, Code Blue in room 222." Suddenly, several nurses come rushing into the room while my mother and I continue to hug and cry. They ask if everything is okay. My mother exclaims, "Ev'rythang is jus' fine. 'Cause dis girl right here goin' ta college!"

- - — —— ∘○∘ —— — - -

College admission letters continue to roll in. They all say the same thing: accepted. Ohio University, Wesleyan University, even Harvard University: accepted. I am overwhelmed by the response. I can't believe it. Deep down, I knew I would get accepted to at least one college, but so far I have not received one rejection letter. My heart is still set on Dartmouth, the winter wonderland in the North, but I haven't received a letter from them yet. Their brochure has convinced me I belong on their campus with the other smiling, well-placed minorities and colorful trees. I reread their brochure over and over while spiraling my hopes and prayers deep into the fabric of the universe. I especially love that the brochure says, "At Dartmouth College, we truly value inclusion. Our students come from diverse backgrounds and communities around the world. Like the Statue of Liberty, we also ascribe to the creed of 'Give me your tired, your poor,' and we will provide a first-class education so that they might go out and become lighthouses in an often challenging world." I'm always tired, and poor, so I feel like they are talking directly to me.

My Dartmouth College response letter arrives exactly two and a half months before graduation. I get home one day and see the letter lying in the middle of my bed, where Mrs. Delaney leaves them each time. I sit next to it and stare at it for several minutes. I try to prepare myself for disappointment. For the shock of having not attained. I hold the letter up to the light to see if I can make out any words like "we regret to inform you" or "unfortunately." Like all the other college response letters, the paper is completely folded over the text, preventing any hint of what might be enclosed. I get up and shut the door in case I need to cry. I don't want Mrs. Delaney to see me crying. If the answer is no, I will tell her I haven't opened the letter yet. I rip the envelope open and begin reading. "Dear Ms. Echo Brown"—I love that they all call me *Ms*. It makes me feel like a full-blown adult—

> "In my fifteen years as an admissions officer, I don't
> think I have ever come across an application like yours.
> The admiration with which all your teachers speak
> about you (and several of them wrote letters for you
> even though only two were required), the depth of your
> perseverance despite truly untenable circumstances,

On the night before my valedictory speech, my mother and I are sitting at the kitchen table in our apartment. I'm waiting for her to give me the gift she says she got for me before I "grow all up and leave for dat fancy college up north." My mother sees me staring up at Jesus and says, "He changes position based on what's happenin' in ya life. I done had dat picture since I was a lil girl and always know when somethin' comin' based on da look on his face. You can take him wit' you if you want. I hear you in here talkin' to him sometimes." I smile and look back up at Jesus's new position, which is him coyly smacking his teeth and pointing his finger like in my dream. My mother and I will be leaving to go to the Heart of the Black Man sermon at Mr. Delaney's church soon, which I decided to attend after mentioning it to Dre and Rone and seeing how much they wanted to go. Davante and my father will also be joining. I already know that, out of everyone, Davante will probably love it the most.

"We been talkin' 'bout forgiveness a lot in my AA group," my mother says. "I was thankin' 'bout how hard it was for me to forgive myself. And not just myself, but all of 'em dat did me wrong, 'specially da mens. I been mad at men my whole life. Shit, I hope dis sermon tonight ain't about worshippin' and praisin' da mens, not afta all da havoc dey done caused. If dat's da case, I will be showing myself to da door." My mother grabs a small black box out of one of the kitchen cabinets and sets it on the table in front of me. "Open it," she says. I gently lift the plush velvet top and see there is a silver necklace inside with a small blue crystal heart attached. "It ain't much," my mother says. "I got it ova at Walmart, but I wanted you to have somethin' when you go away. For when thangs happen dat you cain't control. I'on' want you to live in a prison of rage and pain like I done most of my life. When da hard times come up, you can 'member me and squeeze it and ask fo hep letting go of anythang dat's botherin' you. I know you cain't see it right now, but it's gon' come a point when yo life ain't gon' be so brand-new and you might find yo'self full of big ol' mountains of pain, regret, anger. One day you might wake up, look 'round yo life, and wonder where all da sunshine went. I know you already done been through it, done had to deal wit' one or two mountains already, but life has a way of stackin' on mo and mo until you ain't got no choice but ta let it all go and surrender to da beyond. In AA, da second step says we came to believe dat only a Power greater dan ourselves could restore us. Dat Power is da beyond, and I hope ya surrender sooner ratha dan lata, is all I'm sayin."

This happens to be the eighteenth lesson of wizard training. Nothing is worse than a wizard who is trapped in a pattern of emotional exhaustion or trauma. Your highest potential can only be achieved if you manage to surrender whatever baggage no longer serves you.

My mother and I head to Mr. Delaney's church. My father, Dre, Rone, and Davante join us on the bus ride to the West Side, where Mr. and Mrs. Delaney are waiting for us outside the church. After the service, I'll spend the night at Mrs. Delaney's house, where my cap and gown are, and practice my valedictory speech one last time.

We all head inside and squeeze ourselves into an empty pew in the middle of the church, watching as the space slowly fills up. Dre, Rone, and I poke and prod one another like we always do when we come together. "Stop touching me," Rone yells playfully even though no one has touched him. I smack him on the side of his arm and tell him to shut up. "I cain't wait fo dat buffet," Dre says. I start to wonder if the buffet, which will include fried chicken, greens, yams, chitlins, and pound cake, is the real reason they were both so eager to come. Davante leans over and says sarcastically, "Heard you got in ta Dartmouth, Ms. Valedictorian. Congratulations. Good luck surviving the oppressor's institutions and halls of knowledge. Hope you enjoy it." I roll my eyes and respond, "Davante, for real? In church? Don't worry about my life choices. Hope Howard turns out to be everything you dreamed, and more. Hope you don't end up accidentally enabling the patriarchy and misogyny."

The lights begin to dim as I playfully smack Davante on the back of his head. The only lights that stay on are highlighting the stage, which is empty except for a drum set and two microphone stands. Suddenly, a woman starts singing the words to what sounds like an old Negro spiritual from somewhere offstage. I am immediately arrested by the power of her voice. I can see the rest of the church is also affected because everyone leans forward as soon as she starts singing. A few lines into the song, Pastor Eweku emerges onstage, while the singer, who I later learn is named Sara, follows him. They walk over to the mic stands. Sara clips in her mic while Pastor Eweku removes his. I am struck by Pastor Eweku's skin. He is so dark. He would be heavily made fun of if he went to my high school. They would call him "tar baby" or "purple" or "black-ass nigga." I wonder if he was ever made fun of for that in Africa, if that's where it started or if it started after they made us slaves.

Everyone is on the edge of their seats, waiting for him to speak, but he stands there without saying anything, just looking out into the darkness of the church. Then he quietly speaks into the mic, "And so here we are. On a beautiful day in a beautiful church. I want you to take a minute to think about everything that has brought you to this moment in your life. All the pain and sorrow. All the joy and triumphs. I ask you: Who is more triumphant than black people? Who walking the earth has been more triumphant than the children of the sun? And so before we were here, we were back there, in our original homes, the place that made us. There we were

"stepping over crack needles, dodging bullets, watching our loved ones succumb to devastating addictions, and dealing with struggles no child should ever have to deal with." I pause and look to my left at the 2002 graduating class of Henry E. Tarver. Everyone in the auditorium stares silently at me, waiting for the next words to fall out of my mouth. I look down at my notes and continue. "I want you to know, I know where you come from. I'm standing there with you. Like many of you, it all started in turmoil for me. At only six years old, there I was in a burning apartment. An actual burning apartment. As the smoke poured in and my brothers cried in their cribs. And my mother—who is here today, right there, and I've asked her permission to share all this with you—she was passed out on the bathroom floor from having ingested too much crack cocaine. As I stood there in the middle of all that chaos, I knew that what happened next—whether I made it out of that fire or not—was out of my hands. I didn't know if I would emerge from those flames or if I would perish before my time, like so many of us. All I could control in that moment was my will to not give up and my ability to

rise triumphantly up out of the good earth," Pastor Eweku says. "The black man, like the mighty African redwood tree in the forests of Angola, like the powerful beanstalks of Namibia, like the vast cotton in the fields of Alabama, and like the stout sugarcane in Jamaica, the black man rose up proudly, resolutely out of this earth. And everything in existence supported his existence. I'ma say that again, 'cause I don't think y'all heard me. I said, everything in existence supported his existence."

Someone in the church shouts, "You betta tell 'em preacher. Tell 'em!"

"Sing to 'em, Sara," Pastor Eweku commands.

And Sara begins again, hypnotizing us with her voice. "We're searching for da glory," she sings. Then suddenly the full choir enters the stage and stands behind her and Pastor Eweku. She sings "Sweet glory," and they sing "Glory, glory, glory" in the background while swaying.

"I'ma say that a third time, 'cause I know some of y'all is hard of hearing. And I know some of y'all just don't listen good. Only hear what you want to hear. I said, everything in existence supports the existence of the black man." Pastor Eweku says the word "black" with such emphasis and power, he makes it sound regal and grand instead of demeaning, like I am used to hearing. "Everything in existence," he continues, "except the white man." I look over and see that Davante has a wide grin as Pastor Eweku says this. He starts nodding yes and clapping his hands powerfully in agreement. I peek at Mrs. Delaney from the corner of my eye to see if she is uncomfortable. Most of the people in the church are black, except for two or three other white women who are married to black men. Mrs. Delaney looks moved also and squeezes my hand to indicate she understands exactly

"the obstacles in front of you," I say while looking out at the audience, including the front row, where Rone, Dre, our parents, Elena, Jessie, and Mr. and Mrs. Delaney are sitting. Elena already graduated last week, and Jessie's wheelchair is nestled on the side of the row next to my mother. I can see that Mrs. Delaney and my mother are already crying and I haven't even finished my speech yet. "And though there will be tragedies and injustice along the way," I continue, "there will also be many gifts and lessons to be learned. Lessons like discovering how unbreakable our spirits are. As Pastor Eweku said in his sermon at church last night, I want to ask you: Who is more unbreakable than black people? Or anyone who comes from where we come from? Only cockroaches and mosquitoes, I'd say. Just like them, we'll be here till the end." The audience laughs and bursts into applause. "There are more lessons. Lessons like unburying everything you have choked down to survive. No one survives what we have without being excellent gravediggers. And yet, in due time, all those skeletons must be dug up and confronted— and that takes courage and bravery. Or lessons like choosing your own purpose regardless of what society says you can or can't do. And lessons like forgiving yourself for everything: all the mistakes you make, all the people you hurt, all the ways you keep falling down." I pause and then look at my mother, who is sobbing quietly. "Let it go, surrender to the beyond, and forgive yourself for all the unhealed pain

in our community, in our hearts, in our minds, in the very fabric of who we are as a people," Pastor Eweku says while looking intently at the congregation. "We have truly been beaten down as a result of colonialism and white supremacy. And no one has been more beaten down, more forgotten, more shamed than black women, even by our own hands, brothers." Pastor Eweku speaks softly now into the mic, almost whispering. "Many of you came here today to hear me preach about the heart of the black man. Well, I'm here to tell you that the heart of the black man is the black woman. And that heart has been broken by so many sins. Our sins. The sins of rape. The sins of betrayal. The sins of patriarchy, physical abuse, isolation, shaming. And now a penance must be paid, brothers. For breaking our own hearts. A penance must be paid, the score must be settled, for when the glory comes, you gotta be right in your soul, brothers. And then the glory will really be ours."

I have never heard a black man speak like this about the burden black women have carried. I am in awe and wonder at how he figured it out. I want to rush the stage and thank him for his words. I look around and see that many other black women in the church are moved by what he says and nod their heads in agreement. The men seem much more hesitant to soak in this part of his sermon, even though they were totally engaged when he was talking about the sins of the white man.

I look down and see the small heart at the bottom of the silver necklace around my neck flashing intensely. I wrap my hand around it and suddenly feel some kind of filter drop down over my eyes, which causes me to see everything differently. A filter that causes me to see a bright white light glowing in the heart centers of all the men. Inside the light, the story of each man's path is archived, their ups and downs, joys and pains. Some people glow brighter than others. From Mr. Delaney's story, I learn how he never truly felt loved or seen, so he hid behind a wall of stubborn defensiveness. I guess this is the heart Mrs. Delaney was talking about that night I eavesdropped on them. I scour around the church, trying to read more words inside more hearts as Pastor Eweku continues speaking. "Brethren, the time to apologize is long overdue. The time to atone for our own sins is now. It's always now brothers. Look within your own hearts

and discover the truth about who you actually are. They have called us low-income, underprivileged, and low-performing. They have set their expectations for us so low, they can't actually see what is possible for us, so they tell us it's impossible, that our journeys are impossible. But I'm here today to tell you that the journey forward always seems impossible. Anything we set out to do in life looks impossible at first, and yet we must keep going, listening only to the small voice inside that tells us to press on, to keep reaching and prove them all wrong.

"I want to tell you that they are wrong about us and what we are capable of because they don't really know us. We are not statistics or stereotypes or lost causes. We are wizards, transforming every obstacle into hope, into new paths forward. We are wizards of the light, and we do not yield. We are wizards of the dawn, and we know the daybreak always follows even the darkest of nights. We are wizards of the horizon, always ready to sail forward, unstoppably forward. So I want to encourage you to take these high school diplomas and set sail. Don't wait for anything—permission, perfection, or less problems—to sail toward the life that is out there waiting for you."

The entire auditorium erupts in applause. I look out and am shocked to see the black veils over many people begin to rise, again. I look down at my mother and Mrs. Delaney in confusion, but they are both so enthralled with what's happening, they don't notice me trying to get their attention. I listen as

apologies ring out all around the church. It sounds like a crescendo of voices all chattering at once. Dre, Rone, and my father all say, "We sorry, Echo. We sorry," which dissolves me into a heaping puddle of sobs that defuses some of the rage and anger I have carried for so long. I read the stories written in their glowing hearts. I am reminded of the essence of who they are beneath all the pain. "And to yo momma, too," my father says as he turns to my mother. "I'm sorry, Aprah, for ev'rythang I done put you through. I'm so sorry."

"Glory, hallelujah," Pastor Eweku cries into the mic while Sara and the choir sing in the background. The church erupts into chaos, with people crying and embracing all around the room. I peek over at Mrs. Delaney and see that she is wiping away the tears falling down her cheeks.

— – — ——o○o—— — – —

On the drive home, we are all mostly silent. No one has words to follow the enormity of Pastor Eweku's sermon. When we come to a stoplight, Mr. Delaney reaches back and grabs my hand and squeezes. I know what the squeeze means. I understand. In that moment, I release and all is forgiven.

Becoming Fearless in Your Pursuits

I am running down the sidewalk in a frenzy. I'm already fifteen minutes late. This was my idea, and somehow I've managed to still be late. I wave when I see Elena standing in front of Jessie's apartment building. The Tarver Six, Elena, Jessie, Dre, Rone, and I have decided to plant wisdom trees and leave inspirational notes in the field for unsuspecting strangers who might need hope. We decide that the perfect way to celebrate our graduation is to leave something behind about what we've learned so far. I've always had a love affair with trees and what they represent: renewal and possibility. "Oh my God, this is so sappy," Elena groans. "But I'm sure whoever finds these notes will be inspired." I glance over at Elena, smile, and think about the first time I met her. She now has only one veil, the hijab, which strengthens rather than depletes her.

Elena smiles back knowingly before giving me a hug and promising to email me often about how she's doing at Yale, which has top-notch drama *and* medicine programs. She plans to take a few pre-med classes to make her parents happy, but she will ultimately study theater and acting. Elena and I grab Jessie and race to the open field, where the rest of the group is waiting. Ms. Patty yells at us as we roll by, "Lawd, y'all almost grown and still runnin' down da street like y'all done escaped from Shaka Zulu's tribe. Slow down! You'a get dere soon enough. Ain't nobody chasin' y'all." She cackles to herself before drinking from her purple cup. For a moment, a wave of nostalgia passes over me and I remember when my brothers and I used to sit up there with her, watching everyone walk by. I marvel at how quickly the time has flown, at how quickly I have arrived at adulthood.

We stop at the penny candy store and see Tiffany inside. When she sees us, she comes rushing out of the store and says, "Jessie! What are we gonna do tomorrow?!" Jessie looks up and smiles before saying, "The same thing we do every day, Pinky—try to take over the world!" Tiffany cheers before leaning down to give him a hug. I smile, grateful for the unexpected reunion, for the homecoming of old friends. I ask Tiffany when she starts community college and about the development of her abilities. We all speak in code so that others passing by don't know what we're talking about. She tells me she's been trying to perform miracles to see if she can use any of it to help Lil Man turn his life around.

Elena taps me on the shoulder, interrupting my train of thought, and tells me we have to go because everyone's waiting. "Remember, this was your idea," she says with warm sarcasm. We say goodbye to Tiffany and quickly run into the store, buy a bunch of candy, and then head to the field. When we get there, all our friends and my brothers have already started digging. We join in to dig a circle of ten holes. Once that's done, we pick up the small potted trees that will one day become large ancient trees, and write inspirational messages on the side of each burnt-orange pot.

"Man, Echo, somebody gon' cut dese trees down," Rone says. "How many ghettos got a circle of trees right in da middle of 'em? Dis some funny shit for real. Niggas gon' be walkin' by and be like 'Where da hell did dat circle a' trees come from?'" Rone laughs to himself while continuing to dig. "And I ain't got nothin' inspirational to say. So I ain't writin' no message."

Dre rolls his eyes and smacks his lips before saying, "Man, jus' try ta be positive, nigga. Dis fo Echo, our sister. She gon' be gone soon, and dis what she wanted for her graduation gift, so jus' do it and chill out." Dre's scolding and reminder that I'll be leaving soon sink deep into Rone. He suddenly becomes sullen while picking up a marker to write his message. He holds the marker in his hand for several minutes, trying to think of what to say.

Elena notices and says, "Think about it as your warrior cry, your own unique message to the world that will live on long after you're gone. An imprint of who you are in this moment and what you've learned so far. You've come a long way."

Rone smiles chummily, as he always does when he gets his way or when a pretty girl pays attention to him, and says, "A'ight, Laina"—his nickname for Elena—"let me figure it out." The mood shifts from jovial anticipation to pensive focus as everyone crafts their own personal message on the sides of the pots, except Jessie, who instead draws a picture on the side of his.

Once everyone finishes writing, we drop all the trees into the holes and bury them carefully. We put a little sign in the middle of the circle of trees that says "May the wide open fields of the journey ahead fill you with wonder and may you always find your way back home. Love, the Tarver Ten."

We also write all our messages on the back of the sign and in the shack to the right of the tree circle, which we assume will stand forever in this place. I tell myself that I will come visit this shack and field each time I come home from Dartmouth. *I will always come home*, I think.

After we all finish writing, I shout, "Wait! We should read our notes to each other." Everyone unleashes a collective outburst of exasperation, embarrassed at the thought of having to share something so personal. "No, no, it will help seal the energy! I'll start!" I shout gleefully. "Just trust me. You're all gonna appreciate this moment later in life and you'll have me to thank for it." We stand in a circle in the middle of the trees, Jessie in his wheelchair between Dre and Rone. I walk to the middle of the circle and pick up the sign. I find my message and begin reading:

> *Once you find the light inside, you can do anything,*
> *even rise from the dead like Jesus. I know because I*
> *did it. I'm writing this to remind you that anything*
> *can be survived. I hope you find the courage to*
> *cultivate the dark and grow the light.*

"Dat was deep," Rone says. "Dat's a good message, fo sho." Everyone nods in agreement as I pass it to Dre, standing to my left. He holds the sign and begins:

> *Just like in da movie* Titanic, *find something to hold on to in life so you don't sink. And if yo bitch-ass friend won't let you up on dey raft when times get tough, dey ain't really yo friend. Other than that, remember dat it's all love. It's always only love, even out here in dese streets. Don't let yo hood make you so hard dat you foget dat.*

Everyone laughs and Elena and I look at each other, remembering the Miracle at *Titanic* and noticing all the small changes it has awakened in my brothers.

Rone goes next:

> *All I can say is, dis shit is not a game, but ya gotta keep goin', gotta wake up, gotta find a way, and gotta lean on da people around you. Pray you get a sister like mine in da next life. I'on' know how she does it, but I swear she be makin' me see things differently. Stay up and stay humble, my niggas.*

I reach over and pat Rone on the shoulder until he smiles chummily again. "Was dat good enough, sis?" he asks.

"That was perfect," I say. "Perfect."

Davante clears his throat and begins reading:

*The heart of any man is the woman. It took me a long time
to understand that because I was so focused on myself.
Do right by the women around you and your life will
flourish. A woman is the only seed on earth that multiplies
everything she touches. Also, don't forget to dismantle
oppressive structures of white supremacy before you leave
this world. That will always be your responsibility.*

Davante looks over at me while holding the sign and says,
"I'm sorry if I was judgmental or put too much pressure on
you. You one of my best friends and I'm always here for you.
I love you, girl." I grin before breaking the circle and giving
Davante a hug. "I'm always here for you, young fella," I say
playfully before returning to my spot.

Jin walks into the middle of the circle, channeling an
imaginary runway:

*When life invites you to a battle to test whether you
are ready, whether you are brave enough, there is only
one thing you can do: Dress to the nines, stand up, pull
your shoulders back, sashay down that runway, and
lip-sync for your life, as fairy godmother RuPaul would
say. Demand they hear and see you. Be unforgettable.*

Alexis, who's going to Northwestern University, reads hers
next:

Compete only with yourself and never compare your journey to someone else's, because it can make you bitter. Like Dr. Maya Angelou says, "You must not be bitter. Bitterness is like a cancer and it eats upon the host." Choose not to be a host to any negativity or pettiness.

Rodman and Karen decline to read their messages, saying they only want whoever finds them to read them. So Elena grabs the sign and starts reading:

My name is Elena Farahmand, first of her name, badass quantum wizard, hijabi Lady Neo of the Cleveland Matrix, daughter of immigrants from Iran, and lover of women and Kool-Aid (thanks to my best friend). I killed the imposter, and so can you. Remember where you came from, honor your roots, but choose to walk your own path no matter the consequences.

Everyone laughs and claps at Elena's bold words. Jessie shouts several times, "Lady Neo!" I tell her, "Thank you . . . for choosing the red pill." Tears well up in her eyes, and she nods knowingly, before grabbing my hand again.

After a few moments of silence, we put the sign back in the middle of the trees and stand awkwardly for a while, not wanting to look at one another. Not wanting to accept that we, too, are all floating away in different directions. "Stay in touch," we say one by one before scattering into the horizon.

I watch the horizon line for the entire drive to Dartmouth, waiting for its red and white brick buildings to rise like something out of a movie and come rolling toward us. The drive takes an agonizing twelve hours over two days, and when we finally arrive, I am asleep, snoring in the back of the car, having entirely missed the prodigious rising of Dartmouth on the skyline. I wipe the sleep from my eyes as Mrs. Delaney claps gleefully and yells, "We're here!"

My mother says, "Praise all that is holy 'cause I gots to use da bathroom." Only my mother has joined us for the drive, since there wasn't enough room in the car for my father or brothers.

We find my dorm and Mrs. Delaney, Mr. Delaney, and my mother help me unpack and set up my room. I will be sharing a room with three white girls from different places around the United States. They are all Christians and talk about how they can't wait to go to Bible study together. They ask me what denomination I am when they notice the picture of white Jesus, who I have brought with me, hanging over my desk. I see Mrs. Delaney smiling out of the corner of my eye as I tell them I'm not Christian, but "I got a thang for Jesus."

They laugh uncomfortably, uncertain about what exactly I mean before one of them breaks the tension and says, "Cool, well, really nice to meet you."

I am stunned by how rich and white the people are at Dartmouth. They drive Lamborghinis and wear funny brown shoes that look like canoes. I wonder if there has always been this much money in the world, and why so little of it managed to make it to me and my brothers. I am fascinated and enraged all at once. Though I feel deeply out of place, like when I first walked into Mrs. Delaney's house, I still feel prepared somehow. I am ready for what is to come.

Mrs. Delaney, Mr. Delaney, and my mother all stay glued to my side while helping me settle in. They ask how I'm feeling and if I need anything. They diligently circle my room, making sure everything is in order. Mr. Delaney hangs a shelf on the wall above my bed. My mother takes out newly purchased sheets and makes my bed. Mrs. Delaney unpacks my school supplies and places them carefully on my desk. She puts the pencils in the cup holder and the notebooks in the drawer. Then she stops to look at the desk and ponder if anything else needs to be done. Ah, yes, she decides before moving the mouse pad from the left of the computer to the right. Watching all three of them, I come to internalize what love is. I come to understand that at the same moment the universe set circumstances in motion to allow for my life, it also set circumstances in motion to allow for this moment. I wonder whose lives I'm being prepared to impact down the road. I think again about all those little girls. *I'm coming*, I say quietly to myself.

On the final night, after they have organized all my stuff and inspected every area of campus, Mrs. Delaney and Mr. Delaney take my mother and me out to dinner at one of the highfalutin seafood restaurants near campus. I look around and see other students, mostly white, out to dinner with their parents. All the parents have the same look in their eyes as Mrs. Delaney, Mr. Delaney, and my mother. A kind of sorrow-infused proudness. I scan the menu and once again see several items I've never heard of. Mrs. Delaney tells me to get whatever I want, even if it's a cheeseburger and fries. She winks at me before glancing back down at her menu. I decide I'm going to try something new. I glance over at my mother and can tell by her look of terrified confusion that I'll be ordering a well-done cheeseburger for her. The waiter comes and takes our orders, then rushes off to the kitchen.

I notice Mr. Delaney looking wistfully across the room. I ask him what he is thinking about. He says, "Well, I was just thinking about my first night at college. How petrified I was. Those were different times, of course. I was at a mostly white school in the South, so I kept waiting for one of those white boys to say something to me. Call me a nigger or something. Mine was the first class to admit black students. And I remember my mother and father took me out to dinner that last night. My father must have seen the fear in my eyes 'cause he said, 'Son, I know I have been hard on you at times, but I want you to know that no matter how hard it gets, you can always come home. If the battlefield grows too weary, come home to gather your strength before you get back out there.'" Mr. Delaney pauses and then continues, "That's what I want to say to you right now, Echo. I know I didn't do everything perfectly. I know I caused you pain out of my own ignorance, but I want you to hear me clearly: You can always come home.

No matter what. No matter where you find yourself in this big, bad world." Mr. Delaney hangs his head. Mrs. Delaney places a hand on his back, then he looks up and musters a smile to try and mask the vulnerability of the moment. I understand the courage it has taken for him to speak these words, and I am bursting with gratitude at having received them. I stand up, practically lunging across the table, to give him a great big hug, the biggest one I've ever given.

We feast and laugh throughout the night. After we take our last bites of dessert and our last sips of water, we stand up and look at each other, still lingering around the table in a circle, like the day my mother and I visited Rone at the juvenile detention center. We each nod silently before walking to Mr. Delaney's car behind the restaurant. None of us can look at one another again for fear that we might all burst out into tears simultaneously and drown the whole campus. We all understand the journey that has been undertaken. I give each of them a hug: Mrs. Delaney, Mr. Delaney, and finally my mother. I hold on to my mother the longest. Sensing that we need a last moment together, Mr. and Mrs. Delaney give us space.

I stand there in the middle of the sidewalk, holding my mother's hands. "Well, you did it, gurl," she says. "You did it all by yo'self, too, 'cause I wasn't hardly dere fo ya." My mother looks down in shame.

"You were there when it counted, Mom, and I'm grateful for that."

My mother smiles and says, "Awright den. Well, you can

call me anytime. Day or night. Morning or evening. You call me if anythang comes up. I'm heah now. You undastand me? I'm heah now."

We stand for a few more seconds, fighting tears that threaten to turn into full-blown wails, fully looking at each other for the first time in our lives. We see the entirety of each other's beings. When it's finally time to say goodbye, when the moment releases and propels us forward, we nod at each other, and then she turns toward the car. I stand there watching my mother's back, her being, move farther and farther away until it disappears into the belly of the car. I stare as the car dissolves into the horizon, back to the place that made me.

In the morning, when the sun starts rising, I walk toward the middle of campus and stand there trying to sense something about my new life. Trying to understand the way of things. I watch the last of the mist roll away over the New Hampshire mountains, welcoming the rays of a new dawn. I ask the particles around me if there are any messages for me. If there is something I need to know right now for the path ahead.

Only one message appears, the final lesson of wizard training: *You are unlimited. Be fearless in your pursuits.* I nod knowingly and walk back to my dorm room, where three Christian girls and white Jesus are waiting for me.

ACKNOWLEDGMENTS

Black Girl Unlimited asked to be written. From the very first line, this book poured out of me onto the page. There was no struggle or fight, there was only an allowing. I am deeply grateful to be the one it chose.

I am firstly grateful to my editor, Jessica Anderson, who understands my voice and vision and is a wonderful ally. We were truly the right partners for this. I have come to understand the importance of having allies in the creative process, which can make or break the spirit of a project. Jessica Anderson, part of your spirit is now here, too, in these pages. Thank you for everything, especially for convincing me to write for young adults—something I would not have done were it not for you and Christy Ottaviano. I would also like to thank Lindsay Wagner and Carol Ly for their dedication, insight, and efforts in ensuring the flawless design and production of *Black Girl Unlimited*. Thank you to Noa Denmon for her stunning cover art. You all helped this book find its perfect creative expression.

My biggest cheerleader has always been my mother. She is the most powerful wizard I know. She did her best to protect me, and that protection is the only reason I'm still here. Thank you is not enough for mothers. So I simply bow to her and all that she has given me. She always knew I'd write a book one day. You were right again, Momma.

I have been lucky enough to have more than one mother on my journey, many of whom were teachers. One teacher in particular profoundly affected my life. She restored my sense of hope and possibility and, most important, she made me believe I was worthy of love. There is no greater gift one human being can give another. That seed will forever blossom in me. I bow to her also.

This book is really an ode to the childhood I shared with my brothers. Though there was chaos all around us, we still found the magic. That's the power of children: They are connected to the divine unseen. Those initial days of innocence shielded us from the future's harsh realities. To my brothers, I hope I did you justice here. I hope your voices and visions ring through as clear as mine. I hope I told your stories, too. I love you endlessly. Forever.

To my dad, who said yes to raising a daughter that was not his own, who crawled up out of the hot, oppressive South in search of opportunity in the North, your story is here, too. The tenderness, authenticity, and good spiritedness with which you have lived is infused in these words. May your journey live on in these pages. And may your body get the one hundred and fifty years—"I wanna live to be a hundred and fifty-four, if da good Lawd see fit"—you've been asking for. May it be so.

To David Ford: When I first walked into your solo performance class, I told you I wasn't an artist but had a story to tell. You saw the artist behind all my fear and insecurity, nurturing her with your gentle guidance and unquestionable brilliance. You are the greatest mentor a very sensitive artist could ask for. I bow to you, also, with deep respect and gratitude.

Finally, to myself, the girl who never gives up. The girl who believed she could, so she did. The girl who listens to the spirits and completes the mission. The girl who has finally discovered her unbreakability:

Well done.

PS: To my cat Baba Baby, you are the wind beneath my wings. Thanks for being there when no one else was. Cats are majestic, otherworldly creatures. Honor them.